Also by Kate Parker

The Victorian Bookshop Mysteries
The Vanishing Thief
The Counterfeit Lady
The Royal Assassin
The Conspiring Woman
The Detecting Duchess

The Deadly Series
Deadly Scandal
Deadly Wedding
Deadly Fashion
Deadly Deception
Deadly Travel

The Milliner Mysteries
The Killing at Kaldaire House
Murder at the Marlowe Club

The Mystery at Chadwick House

DEADLY DECEPTION

KATE PARKER

JDP Press

Deadly Deception copyright © 2019 by Kate Parker

ISBN: 978-0-9976637-4-7 {ebook}

ISBN: 978-0-9976637-5-4 {print}

Published by JDP Press

Cover design by Lyndsey Lewellen of Lewellen Designs

Dedication

To John, forever

London, late October 1938

CHAPTER ONE

My father had done it again. How dare he?

It was bad enough when my father's housekeeper, Mrs. Johnson, had whispered to me before the church service that they'd be thrilled to attend my wedding. She was so happy for me, she told me, and when was the big day?

It was worse, much worse, when Lady Gordon and her social-climbing acolyte, Miss Winterbottom, cornered me in the churchyard after service and asked when they would receive their invitations. My father had kindly informed them they would be invited to the nuptials, but he wasn't clear on the date. They told me with much *humpfing* and "I'm sure you understand, dear Olivia" that they did have rather busy social calendars.

My smile weakened as I said no date had yet been set.

Their eyebrows went skyward.

I stammered something about Adam's schedule being at the mercy of the army and excused myself. I crossed the churchyard to walk to my father's house. As soon as I was out of sight of the church, my stroll turned into a stride.

He was supposed to meet me at the church. Where

was he?

Heels clicking a staccato beat, I trotted down the pavement toward my father's house. Past large red-brick homes built before the Great War, around the curve in the road, then past the huge oak I'd hit learning to ride a bicycle, and finally the massive evergreen he and my mother had planted as a twig. With the house now in sight, my list of grievances was ready.

Stomping my pumps as I stormed up the short walk from the street to my father's house, I beat on the front door with my knuckles. The more I thought about his impertinence in inviting people to my wedding without asking, the angrier I became. I stabbed my finger on the bell. Too impatient to wait for him to answer, I fished my key from my bag and unlocked the door.

"I know you're in here," I shouted as I marched down the front hallway, shoving at the door behind me. It didn't completely close and I didn't care. "What do you think...?"

And what was that smell? It was familiar.

My voice trailed off as I stared into the front drawing room. My father knelt beside a man lying in the middle of the room on the large Oriental carpet. My father's ornate Serbian dagger stuck out of the man's chest.

Father gave me a single glance as he let go of the man's shoulder and said in his stuffiest tone, "Olivia. This isn't what it appears."

My anger fizzled away into shock and dismay. "Father. We must call for a doctor. Or the police."

"Oh, he's dead. Has been for over two years."

"What?" If I thought my father had lost his mind before

I entered the house, I was certain of it now.

"Don't you recognize him?" Father sounded surprised that I didn't.

The face, now slack with death, looked vaguely familiar. I shook my head, my eyes never leaving the dagger. And the blood on my father's hands.

"It's John Kenseth."

"Mr. Kenseth?" I remembered him from my childhood. He'd vanished, presumed dead, in a sailing accident off the Isle of Wight in the summer of 1936. My father had been struck hard by his old friend's passing. "What's his body doing here now? And why does he look so," I swallowed, "so fresh?"

"I don't know, and I have to find out. I owe it to Louise. Damn fool shouldn't have left her that way." Faced with the second death of his old friend, my father sounded annoyed.

"No." Mrs. Kenseth would have to wait. "What you need to do is call the police."

He acted as if he hadn't heard me. "If we wait until after dark, we can—"

"We're not going to hide a body, Father." I could only imagine what he would say if I suggested such a scheme.

"Take him out of the back door to the car, and drive to—"

"I'm calling the police." He couldn't have killed his friend. His long-dead colleague. Could he?

"Don't you see? He was Foreign Office, like me. If he staged his disappearance, he must have been working on something so hush-hush he had to vanish. The fate of our nation could be at stake." My father began to assume his lecturing tone.

"With Hitler running mad all over Europe, everything puts Britain's future in jeopardy." How often had I heard that phrase lately? My tone was dry with sarcasm.

I heard a bang on the front door and then "Police!" as heavy footsteps sounded in the hallway. I flinched as a man stepped into the doorway. "Move away from the body, sir."

"Who are you?" I asked as my father stiffly heaved himself to his feet.

The man pulled out his warrant card. "Detective Inspector Jones. And you are?"

"Mrs. Olivia Denis. This is my father, Sir Ronald Harper. This is his house."

"And the dead man?" As he spoke, two constables entered the room. The younger one stood by the body and my father. The older one stood next to the inspector. The detective spoke a few words to him and the constable left, banging the front door behind him.

"John Kenseth. He's a long-dead corpse." I was still having trouble taking in the memory of my father kneeling over a murdered man. Especially a man who'd been dead for years.

"Don't try to be funny, miss."

My father walked over to us, absently wiping blood off his hands onto his handkerchief. "She's not, Inspector. This is John Kenseth. He was believed to have died over two years ago."

The detective looked closer at the dead man and scowled. "Why does his body look freshly killed?"

"Obviously he's been alive and in hiding," I said,

staring at Kenseth. Then I turned to the policeman. "Why are you here? We'd just found him like this. We hadn't had time to call yet."

"No? Well, someone did. Told us a man had been murdered at this address."

"Who called? The murderer?" Who had been in my father's house?

The detective glanced at the notebook in his hand. "A voice identified himself over the phone as Sir Ronald Harper. He said the body was in his drawing room."

"Nonsense. I didn't call." My father sounded annoyed rather than worried.

"How do you explain someone calling Scotland Yard and identifying himself as you? This person was correct about the presence of a murdered man."

"Well, it wasn't me. I'd just returned and found—him." My father now sounded both annoyed and upset.

"Is that your pipe, sir?"

My father looked over his shoulder. "No, that's Kenseth's."

Of course. The smoldering pipe was giving off the stink when I came in. I remembered the French, expensive, horrible-smelling pipe tobacco that Mr. Kenseth had used for years before what I now thought of as his first death.

"Where have you been, sir?"

"Am I going to be questioned in my own house as if I'm a criminal?" my father demanded.

Where had he been? He hadn't met me at the church as we'd planned. Before the situation got worse, I said, "Shall we go to the kitchen and talk while I make some tea?

I'd really not like to spend any more time looking at a dead body."

"That sounds like a very good idea, miss. Er...Mrs. Denis." Inspector Jones escorted us to the kitchen, where I put the kettle on.

The inspector and my father sat across from each other at the scarred kitchen table. The sturdy, plain wooden table had rested in the same spot as long as I could remember. Meals had been prepared, jams made, and pastry dough rolled out by the lorryload on a surface now scrubbed nearly white. This day it would be used for taking tea with policemen. I took a seat at the end closest to the stove with a view of the front hall and the doorway to the drawing room.

"Let's start with you, Mrs. Denis. Where had you been?"

"Church. St. Matthew's C of E around the corner. I walked here directly after the service." Which reminded me of my grievance when I had rushed over here, making me angry all over again.

"Can anyone confirm this?"

"I spoke to Mrs. Johnson before the service and Lady Gordon and Miss Winterbottom afterward." I glanced at my father. "They all wanted to know when they would receive invitations to my wedding."

My father winced.

Inspector Jones frowned as he watched us. "Why has what should be a joyous occasion led to a family argument?"

"We haven't set the date yet, making any discussion of

invitations premature," I told him.

"I don't know what you're waiting for. You two might as well be married. In my day..." my father said, warming up to a familiar topic.

The inspector interrupted. "Is this why the man was murdered? Was he to be the bridegroom?"

"Good grief, no," my father said. "When Kenseth died, well, when he was supposed to have died, he was married to Louise and Olivia was still married to Reggie."

"The late Mr. Denis," I said. I could tell my father was upset. He would never have made such a confusing explanation otherwise.

Jones frowned more deeply. "What happened to your husband?"

"He was murdered, but his murder was solved. And neither of us found that body. Meanwhile, I went to work at the *Daily Premier* and ever since then, my father has been trying to marry me off." I wiped his death away with one sweep of my hand. I felt my explanation cleared us both of any involvement in my poor late husband's killing.

The look on the inspector's face told me otherwise. He jotted a line in his notebook and said, "So you both knew this victim?"

"His name was John Kenseth, Inspector," my father said, sounding irritated. He hated having to repeat himself, and he'd already given Kenseth's name to the police inspector.

"Yes, we both knew him," I said.

"When did you last see him?"

"Just before he went on a sailing holiday. In the

summer of 1936," my father told him.

"He supposedly died on this sailing excursion?"

"Yes." My father sounded as though he might start grinding his teeth.

"He was thought lost in the Channel in a squall," I added. "The body was never recovered."

"Where has he been all this time?" the inspector asked.

"That's a very good question," my father replied.

At that moment, the front door banged open and men with heavy footsteps came in the front hall. Forensic officers wearing rumpled suits and carrying cases and cameras and notebooks walked into the drawing room.

"Suppose we start from the beginning," the inspector said. "What time did you arrive home?" he asked my father.

"Nearly noon."

"Nearly noon. We received the call about the murder at 11:55. Are you sure you still want to tell us you didn't make that call? Someone did."

"I didn't telephone you," my father said.

"Was anyone in the house when you returned home?"

"No."

"Does anyone else live here?" The detective glanced at me.

"I live alone," my father said, stuffiness growing in his tone.

"I have a flat north of Oxford Street," I told the policeman. "Toward Regent's Park."

"Did you hear a back door shut? A floorboard squeak? See someone in the garden?" The inspector seemed to be checking off boxes.

"No. I live alone. The house was empty when I arrived." I saw my father's shoulders droop and felt a momentary pang of sympathy for him.

"What did you do when you returned home?"

"I came in the front door. I was going to put the kettle on since I knew Olivia would soon be here, but the front drawing room door stood open. I looked inside, saw John on the floor, and then rushed in to see if I could do anything for him. I was too late."

"The front drawing room door. Is it always shut?"

"Of course."

"When did you arrive?" the inspector asked, focusing his gaze on me.

"I'd guess five or ten minutes after midday. I didn't look at my watch."

"What did you do when you came inside?"

"I called for my father. I saw the drawing room door was open and looked in."

"What did you see?"

"You know what I saw. Poor man." I was still feeling slightly sick thinking about it. I wished the water for the tea would boil.

"Where was your father?" The inspector kept pestering me with questions.

"Kneeling on the floor next to Mr. Kenseth."

"What was he doing?"

"Seeing if Mr. Kenseth was showing any signs of life."

"By his own admission, he'd had nearly fifteen minutes to find out if the murdered man had any signs of life. What was he doing, Mrs. Denis?"

I pictured the scene again. My father was kneeling on the floor. His bloody hands were near the knife. "He looked shocked. He looked as if he was praying."

The inspector kept questioning me, while my father continued to study the tabletop. "Had you ever seen the knife before you saw it sticking out of the victim's chest?"

"It's Serbian. My father bought it while he was on a mission for the Foreign Office."

"It's your father's?"

"Yes."

"Where is it normally kept?"

"In my father's study." I flinched as the kettle whistled.

The inspector rose and walked into the drawing room, from where I could hear low voices and see occasional flashes from a camera bulb light up the hallway.

I went to the stove and made tea. It wasn't until my father and I both had cups of tea warming our hands and no policemen had reentered the kitchen that I asked, "Who else was here?"

My father glared at me and took a sip of his tea.

Either he was lying and he'd seen someone or he was bothered that I didn't believe him.

CHAPTER TWO

"What do you plan to do?" I whispered. I didn't want to share my thoughts with the police.

"Speak to Louise. And General Alford," he murmured back.

We heard footsteps above us. Someone, presumably a policeman, was searching the house. I hoped he'd find the killer I suspected my father was protecting.

"You think he was working for Alford?" I had recently been involved in identifying the French assassin on behalf of the general. Alford seemed to be involved in every clandestine move Britain made against the Nazis.

"This reeks of someone's involvement." My father sounded bitter. Not the reaction I'd expect from someone who was a dyed-in-the-wool patriot.

"What's wrong?" I asked so only he could hear me.

I heard a floorboard creak outside the kitchen doorway as my father mumbled, "Later."

Inspector Jones came into the kitchen with another, older man. The older man walked up to my father, hand outstretched. "Sir Ronald? I'm Sir Malcolm Freemantle."

In that instant, my father rose with an awed look on his face. "Pleased to meet you, sir."

I looked the stranger over. Heavy-set, with silver-framed glasses, and dressed in an expensive suit. I pegged him as upper-echelon Whitehall.

"And this is Mr. Whittier." Sir Malcolm gestured toward the doorway, where a nondescript man of average height wearing nondescript clothes stood. "You need to come with us, sir."

I half rose from my seat. "Where are you taking my father?"

"This is nothing to concern yourself about, Mrs. Denis."

"Where are you taking my father?" I repeated, on my feet now with my arms crossed.

"There's nothing to fret about. He should be home in a day or two." Sir Malcolm's tone was dismissive. Patronizing. Really annoying.

"In a day or two? Where are you taking him?" At this point, I was keeping my voice level only by a great deal of effort.

Sir Malcolm said in a hard voice, "That is none of your business."

My father said, "It's all right, Olivia." With the nondescript Mr. Whittier on one side and the taller, bulkier Sir Malcolm on the other, my father was marched out of the house. I followed them as far as the front porch, where I watched all three climb into a large black saloon car. As soon as they were inside, the automobile sped away.

I went back inside and found Inspector Jones instructing one of the constables. "Where is the chief constable taking my father?"

"He's not the chief constable. He's not even with Scotland Yard."

"Then who is he?"

Jones shrugged. "He said he works for Whitehall."

"Are you certain that's who he works for?" I felt Sir Malcolm was the least trustworthy of men. Certainly the least accommodating.

"He had the proper credentials," the inspector said, staring at me.

I stared right back. "So does my father."

"Then they should get along well." The inspector went back to directing the policemen, leaving his ominous words hanging in the air. Get along? My father was his prisoner.

Nobody was willing to tell me anything, and Adam was off training with the British Army. How I wished I could telephone him. Adam would know how to reach my father. Even if he didn't, I'd be happy just to hear my fiancé's voice.

* * *

Once the body was removed, the police wrapped up their examination of the house and finally left me alone.

My first task was to search for my father's current leather-bound notebook where he kept addresses and phone numbers in a jumbled fashion along with reminders of appointments, invitations to parties, and notes about housekeeping arrangements for Mrs. Johnson. Once I found the notebook under a thick volume of maps on the desk, I sat in my father's swivel desk chair and began to read.

I found my birthdate on the same page as the phone

numbers for St. Agnes School for Young Ladies along with an Ealing butcher. It took me a while, but I finally found the phone number for General Alford. If anyone had been involved in hiding an ordinary bureaucrat for over two years, it would be General Alford.

I dialed his number and let it ring for over a minute. It was Sunday afternoon, and this was an office number. I was going to have to be patient to find out where they had taken my father.

Unfortunately, patience was never one of my best qualities.

Next I dialed a number I knew by heart. After two rings, it was answered by a maid who passed me to Sir Henry Benton, the publisher of the *Daily Premier*. "Livvy, how did you hear so quickly?"

"Hear what?" Had something else happened to my father?

"Esther's grandfather died."

"I'm sorry to hear that. Will the funeral be in Berlin?" Sir Henry's late wife was German and her parents still lived in Berlin. Since her family was Jewish, living in Berlin with Hitler in power seemed to be an oxymoron.

"Yes, and then we're going to want you to go to Berlin to help Esther's Aunt Ruth leave with Grandmother Neugard."

"I'm sorry, but I won't be able to go." I briefly told him what had happened to my father. "Can you find where this Sir Malcolm Freemantle has taken my father?"

"I'll put Colinswood on it. He can assign a reporter from the national news desk to find where they've taken your father and what's going on with this police investigation."

"Thank you." I felt relieved. Through tricks and bribery, there wasn't much Sir Henry's reporters missed.

"I'll see you tomorrow morning at the office. By then, your father may have been released."

"I hope so." The sooner he was home, the happier I'd be.

As Sir Henry hung up, I considered how much of a chance my father had of being released quickly. Not much of one if he was as stubborn as he usually was. I hoped Sir Henry's news reporters had good luck. And I would call General Alford in the morning.

* * *

The next morning, I dressed for traveling across London in a business suit, low-heeled pumps, and a rain-resistant coat and hat before I went to my job on the society and women's page desk at the *Daily Premier.* I didn't expect today to be ordinary.

An hour later, I received a summons from my "official" boss, Miss Westcott, to go to the top floor and see Sir Henry. "We'll be losing your services so soon?" she said drily.

"I don't know," I replied. Miss Westcott had been taken into Sir Henry's confidence about my secret assignments after he found he could no longer hide my activities from her. She had let me know she wasn't pleased about sharing my services. "Let's hope not."

I went upstairs and was waved into Sir Henry's office. I took a seat across his mammoth desk from him as he finished a telephone call. When he hung up, I said, "You wanted to see me, sir?"

"I thought I had the best news hounds in London. I was wrong. No one has been able to find out a thing about your father or where he's been taken."

"What about Sir Malcolm Freemantle?"

"Claims to know nothing about your father or any murder." Sir Henry leaned forward slightly. "What is this? Ordinarily, you're fighting with your father."

"These aren't ordinary circumstances. He's the only relative I have left." I stared at Sir Henry. "I won't have some mystery man take my father away for a crime he didn't commit."

I had another thought. "Has anyone spoken to Detective Inspector Jones?" He was from Scotland Yard. While the police hadn't taken my father away, he might know if charges were pending or who might have imprisoned my father.

"Now that's interesting." Sir Henry picked up a typed sheet of the poor-quality paper that we used for writing our stories, glanced over it, and then looked at me. "Inspector Jones did indeed investigate a stabbing death in Ealing yesterday. The victim's name was Gaspard Eliot—"

"What?" My shriek was probably heard downstairs.

"A French citizen who was found dead inside a home. The owner is assisting in their inquiries."

"No name of the owner?"

"No."

Thank goodness for that. My father would be so embarrassed if his name appeared in a crime report. Being suspected of murder by the police was not as big a social *faux pas* in my father's eyes as appearing in the news section of the newspaper. I leaned back in my chair and shook my head, hoping it would make Sir Henry's information make sense.

"Did anyone mention John Kenseth?" I asked.

"Yes. Inspector Jones said John Kenseth died in a boating accident in 1936. He said he had heard that story, and while there is a vague similarity in appearance, Kenseth and Eliot are two different people. No relationship between the two has been found."

"Did anyone mention Sir Malcolm Freemantle to him?"

"He said he'd never heard of the man."

"He spoke to the man yesterday in my father's house. Has anyone talked to Mrs. Kenseth?"

"No. One of my reporters went to her house, but no one answered the door."

I rose. "Do you mind if I do some investigating of my own?"

"Not at all. We have plenty of guesses as to what's going on, but no facts. Good luck."

I went downstairs, grabbed my coat and gloves, pinned on my hat, and hurried away from our office before Miss Westcott saw me and could register her displeasure. I took the Underground north into the suburbs to where I knew Louise Kenseth lived.

She and John had no children and their semi-detached house had always seemed overly large to me for two people to rattle around in. I wondered why Louise had stayed there. My father visited her once or twice a year after John died, but I hadn't been there since shortly after the funeral.

I walked past a tiny, unruly garden and knocked on the door, which needed a coat of paint. No sound made its way to me on the steps and I didn't see any of the lace curtains twitch. As I was about to give up, the door opened a crack. "Yes?" an elderly voice said.

"I'm looking for Mrs. Kenseth. Her husband was a friend of my father's."

"Louise," the old female voice called.

Brisk steps echoed on bare wooden floors and a moment later Louise Kenseth faced me through the crack in the door.

I put on a big smile. "Mrs. Kenseth, I'm Livvy Denis. It used to be Livvy Harper."

"I know who you are." Her tone was not friendly.

No sense dragging this out. "My father thought he saw your husband yesterday."

"Nonsense. My husband is dead."

"John?" the old woman said. "John?"

"No, Mother. It was a mistake. A silly mistake." Louise sounded weary.

"Is this your mother? I don't believe we've met. Hello, ma'am." I tried to sound both cheery and polite.

"Hello," the old woman said with rising hope. "Are you Dotty?"

"No, ma'am, I'm Livvy."

"Oh." I could hear the hope fade in her voice.

I looked at Louise Kenseth. "Who's Dotty?"

"My sister. You won't see her around here when

there's any work to be done." Bitterness poured out of her.

"Do they live with you?" I asked, trying to sound sympathetic.

"Mother does. Not Dotty. Not Miss High and Mighty."

"Did my father try to help you with your mother?" I don't know why I asked. It didn't sound like something my father would do.

I was shocked when she immediately responded. "She loves him. Thinks he's John. He comes around every month or two to keep up the pretense." Her expression softened. "He helps."

"Some men from Whitehall took my father away after he saw John, and I don't know where. I was hoping you might know something about where your husband has been and who he's been working for."

"John is dead. I get a pension once a month from Whitehall that keeps us fed and clothed and not much else. Otherwise, I have nothing to do with that lot anymore. I don't know where your father might be and I don't want to know. And I certainly don't know why anyone would think John is still alive."

I pressed her, wondering if her husband would have gone into hiding and not told her. "Do you know where John's been the last two years?"

"At the bottom of the Channel. Come on, Mother." With a quick movement, she shut the door in my face.

I refused to be put off. I walked to the high street and found a telephone box. Putting in my coins, I called the familiar War Office number.

In a minute, they put me through to General Alford.

"Mrs. Denis. What can I do for you?"

"You can tell me where they've put my father."

"Sir Ronald?" He sounded genuinely surprised. "What happened?"

"John Kenseth came back to life long enough to show up in my father's drawing room, where he was found stabbed to death."

There was a slight pause. "Are you sure it was he?"

"Yes. So was my father. A Sir Malcolm Freemantle took my father away and no one can tell me where he's gone."

"Freemantle? Well, there's your problem." General Alford spoke as if the name itself explained everything.

I didn't like the way our conversation was going. "What do you mean?"

"We can't talk on the telephone," came out in a rush, but also as an order.

"I'll be right over," I told him before I hung up the receiver.

CHAPTER THREE

"How could Sir Malcolm Freemantle be the problem?" When I was finally shown into his office, I looked at General Alford, hoping he'd clear up my confusion.

He stared at me across the tidy stacks of paper on his desk, his back straight, dressed in his pristine uniform. "He's a law unto himself. Probably because he takes his work to heart."

"What work? And what has he done with my father?"

He held up one hand. "Why don't you leave it with me, Mrs. Denis? Government types can be a bit reticent with civilians. I'll make a few calls and find out what is going on."

He rose from his seat and I had no choice but to do the same. And leave my gloves on my chair.

He hit a button on his intercom and a uniformed officer opened the door to escort me out. I thanked the general, shook his hand, and walked out of the office. The officer shut the door and moved in front of me to guide me out.

I followed him for three steps before I said, "Oh, dear. My gloves." I turned and rushed back in before the officer could stop me.

General Alford was saying, "Get me Section C," into the telephone. He looked up and glared at me as he hung up the phone.

I walked over and picked up the gloves on the chair. "Sorry. I forgot these. What is Section C?"

"Forget you ever heard that, Mrs. Denis. Official secrets."

I'd heard my father say that. I suspected it was a holdover from the Great War. The Official Secrets Act meant you couldn't divulge government information or you would risk imprisonment.

I had just discovered one of those things. But what was Section C? I nodded and said, "Please find my father."

By then the officer had a grip on my upper arm and forced me out of the building. I moved at a near run to keep up with his longer strides, my heels clicking on the tiled hallways.

I went to the *Daily Premier* building and headed straight up to Sir Henry's office, where his secretary showed me in. "Any luck?" he asked.

"Sir Malcolm Freemantle is definitely a high-ranking government employee. There's been no word on my father."

Sir Henry frowned. "I'm sorry."

I studied him for a moment. "Can we go about this another way? Could you have someone look into Gaspard Eliot?"

"The stabbing victim in Ealing?" Sir Henry looked puzzled.

"Yes. Whoever looks into him only needs to go back

two years. I'm sure there's nothing before then. I suspect this was an alias John Kenseth used while he was presumed dead."

"What do you expect for them to discover?"

I gave him a smile. "If we find out what John Kenseth has been doing the last two years using the Gaspard Eliot alias, maybe we can find out who killed him and thereby gain my father's release."

Sir Henry sent me back to work, assuring me he'd have someone look into Kenseth's alias.

I found it hard to concentrate. Miss Westcott was kind enough to take me off posted notices and send me to cover rehearsals for a Remembrance Day concert featuring a women's college choir. She sent Jane Seville with me to take photographs, muttering, "One of you had better keep the other out of trouble."

Jane raised her eyebrows before she handed me some of her camera cases.

Once we were out of the building, I told her about the body and my father's disappearance.

"Have you checked Brixton Prison?" she asked as we climbed into a taxi.

"Why?"

"That's where they send the remand prisoners." She blushed before she added, "I have an uncle who ends up there too often."

Finally. A useful suggestion. My father could be on remand awaiting trial and I wouldn't know. "How would I do that?"

"The easiest way would be to call the prison office and

ask if anyone by your father's name is being held there on remand. They hold all the male prisoners from all over London at Brixton until their trial." Jane had been giving me pointers since I began working with her over a year before, and they'd all been helpful.

"Thank you. I'll call as soon as we finish at the women's college."

Working fast, we finished everything we needed to do and heard one of the choir's songs before we raced back to the *Daily Premier*. Jane went to develop her film and I went up to the office of Mr. Colinswood, the head of the national news desk.

As usual, a cigarette burned in his overflowing ashtray and the phone receiver was cradled between ear and shoulder while he typed. I waited until he was off the telephone and had picked up his cigarette.

"Mrs. Denis. What can I do for you?"

"I need a telephone book and a telephone."

"Calling anywhere special?" Colinswood had known about my assignments for Sir Henry since the beginning.

"Brixton Prison remand section."

"I heard about your father. I'm sorry. We already tried Brixton in our search. No luck."

My shoulders drooped. "You're certain?"

"Yes. And I have one of my best reporters chasing down Gaspard Eliot as we speak."

"Thank you." Giving a top-notch reporter this assignment was generous, since there would probably not be anything they'd be allowed to print in the *Daily Premier*. I lowered myself into a chair without invitation. "If they didn't take him to Brixton on remand, where could they have taken him?"

He stubbed out his cigarette and ran a hand through his thinning sandy hair. "You're certain this was the government and not some thugs?"

"Yes. I verified Sir Malcolm Freemantle works for His Majesty. I saw him and another man named Whittier take my father away."

"What did they take him away in?"

"A big black car. It looked very official." Another reason I'd been certain from the beginning that my father hadn't been taken away by thugs.

"Not a police car?"

"And not by policemen." I held Mr. Colinswood's gaze.

"No reason to believe he'd be held in Brixton, then." Colinswood lit another cigarette. The air was oppressive with smoke. "There are rumors..."

When he paused, I said, "Rumors of what?"

"An old army base from the Great War. Used now for detention."

"Who are they detaining?" I nearly shouted, frantic that my father was in a crowded cell, seemingly forgotten by the world.

"Spies. Traitors. Enemy agents the government wants to turn. This is all rumor. If it does exist, it might explain what Freemantle is up to and where your father is being held."

There was something in the way Mr. Colinswood spoke that made me ask, "You've heard of Freemantle before?"

"One of my eager young reporters was working on a piece about him. Strictly on his own time, to be considered if it amounted to anything."

"Was? What happened?"

"He disappeared."

Something cold ran down my back. "Like my father?"

"He left one day after work and never returned."

"Did you look for him?"

"Of course. We spoke to Freemantle, too. Nothing. No one saw anything. Heard anything. Knew anything. Nothing."

"What did his family say?" They must have been as outraged as I was.

"His parents are dead. He's an only child. Never married. He lived in a boardinghouse where he had several acquaintances, but no one worried when he didn't return one night."

"Who took his possessions?" I hoped no one threw them out.

"The landlady boxed them up and is storing them in her basement until it is decided whether he is alive or dead." Mr. Colinswood looked gloomy. "He was a good, young journalist. I miss him."

"How long has he been missing?"

"More than two months."

I shook my head. "What is his name?"

"Michael Littleshaw."

"Well, when I find my father, maybe I'll find your reporter, too. Can you let me know as soon as you find out anything about Gaspard Eliot?"

He nodded. "Of course. It shouldn't take too long to find out the basics." He reached across the desk and patted my hand. "Don't worry, Olivia. With all of us working on it, we'll find your father."

I smiled at him. "Thank you. In the meantime, I'll be down at my desk. Please, give me a ring when you uncover something." At the moment, I was out of ideas.

I went back to work writing up my notes on the choral practice for Remembrance Day. When I turned it in, Miss Westcott looked surprised. She had to study it closely to find any mistakes in my copy.

It wasn't until late in the day that I was called to the telephone. I expected to hear from Mr. Colinswood and was momentarily disappointed to hear the voice of Sir Henry's daughter, Esther Benton Powell.

She heard the frustration in my tone and asked if she'd called at a bad time.

"No. It's just that I was hoping it was word from my father. Or about my father. And here you've just lost your grandfather and I haven't even called with condolences. Please accept my apology." I was so wrapped up in my own worries I hadn't thought of Esther, and that made me feel worse.

"Livvy, don't worry about it. My grandfather is at peace. Your father is missing and just now that's more important. Can I do anything?"

"I don't know if any of us can do a thing. He's not in police custody. Someone else has him."

"That's terrible. Come to dinner tonight at my father's. We'll put our heads together and see what we can think of."

"I've already taken up enough of Sir Henry's time and patience over this—this insanity. He'd probably get mad at you for suggesting it."

I could hear Esther smiling over the phone. "Since James is out of town, Father suggested it."

"And how is his grandchild?" I said the last two words the way Sir Henry said them. He made it sound as if Esther and James had nothing to do with the baby. It was amusing to see a rough and tumble Captain of Industry so besotted with a baby who hadn't even arrived yet.

"Kicking. Doing somersaults. Keeping me up at all hours of the night."

"Do you want the bother of meeting me and your father when you could be resting at home with your feet up?" Much as I wanted to see her, Esther sounded uncomfortable.

"I'm bored silly." Her annoyance sounded through the wires.

"Then your father and I will entertain you with tales to keep you and the baby up all night."

A glare from Miss Westcott quickly ended our conversation.

A few minutes later, a caller again asked for me. Miss Westcott scowled as I rose and walked to the telephone.

"We have some details on Gaspard Eliot, including his address outside Etretat, France," Mr. Colinswood told me.

"Where is that?"

"Just up the coast from Le Havre. Etretat is a small port on the Channel."

"That's good to know." And handy, since I wanted to investigate this myself.

"There's more," Mr. Colinswood told me.

* * *

After work, I went home and looked through the post. Nothing from my fiancé, Adam. Nothing from my father. Nothing else seemed important. I dressed for dinner in a long-sleeved green gown with a long graceful skirt and a plain, scoop-neck style that screamed "matron."

I alighted from a taxi in front of Sir Henry's home at eight on the dot. When I rang the bell, a maid answered the door.

She didn't look familiar, but her accent was German. I knew immediately she had to be one of the Jewish refugees being aided by the committee Sir Henry and Esther belonged to. Domestic service was one of the few positions open to the refugees.

When I gave my name, she took my coat and then led me to Sir Henry's study. Once inside the paneled, book-lined room, I hugged Esther, noticing her stomach had grown in the week since I last saw her.

Sir Henry handed me a glass of sherry and said, "Please sit down. I saw Colinswood in passing. He said he'd filled you in on Gaspard Eliot, whom we all suspect was John Kenseth."

"I want to take some time off and go to Etretat and see where John Kenseth has been living for the past two years. See what he's been doing. I hope I can find a clue that will help find my father."

He shook his head sadly. "I can't do that. I need you

here so I can send you to Berlin to help Ruth and Mrs. Neugard leave."

"Will his widow be willing to leave now that Mr. Neugard is dead? She was determined to stay in Berlin when I met her."

"He was the one with the strong will and the determination not to leave his home in Berlin. Ruth is already working on her, and Esther is telling her grandmother she wants her here for the birth of her great-grandchild."

All I could think was *God help Esther's husband.* James Powell was a patient man, but between Esther's German-Jewish family on one side and Sir Henry, a bullheaded, self-made man from Newcastle on the other, James was liable to be pushed aside when his first child arrived.

"The rest of the family is here now," I said. "I don't think Ruth will have too much trouble convincing her mother to come to England. Do you want me to help them get their valuables out of Germany?"

"Yes."

I sat up straighter in my chair and put on my sternest face. "But they don't need me to exit Berlin, while my father isn't free to go to Etretat. I'll resign if I have to, but I must go there now. It'll only take a couple of days."

"No."

His firmness surprised me. "I won't be gone long, and I can be easily reached so I can head straight to Berlin from Paris."

He stood up and glared at me. "No. You wouldn't have known where Kenseth was hiding if my reporters hadn't told you."

I rose as well, puzzled by his refusal and determined to discover what I could learn in France. With or without Sir Henry's blessing. "Why are you so against this? I need to follow in John Kenseth's footsteps to learn about his double life. I need to free my father."

CHAPTER FOUR

How could Sir Henry be so unreasonable? I set down my sherry glass, ready to walk out and not come back. I could drop whatever I was doing in Etretat to help Esther's aunt and grandmother. Being in London wouldn't get me to Berlin any faster, and I saw no need to rush. How could Sir Henry regard traveling to John Kenseth's hiding place as a difficulty?

Meanwhile, I had a big problem. I needed the information from Etretat to help my father.

Esther sprang to her feet with surprising grace, considering her condition. "Livvy, wait. We need to sit down calmly and talk about this."

"There's nothing to discuss," her father said. "We've had one man killed and two more disappear chasing after whatever John Kenseth has been doing for the past two years. I don't want to lose Livvy, too."

I looked into his eyes and saw fear. I was too angry, too determined, too headstrong to be frightened, but I could accept a need to be cautious. And then I realized what he said. "Two men disappear? There was someone besides my father?"

"One of our reporters," Sir Henry grumbled. "I don't

want you to be the third missing person."

And then I had what I considered to be a brilliant idea. "If I could get Adam to go with me to Etretat, would you relent?"

"I would feel better if there were two of you going," he admitted.

"Is that why you told me to stay in London?"

Sir Henry nodded as he slumped into the chair. "I'd never forgive myself if you disappeared, and Esther would blame me forever. Do you want me to see if I can find someone to grant a spot of leave for Captain Redmond?"

"I'd love it." I could barely keep from jumping for joy. I hadn't seen my fiancé, Captain Adam Redmond, in what felt like ages, and I didn't know when I might see him again. He was off with the army doing training exercises. What kind of training the army was doing, with Hitler changing the boundaries of Europe, I didn't want to imagine.

"Let me see if I can arrange a few days' leave for him. There must be some way to make his trip to France useful for the army." Sir Henry smiled. "Now, shall we go in to dinner?"

* * *

The next two days were spent waiting. There was no word from or about my father. When I stopped by and let myself in, the interior of his house hadn't been disturbed. I had told Mrs. Johnson my father had been called away for a few days so there was no need to clean until he called her. The dust was slowly covering every surface.

Work at the newspaper was boring for a change. News from overseas was no more ominous than usual. The weather was wet, chilly, and gloomy. Autumn was here and winter was threatening. I was ready to give up and tell Sir Henry I quit and that I'd go to Etretat alone. Finally, he phoned down to the women's features desk.

"Livvy, I've had some luck getting your young man leave, but only until Monday. Go straight home after work tonight and wait for him. We'll expect you back here and at work on Monday."

"Thank you. That's the first good news since my father vanished."

"Do what you have to do, but Livvy, please be careful." He cleared his throat and added, "I don't want you disappearing, too."

His unexpected concern nearly moved me to tears. I could barely get out, "I won't."

After that, the hands of the clock on the wall barely moved. Finally, the other women began to take out handbags and touch up their lipstick. I considered it my signal to jump up, pin on my hat, pull on my coat and gloves, grab my umbrella, and dash out of the door.

Out of the corner of my eye, I saw Miss Westcott shaking her head.

I stopped at the butcher's and the grocer's, wishing our plans were firm enough that we could make reservations to go out for dinner. In the morning we'd be off for France, and who knew what we'd face.

Rushing home, I found Adam hadn't arrived yet. I picked up the flat, brushed my hair, and packed for the trip to Etretat. When I thought it time, I started the chops. I flipped through magazines, filed my nails, and kept glaring at the clock on the mantle. After a while, frustrated by Adam's continued absence, I began to pace.

Adam arrived about nine o'clock, looking travel-weary and incredibly handsome in a scruffy way. Claiming he was ravenous, he dropped his suitcase off in my guest room. After a fond greeting, we eventually went to the dining room. It wasn't until we were seated with a bottle of red wine, overcooked chops, undercooked greens, and rolls, that he asked, "What is this mysterious assignment?"

"My father found one of his old friends dead in his drawing room on Sunday. The friend supposedly died in a sailing accident two years ago." I raised my eyebrows. "The police claim the dead man was really a Frenchman named Gaspard Eliot who lived in Etretat. We're going to Etretat to find out what my father's friend was doing there."

"Why doesn't your father do this?" Adam asked, smearing butter on a roll.

"He's been taken off by a man named Sir Malcolm Freemantle and no one knows where. He hasn't been heard from since."

"Who is this Freemantle? Does he work for Scotland Yard?"

I was glad no one was around to hear what I was going to say. Still, I whispered, "Have you ever heard of Section C?"

Adam sat back. "No, Livvy. Leave it alone."

I frowned at him. "Why?"

"I can't tell you. Official secrets and all that."

How often had I heard the phrase *official secrets?* "All right. I think that's who Freemantle works for, so he must have my father in some secret prison. But that doesn't explain a murdered man on the drawing room floor. We're going to Etretat in the morning and I'm going to look for this dead man's home."

"So you find this man's house. Then what?" Adam asked.

"We'll decide that when we find it."

Several bites later, Adam slowed down his eating enough to say, "This may be a short trip. If there's anything funny going on, whoever is in charge will have removed anything incriminating."

I shrugged. "We won't know until we get there."

"You're just planning to go there, find his house, and knock on the door?" Adam sounded unconvinced.

I knew he was more cautious and more of a planner than I was. "Yes. Unless I see something more promising on the way there."

* * *

The next morning, dressed as ramblers and carrying rucksacks, we caught the early train from Waterloo Station to Portsmouth. All we had time for was a cup of coffee. That turned out for the best, since the crossing from Portsmouth to Le Havre was rough, even for early November.

We reached Le Havre in early afternoon, the sunlight failing to warm the chilly breeze off the Channel. Walking to the city center while serenaded by seagulls, we found a café where we had lunch and obtained directions to Etretat. The simplest way, we found, was to ride the train bound for Dieppe, get off at a station near Etretat, and walk.

It was still light out when we reached Etretat. It consisted of a pretty village hugging the chalk cliffs and a small harbor full of fishing boats. We found a guesthouse overlooking the water and went in to book a room. The landlady gazed at the absence of rings on our fingers, stuck out her hand, palm up, and informed us we needed to register separately for single rooms. And we needed to pay in advance.

Once installed, we strolled down the street toward some cozy restaurants. Adam muttered, "In the summer when she has more business, that landlady would have thought nothing of renting us a double, being certain to have customers for all her rooms."

I suspected he was right.

"Of course, nothing says we have to stay separated all night," he said as he wiggled his eyebrows, making me laugh.

We went into a bistro and were seated at a table in the front. The fresh seafood was good and plentiful, there was no traveling planned for the morning, and Adam was soon in a better mood.

Since we spoke to each other in English, the staff kept their distance from crazy tourists visiting in the off season. As we were readying to leave, the waiter hesitantly asked in French if we'd ever been there before.

"No," I answered in fluent French, "but I know someone who lives here. Gaspard Eliot."

"Oh, no. You're too late, mademoiselle." His face sagged in sorrow.

"Too late? Why?"

"Gaspard died in London last weekend."

"What? Oh, no. Dead? That is so sad. And to die away from this beautiful place that he loved." I hoped I hadn't overplayed my fake surprise.

He nodded. "Elise is devastated."

"I would imagine so." Who was Elise? I didn't want to make a mistake now. "How do I find the house? I want to pay my respects."

"I don't know if Elise will be there."

"We'll leave her a note if she's not."

"Go up to the top of the cliff and follow the track to the left until you come to a hardwood grove. The cottage is there."

I nodded.

It was full dark on the narrow street outside when we left the bistro. We made plans to go up to Kenseth's house just after dawn to look over the area. And hopefully gain entrance to search the house.

After a night on a lumpy mattress, I met Adam for coffee and croissants. Then, wearing sturdy boots and thick socks, we hiked up the steep hill and listened to the cry of sea birds as they circled overhead in the wind. We found a track that wandered off to the left. It soon was lost in a pasture, and there were no cottages in sight.

We backtracked and went farther along the road to another track. Adam grumbled when I started down that farm lane, but he followed me. This track went farther than the other had between fenced pastures of dry, autumn grasses and bare, gnarled trees.

The wind was cold and no longer carried the tang of salt from the Channel. There wasn't a person around to give us directions. I was about to quit when the track dipped down behind a rise where the wind was no longer fierce. In the distance, I could see where next to a woodland there was a one-story stone cottage with an attic.

Adam stopped grumbling and started taking longer strides, making me hurry to keep up with him. We were still fifty feet away from the cottage when he stopped and said, "Look up."

I tried to make out what I was seeing in the branches. "What is it? A vine?" It didn't look quite like one I'd seen before.

"A large antenna. The kind they use for shortwave."

"Well, we now know Monsieur Eliot was a shortwave radio enthusiast."

Adam walked forward, past the cottage and into the woods. The antenna was close to the house and rose a little above the tops of the trees. Even with the leaves off the trees, the silvery wire was hard to spot.

Using my boot to shove aside the unraked leaves, I found a cable that ran from the antenna, down a tree, and across a short distance to the cottage.

Adam returned and gestured toward the front door with his head. "Shall we?"

He didn't need to ask me twice. My goal had always been the cottage. If Adam hadn't spotted it, I would have missed the antenna. I walked up and knocked on the dark-stained door, relieved that I didn't see any smoke coming from the chimney.

I waited on the single step, hoping no one would open the door while Adam walked around the side of the cottage.

When no one answered, I knocked a second time, and a third. As much as I wished to discover what Elise could tell me, I wanted to explore the house on my own. I was looking for a way to break in when the door opened.

I nearly fell off the step.

Adam stood in the doorway. "The back door was unlocked. No one is home."

It took me a moment to slow my heartbeat and find my voice. "You scared the life out of me."

He bared his teeth in a playfully fierce smile and stepped back into the house. I followed, shutting the front door behind me.

The old cottage had exposed beams and white plaster walls. The ground floor consisted of a small living room, a kitchen crowded by a scarred, solidly built table and chairs made by a farmer long ago, and a bedroom with a double bed covered by a colorful quilt. A fireplace between the drawing room and kitchen, cold and swept, was the only heat source.

I sniffed the air, but the only smell was the lingering odor of a horrible French pipe tobacco, a familiar stench. A brand favored by John Kenseth for all the years I knew him.

We walked up the steep, narrow stairs to the upper story tucked under the eaves. A large shortwave radio sat on a sturdy table like the one in the kitchen. Stacks of papers with notes surrounded the machine, and a bookcase nearby held maps and charts and more stacks of papers. I started to look over the papers and found sketches and maps drawn in a familiar hand. John Kenseth's.

Just inside the window facing the sea was a large telescope. An oil lamp sat behind the only chair on a small table all its own.

An oil lamp. Then how…

As if Adam read my mind, he said, "There's a small generator out back. The only thing it seems to run is the radio. A tidy, compact system. Was John Kenseth mechanically inclined?"

I ran my mind over the memories of a man I'd known since childhood but hadn't really thought about. "Yes, I suppose he was."

"And being a sailor, he'd have been able to read these charts." Adam peered through the telescope. "Great view of the ships in the Channel. Come and look."

I peered into the telescope, but all I focused on was the white cliffs across the Channel. Britain. Home. Where my father was missing.

Then I realized some of the papers spread out on the table were maritime charts, but I couldn't tell exactly which part of the Channel they mapped.

Adam looked over the papers I'd spread on the table and said, "He had a lot of artistic talent, too. Look at these maps he drew."

"He used to draw silly things that made me laugh. Since I liked to draw, too, I recognized how much talent he had. My father shrugged off his drawings, and mine, as foolish."

At that moment, we heard someone come in the front door. Adam put a finger to his lips. I shifted my weight and a board squeaked, giving us away. Light footsteps ran up the stairs. "Gaspard? Is it really you?"

CHAPTER FIVE

A woman with curly, dark hair stared at us from near the top step. She was petite with an elfin face, although I'd put her age at closer to forty than thirty.

"No, madame, we are not. Gaspard, or John Kenseth as I knew him, is dead," I answered in French.

She lowered her head and nodded. "They told me, but I didn't believe it. Gaspard was so clever. I thought perhaps he'd escaped again."

"Again?" What had Kenseth been doing?

"A woman came looking for him two weeks ago. She had a gun." She shuddered. "Her shots must have missed. Gaspard disappeared for a week, as did the woman. I was very worried, but he returned without a scratch on him."

"Were you a witness to the shooting?" Adam sounded amazed.

"Yes. He'd dropped something and as he bent to pick it up, the shot went over him. He ran into the back garden. There were two more shots outside."

"Did you see this woman?" I asked.

"For an instant. She was standing outside and then she ran. Dark hair, in her thirties or forties. I thought it might be his wife."

"You know he had a wife?" I asked.

"He mentioned her once. I did not care. I loved him." There was defiance in her tone.

"Your description doesn't match his wife." Louise was a little older. And her coloring was washed out. Besides, Kenseth would have made sure she didn't know where he was.

"Two days after Gaspard returned, we saw her again. The next day, Gaspard left. He said he'd seen her that morning. She hasn't been in Etretat since then."

"So, this mysterious dark-haired woman has been here looking for him twice?"

"*Oui.*"

"Did he say why he thought she was there?"

She shook her head. "Have you come for his radio?"

"No. Who was he calling on the radio?" Adam asked, a puzzled look on his face.

"No one. He only listened."

It was unusual to only listen in on shortwave communications. What was he up to? "Why would you think we have come for the radio?" I walked slowly toward her, not wanting to frighten her into not answering.

"It is expensive. And I do not think it belonged to Gaspard. He said it was his boss's."

"Who was he working for?" Adam asked her in halting French.

"That he would not say."

"How did you meet?" I asked. "And why are you not surprised that I knew him by another name?"

"Come downstairs. We will have a glass of wine and I

will tell you."

We followed her down the narrow stairs and into the kitchen. She opened a bottle and pulled out three mismatched glasses. We toasted Gaspard with the rich red liquid and then she looked across the table at us.

"My name is Elise Telfor."

We introduced ourselves.

"We met when I was on the dock buying fish when he came ashore from a local fishing boat. He looked half-drowned and was wrapped in a blanket lent to him by the captain. I'd recently lost my husband and his clothes fit Gaspard. I needed help with my shop, and he went to work for me. Things were nice for a while." She fell silent, smiling.

"What happened?" I asked quietly, not wanting to break the spell.

"Two Englishmen came into my shop one day and walked up to Gaspard. He left with them, but he looked unwilling. Frightened. They walked out of the shop and up the street past the tops of the cliffs. I watched them. Gaspard returned an hour later, alone and in a bad mood. He kept saying, 'I didn't think they'd find me.'"

Adam and I glanced at each other. Did this have to do with Whitehall, or did Kenseth owe someone money? Did he steal something, or did he get involved with another man's wife?

"What happened next?" I asked.

"The men came back three days later and Gaspard left with them again. This time, he appeared determined. Angry. That evening, he met me at the shop and walked me up on the cliffs to this cottage. He took me upstairs and showed me the telescope and the radio and made me promise never to tell anyone. Not about what was up there or the two men."

"Gaspard is dead. Murdered. It's time you broke the promise you made," Adam told her.

She crossed her arms over her chest as if protecting herself and shook her head. "This was his home. He moved in here, but he still worked for me."

I reached out and patted her arm as I spoke quietly. "Did he tell you his real name?"

"No, but I knew then he was not Gaspard Eliot. I knew from the beginning he was not a Frenchman."

"My father and I had known him for many years. Before he died the first time," I told her. "And I was there when his body was discovered at my father's house."

"The first time?" She stuttered over the words.

"We'd believed he'd died in 1936 in a sailing accident. Instead, he came here. To you." I gave her an encouraging smile.

"What did the two men who met Kenseth look like?" Adam said.

"I never really noticed the younger man, because the older man was obviously in charge. The older man was tall, heavy-set, and gray haired. He wore glasses with silver frames. The suit he wore was very well tailored. The younger man was slightly shorter and thin." She shrugged. "Ordinary."

Adam glanced at me and I nodded once. The description sounded like the two men who took my father away.

Sir Malcolm Freemantle and Mr. Whittier.

"Did those men ever come back here again?"

She shook her head. "But they sent him letters every month. Letters with money."

That made sense if Kenseth was still working for Whitehall. I watched her carefully as I asked, "Why did Gaspard go to England?"

"He got all excited about something he heard on the radio. He said he couldn't trust this to the post, he had to deliver this news in person. He told me to be very careful. He would return in a day or two. If he didn't, then he wouldn't be coming back. He'd be dead."

"So, you weren't surprised when you learned Gaspard was dead?"

She poured herself another glass of wine. "It has been five days since the police came to my shop with the news. I was running out of hope."

She must have really loved him. It was written on her face. "Did he say whom he would see, or where he was going?"

"No. Not really. I asked him what he would do if things became dangerous. He said he had a friend who had a house where he could hide. Sir Ronald Harper."

I tried to take a gulp of wine and choked on it. Adam thumped me on the back while Elise found me a towel.

"Does this name mean something to you?" she asked.

"Sir Ronald Harper is my father. Gaspard was killed in his drawing room. My father came back home and found him murdered. And then I came in and found them both."

She reached out and grabbed my hand. "Did he suffer?"

I shook my head.

"What happened? The police only told me he was killed in London."

"He was stabbed once in the chest. He would have died immediately," Adam said when I couldn't force the words past the lump in my throat. When I glanced at him, he added in English, "I read the autopsy report."

General Alford was generous to Adam with the information he was given, which would have annoyed me if it weren't so useful.

Reports... That made me wonder. "How did Gaspard normally report in?"

"By post."

"Did you ever see who he addressed the envelopes to?"

"Yes. He had me post the letters for him on occasion. I copied the address down. It's at my shop."

We left the cottage and walked with Elise to her small, crowded shop full of fishing gear and water-resistant clothing. She pulled out a scrap of paper with the name John Smith and the address of a third-floor flat on a central London street.

"May I take this?" I asked.

"*Oui.* I hope it leads you to the man who killed Gaspard."

We checked out of the guesthouse immediately and traveled back to London. The Channel crossing was rougher than before and, in the dark, I was too frightened to speak. It was so late when we returned that we skipped calling on this John Smith or stopping for dinner but instead went straight to my flat.

The next morning, Adam reminded me, was Saturday, and the office I wanted might not be open. He suggested a leisurely breakfast while we considered our options. I agreed immediately.

Before I started cooking, I called my father's house, hoping against hope that he'd returned and would answer the telephone. Eventually, I gave up after the twentieth ring.

Over a cooked breakfast, I argued we should go to the address and see what there was to be found. It might be an accommodation address and we'd need to question someone to find out who picked up the post for John Smith.

Adam wolfed down half his breakfast before he slowed down enough to say, "I'm sorry. What did you say? An accommodation address?"

"Possibly. I can't believe after someone, Sir Malcolm maybe, had him listening to ship traffic, he would give him his address. What if this information fell into the wrong hands? An address where he could retrieve his post would be safer and more anonymous. Finish your breakfast and then we'll go there."

He didn't need me to tell him twice.

"Don't they feed you?" I asked. "What do you eat when you're away?"

"Nothing you'd want to eat. The coffee's foul, but at least it's hot," he told me when he came up for air again.

We finished our meal and headed toward Whitehall.

The address was on a side street between the palace and Westminster Abbey. When we walked by the building, it looked like a typical block of flats built while Victoria was on the throne. The stonework was grimy with decades of coal fire soot.

When we approached from across the street, Adam stopped me with a hand on my shoulder. I turned to look at him.

"We won't get past the front door."

"What do you mean?"

Adam gestured with a tiny movement of his head. "See the man leaving? He's in uniform. No one wears a uniform on weekends unless they're on duty or traveling for an assignment."

"You think he's a guard for some general in the building."

"No. I'd heard rumors of His Majesty's government taking over a building around here and using it for overflow offices for clandestine departments. I think we just found those offices."

I studied the building. It was four stories above the ground floor, with a wide frontage on the street and a longer length along an alley. A sizable building. The government could put a lot of offices in there. "I'll go in."

"No."

"You stay here, Adam. You could get into trouble with the army for following me in, so wait here for me. If I'm not out in an hour, call the police."

"You think John Smith is Sir Malcolm Freemantle, don't you? You recognized him from Elise's description, and now you're going in to try to find out what he's done with your father." Adam still had his hand on my shoulder with just enough pressure to keep me in place.

"Yes."

"It's not safe, Livvy."

"You're in the army, and you talk to me about safe? We're in London. They're hardly going to shoot me. Throw me out, possibly, but they have no reason to harm me." I liked his coddling, but just now I needed answers more.

Adam removed his hand. "Go ahead, but I'm not certain about this. I'll wait here for half an hour. If you're not out in that time, then I'm going to the police."

I gave him a big smile. "Thank you." There was little traffic on this road in central London on a Saturday, and I was able to cross the street directly toward the steps leading to the door.

The top half of the door held glass panes, and I could see a man at a desk inside the dark interior. When I opened the door and walked in, the man rose. I could now see he wore a British Army uniform. And had his hand on the handle of the pistol in his holster.

I walked forward, my open hands out from my sides. "I've come to see John Smith."

"He's not here." At least the soldier hadn't drawn his pistol. I was more interested in the fact that he immediately recognized the name "John Smith."

"I realize it's a Saturday, but I was hoping I could speak to him."

"Name?"

"Olivia Denis."

The soldier glanced down. "You're not on the list."

I made an inspired guess. At least I hoped it was inspired, since it appeared Adam's rumor must be correct. This was a government building. "Not yet. And if I don't hear from him by four o'clock concerning my father's whereabouts, I'm notifying the prime minister about this location and its connection to Sir Ronald Harper's disappearance, Sir Malcolm Freemantle, and the death of John Kenseth. Do you have all that?"

The soldier scribbled furiously on a small notepad.

"I will be waiting at Sir Ronald Harper's home. Sir Malcolm has the number." I walked out of the lobby before the soldier lost his stunned expression. When I reached Adam, I said, "Well, shall we head out to my father's house?"

He fell into step beside me. "What did you do?"

I gave him a smile as we headed toward the Tube. "I told the soldier on duty that if I didn't hear from John Smith by four o'clock, I would contact the prime minister."

"Chamberlain's going to love that," Adam muttered before he smiled. "John Smith isn't going to be pleased, either."

I kept glancing over my shoulder until Adam said, "Expecting someone?"

"I'm half expecting a thug to come after us."

"I've been keeping an eye out," he murmured as we took the stairs down into the Underground.

We arrived at my father's house without any problems, and I let us in with my key. I looked around the ground floor, but the only thing unusual was an undisturbed, thin layer of dust everywhere. Mrs. Johnson would not be pleased when she once again returned to clean for my father, but he'd disappeared for longer than I had thought possible.

We both found books to read in my father's study to occupy our time, but then I paced while Adam took a nap sitting straight up in a chair. When mid-afternoon arrived without a word, I made us tea and found some biscuits. I apologized for the lack of milk for the tea, which caused Adam to give me a dry stare.

"No one has been here for a week. I wouldn't want any milk that had been left behind," he told me.

"I'd better remember to stock his larder when I know he's coming home."

I wasn't hungry after our large breakfast, followed by threatening to contact Chamberlain, but Adam looked a little sad as his stomach rumbled.

It was nearly four when I heard a key in the front door lock. I jumped up, hoping it would be my father. I rushed into the front hall, but Adam stepped in front of me as the door started to open.

CHAPTER SIX

The front door opened and my father walked in. Close behind him were Sir Malcolm Freemantle and his assistant, Whittier, both of whom I'd met the day my father was taken away.

Elise had described them perfectly.

I stepped around Adam and hurried up to them. "Father, are you all right?"

"Yes, I'm fine." He sounded both annoyed and uneasy.

"Perhaps you can fix us some tea," Sir Malcolm said, as if speaking to a servant.

I glared at Sir Malcolm. "Excuse me, I'm talking to my father."

Then I turned my back as much as I could on Sir Malcolm. "Father, are you all right? Where have you been? Did they treat you decently?"

"You said she was feisty," Sir Malcolm said in an amused tone.

"I could do with a cup of tea," my father said and headed toward the kitchen, shaking hands with Adam on the way. I followed them and heard Sir Malcolm and Whittier behind me.

I filled the kettle and put it on, then realized the men

had taken all four chairs at the kitchen table. As I returned with a dining room chair, Adam took it from me and set it between his chair and my father's. Once everything was set on the table and the tea ready, I sat down and joined the men.

"I'm sorry there isn't any milk for the tea," I began.

"It doesn't matter," my father said.

Everyone was silent. They could remain silent, but I saw no reason to. My father had been missing the better part of a week. Now he'd returned as if he'd been out for a stroll. I was angry with him and frightened for him. "Where were you?"

"I can't tell you."

"Did they suspect you of killing John Kenseth?"

My father studied his teacup.

"Are they letting you go?"

He shrugged. "It appears so."

I turned on Sir Malcolm. "Well, are you?"

"Am I what?" He smiled smugly before taking a sip of tea.

He may have found himself amusing, but I didn't. "Releasing my father."

"Your father is free to go about his business."

"Does that mean you won't arrest him for murder?"

"I have no power to arrest anyone for murder. I'm just an ordinary citizen," Sir Malcolm told me.

"Then why did you take my father away?"

"I didn't take him away. He came with us voluntarily."

It hadn't appeared that way to me. I turned my gaze on my father. "Please look at me."

When he did, I said, "Next time you go someplace with someone for several days, voluntarily, would you please tell me what you have planned? I've been frantic with worry about you."

The tautness in his face disappeared as he looked me in the eye. "I don't want you to worry." He reached out and took my hand, as loving an action as I'd seen from him.

What had happened? And what had they done with my curt, stuffy father? "Where were you and what happened?"

"Do you remember my telling you about the Official Secrets Act, that I signed as part of my work in the Great War?"

"Yes." Where was this conversation going? I gripped my teacup so fiercely I feared I'd snap off the handle.

"My paperwork's been updated to include some things I'll be working on now."

"For Sir Malcolm?"

"Yes."

"You shouldn't have answered that, old boy. You're a little rusty on the Official Secrets Act, aren't you?" Sir Malcolm said.

I glared at him. "He didn't have to. Your presence here is confirmation enough."

"She's very loyal," Sir Malcolm said to my father.

"If she likes you, you won't find a more reliable friend," my father replied.

High praise from my father. Shockingly high praise, considering how badly we got on.

"You've signed the Official Secrets Act?" Sir Malcolm asked, looking at Adam.

"Of course," he replied.

"I requested the particulars of your military record. Quite impressive. We'll be glad to put you to work if we end up in the war we're all expecting. But you," he said, turning to me, "what will we do with you? A reporter for Sir Henry Benton, fluent in German and French, and you identified the French assassin, that dressmaker Fleur Bettenard who tried to blow up Churchill."

"I can be discreet," I told him. I didn't want to be the next member of my family to disappear. I was afraid my father would leave me to my fate.

"No doubt." Sir Malcolm shoved a paper toward me. "Sign."

"What is it?"

"It acknowledges you must conform to the Official Secrets Act."

"I'm a newspaper reporter. How could I do that?"

"Covering teas and concerts and wedding announcements. Hardly the stuff we're interested in." He sounded bored as he patted his mouth as if yawning.

"What are you interested in?" I asked.

"Sign," he replied.

"You know I travel overseas for Sir Henry."

"Helping his late wife's family escape the Nazis. Very commendable."

Good grief. I'd been under surveillance by our government and never realized. "Does Sir Henry know you've been watching me?"

Sir Malcolm shrugged. "I don't know. It doesn't matter."

"It does to me. You've been spying on me." I was growing more annoyed by the moment.

"That was how we learned how useful you can be."

"That's not exactly a compliment." And this brought up another problem. "Will signing complicate traveling?" I couldn't leave Sir Henry in the lurch after all his help to me.

"Your travels might prove useful. You'll have to keep us informed when and where you'll be going."

I tried to imagine a trip to Germany for both Sir Henry and Sir Malcolm. I'd end up in a Nazi prison. My tea soured in my stomach. "Will you ever block my travels for Sir Henry?"

"No. Any cover can be put to good use."

I glanced at my father, who wore a bland expression, and then at Adam, who said, "They'll likely use your adventurous streak, and then we'll have even more secrets between us that we won't be able to share."

"Will that bother you?" I loved Adam. I didn't want to destroy our relationship. And I refused to let Sir Malcolm ruin everything.

"No." He winked as he added, "I'll be able to help you more often, if Sir Malcolm wants to put me to use."

"A double gain. I like it," Sir Malcolm said as he nodded.

I signed.

"Nothing you learn in the course of this investigation or in your work for Section C can ever be revealed," Sir Malcolm began. "You must be very clear about that."

"Yes."

"Very well. We need to put you in the picture about John Kenseth."

When I nodded, he began. "John Kenseth was getting bored in 1936 and wanted more excitement. I think he'd had it with his wife. So, he staged the accident and disappeared. It didn't take us long to find him and put him back to work."

"Watching shipping in the Channel," I said.

"Yes. Elise told us you were there. Very resourceful. But he had a second purpose, too. Certain ships were passing messages, coded messages, to Germany about other ships, including British Navy vessels. The messages were being sent by shortwave radio."

"And Mr. Kenseth was to pass them on to your organization for decoding," I guessed.

"You said she was bright," Sir Malcolm said to my father.

"And I suspect you already have someone else in place." I knew he didn't want me for that job.

"You've missed the most important detail," Sir Malcolm said. "The ownership. The ships that have been sending out the coded messages about other ships are owned by Palmer Shipping. I believe you've met Edmund and Alicia Palmer."

I'd had dinner at their restored farmhouse south of London while visiting Sir John and Abby, my late husband's cousin. Alicia Palmer was a well-regarded artist. Her businessman husband, Edmund, gave me the creeps. "Yes, I've met them."

Adam stared at me as he heard the coldness in my voice.

"Palmer is a known Nazi sympathizer and a good

friend of the Duke of Marshburn—ah, I see you've met the duke," Sir Malcolm continued.

My expression had given away my feelings. "I believe he smuggled the French assassin to safety," I said.

"Can you prove it?" His voice was hard.

"No. By the time I realized Fleur Bettenard, the chief cutter for Mimi Mareau's salon, was the French assassin, she had already disappeared. I believe she was whisked out of town by the Duke of Marshburn in his sportscar." I shrugged as I added, "No one believed me."

"Back to Palmer," Sir Malcolm grumbled. "Some shortwave transmission Kenseth overheard sent him racing back to London. He left a phone message for me to meet him here, at Sir Ronald's house. Unfortunately, by the time I arrived, he was dead and the police were here."

"And you believe what John Kenseth overheard had to do with Palmer and the messages his ships were sending to Germany," I said. Taking it one step further I asked, "Do you think Mr. Palmer had John Kenseth killed?"

"So far, the police have no suspects except your father—"

"Nonsense," my father said.

"And until we know why John Kenseth, or Gaspard Eliot, as he was known in France, dashed back to London, we won't know if Palmer had anything to do with it." Sir Malcolm held me in his gaze.

"Does Elise have any ideas?" Adam asked.

"She knows he was on the radio shortly before he packed up and left. She also says there was a stranger in the village, a woman, that Gaspard was trying to avoid."

"Any idea who she was?" Adam asked.

"How long was the stranger there?" I asked.

Sir Malcolm looked pleased when we both asked questions. "We have no idea who she was. She just showed up one day and then disappeared the next, shortly after Kenseth left. Elise thinks she might have been the woman who took a shot at Kenseth a while before."

"And you want us to find out what this knowledge was that sent Mr. Kenseth running back to London and his death." It sounded as if it were an impossible task, and I had no idea how to begin. My interest had been in freeing my father, and he had been released.

"Not at all, young lady. I know you'll be going to Berlin in the next few days for Sir Henry."

"How do you know that?" Heavens, I didn't know.

"We have our ways. While you're there, you are going to go to a particular shop where you'll ask for a copy of the *Daily Premier.*"

"They won't have it." I'd never seen a copy of Sir Henry's newspaper in Berlin.

"Of course not. Whatever newspaper he offers you instead, buy it and bring it back to London with you." Sir Malcolm used the patient tone one might use on a dimwitted child.

"Will it be safe to open it? Will something fall out?"

"It will be an ordinary newspaper. Nothing will fall out." He sounded as if he was laughing at me.

"Why should I trust you?" I saw no reason to. He'd abducted my father and had been spying on me.

"You mean besides the Official Secrets Act that you

just signed?" His mouth smiled, but the rest of his face showed his annoyance. "Because you can. And you should. You'll never know what you are doing, bringing us that newspaper, but rest assured it is important or we wouldn't have you do this for us. For our country."

"And you'll tell me which shop, and which person working inside that shop?"

"Of course. Nothing could be easier. I don't understand why you're making such a fuss over a little assignment that will take five minutes."

I wasn't making a fuss. I didn't trust Sir Malcolm. "Why have me do it? You have plenty of people at the British Embassy who could do this simple chore for you."

"They're all being watched. You, on the other hand, will be there to help your boss's mother-in-law and sister-in-law leave Berlin. Since they are Jewish, the German government is perfectly happy to see them go, especially because they'll be leaving most of their possessions behind. When they see you buy a newspaper all they'll see is a British journalist buying and reading a newspaper, because that's what journalists do. The German government will see exactly what they expect to see, and they won't pay any attention."

I was about to ask another question when there was a knock on the front door. Adam rose to answer it. In a moment, I could hear him talking to another man. Then three pairs of footsteps came down the hall to the kitchen.

Adam came in first and moved back to his chair, leaving Detective Inspector Jones and a uniformed constable in the doorway. "I see you've returned, Sir

Ronald. I hope you don't mind coming with us," the inspector said.

"Whatever for?" my father asked, not budging from his chair.

"Helping us with our inquiries into Gaspard Eliot's death in your drawing room. Come along, please, sir."

My father wearily rose and once again walked out of the house between two officials. Once again, I was certain they would file a murder charge against him.

How was I going to stop this? I couldn't let them hang my father.

CHAPTER SEVEN

I rose and followed my father and the policemen out the front door. "Where are you taking him?" Once outside, I quickened my steps to catch up.

"To Scotland Yard for the time being, while your father answers some questions," Inspector Jones said, blocking my way.

"Call our solicitor," my father said. The policemen helped him into the back seat of another large black car as a burly constable climbed in on the other side.

I stood on the pavement and watched them drive away, not aware until they were gone that Adam stood next to me. He put his arm around my shoulders, and we walked slowly back into the house.

I went straight into my father's study. "He just came home from who knows where and immediately he's taken away again," I grumbled as I searched through my father's diary for our solicitor's telephone number.

"Who are you planning to contact? You can't tell a solicitor or anyone else about Gaspard Eliot's real identity, or what he was doing in France, or Section C, or anything we discussed today, or where your father has been the last few days," Sir Malcolm said from the doorway.

"I don't know where he's been," I said, glaring at the heavy-set man.

"Well, that's good. You can't let that slip." He stared back at me. "Or anything else."

"What does 'Section C' stand for?" I asked.

"The 'C' is for counterintelligence."

"If there's no one else's day you plan to ruin..." I stood completely still.

"Let me know when you get your traveling arrangements for Berlin. Here's my telephone number. Please don't reveal that, either." Sir Malcolm moved toward the door as he set his bowler on his head. "Come along, Whittier."

I caught a quick glimpse of Mr. Whittier, average height, thin, and sour of expression, following Sir Malcolm out of my father's house. Adam saw them off and then returned to the study.

I found the number for our family solicitor, Mr. Peabody, and dialed. A maid answered, and after a minute his dry, solemn voice came on the line.

"Mrs. Denis," he said when I'd identified myself, "why are you calling on a Saturday afternoon? Is your father unwell?"

"My father is at Scotland Yard answering questions about the murder of a man found in his drawing room. He didn't do it," I added unnecessarily.

Mr. Peabody asked for the bare amount of information, not following up when I told him the murder was late the previous Sunday morning. I'd have wanted to know why my father had waited a week to call his solicitor, and why the police waited a week to bring him in for questioning. Assuring me he'd talk to my father, he hung up.

I looked at Adam. "Why would a solicitor not appear interested in why no one acted on this murder for a week?"

"He probably wants to hear what your father and the police have to say about Kenseth's death." Adam took my hand. "You've done everything you could."

"I feel as if there should be more I can do."

He took my hand and kissed my knuckles. "I have to leave to return to my base tomorrow afternoon, and you'll be off for Berlin soon. Let's try to forget about this and enjoy today."

I felt the weight of the paper I'd signed, and the secrets I'd now have to keep. Shaking it off, I gave Adam a smile. "What do you say to a little dinner and dancing?"

* * *

It was nearing three in the morning when we returned to my flat. Adam flopped into Reggie's favorite chair and undid his black bowtie. I dropped onto the couch and pulled my green satin heels off my tired, swollen feet.

"I don't think we've ever stayed out this late before," Adam said. "Or danced so much."

"But it was fun. That band was terrific." In a burst of candor, I added, "I needed to get my father's situation and all this other—utter nonsense off my mind for a little while. Dancing is good for that."

"I understand. But just now, I need to get some sleep. Tomorrow will be another long day." He rose stiffly with shoulders slumped and shuffled slowly out of the drawing room toward the back of the flat.

He had a good point. I wearily rose in my stocking feet and had just reached the hall when the phone rang. Thinking it had to be about my father, I reached over and picked it up. "Yes?"

"Captain Redmond, please."

"Just a moment." I put the phone down and went back to the guest bedroom. "Adam, telephone."

He hung up his tuxedo as he gave a deep, exhausted sigh and walked out to answer the phone in his undergarments. I knew what the phone call meant, but it didn't stop me from enjoying the view.

I heard his voice, too quiet to make out the words, as I took off my green gown with its tiny sleeves and a deep vee in the back. I had slipped on my nightgown, flannel with a high neck and tiny buttons, and was ready to climb into bed to fight the chill that was threatening to overwhelm me again when Adam plodded to the back of the flat.

"When do you have to return?" I asked.

"I have to catch an early train. I'll try not to wake you when I pack. In the meantime, I have to get some sleep."

I nodded and flipped off the light when he climbed into bed. "Wake me. I'll want to say good-bye."

He was snoring in a minute, but I lay awake. I was going to miss him. I pressed my forehead against my pillow and drifted off to sleep.

* * *

I woke up as I stretched out and realized the flat was silent. My eyes flew open and I sat up, looking around.

Adam stood in uniform in the doorway, his knapsack

in one hand. "I'm sorry. I didn't mean to awaken you."

"You didn't." I put my hand over my mouth to hide my yawn. "What time is it?"

"Half seven."

I was out of bed in an instant, my bare feet hitting the cold floor. "Why are you leaving so early?"

"I have to report in early. I told you. That was the telephone call I received last night. My orders have changed." He walked away from me down the hall.

I ran after him, ignoring the chill. I squeezed past him and placed my back against the front door to the flat. "What aren't you telling me?"

"Livvy, you know I can't tell you where I'm going or what I'm doing." He dropped his rucksack next to him.

"I'd like to know that you're safe."

He smiled at me. "I'll be safe."

"Write to me and let me know you're safe."

"I won't be able to write to you this time." He sighed. "And I probably won't be able to get your letters until I return."

He wouldn't be at some army base or training in Great Britain. If he was being posted in the colonies, he'd be able to write once he arrived. And if he were doing embassy duty, he'd be able to write. This meant only one thing.

"You're going to one of the countries Hitler is threatening under some sort of cover to meet with their military. To set up lines of communications, or intelligence, if they're invaded."

I expected surprise to appear on his face, if only for an instant. But Adam surprised me. He kept a noncommittal expression the whole time I spoke. I couldn't tell if I'd guessed right or not.

"You know I'm not going to tell you if you are right."

I laid a hand on his arm. "Please be careful. I don't want you caught behind enemy lines if Hitler invades while you're there."

He bent over and kissed my cheek. "I'll be careful. My worry is what you'll do for Sir Henry, and how you plan to rescue your father from jail while I'm gone."

"You don't have to worry about me. I'll just be annoying the police and the Foreign Office in my efforts to get my father released." I gave him a big smile. "And they aren't allowed to shoot me."

Shaking his head, he said, "I know about the French assassin. I know the risky things you'll do for Sir Henry. I am worried, but not about the Foreign Office shooting you. You signed the Official Secrets Act, Livvy."

"I had to sign to get Sir Malcolm's help to save my father."

"Save your father. Is that how you see it?"

"Yes."

He scowled at me. "Don't you get it? They can use you for any task they want. Dangerous tasks that have nothing to do with saving anyone you love, or even like." He put his hands on my upper arms and moved me away from the door. "Promise me you'll stay away from any investigations into Mr. Kenseth's death. Let the police find his killer."

"I can't promise you that." I sounded petulant, but I didn't care. "The police are convinced my father is guilty. I have to find the killer, because no one else will even look."

"Have you heard anything I've said?"

"Of course, but..."

With a low growl, Adam picked up his rucksack and opened the door. He was outside the doorway when I threw caution aside and stepped out of my flat wearing only my flannel nightgown.

I reached out and grabbed his free hand. "Please be careful. I love you."

He dropped the sack again, swept me up in his arms, and kissed me until I was out of breath. "I love you. Stay out of trouble." Then he picked up his bag and walked to the lift.

I stood in the hallway, our gazes locked, until Adam disappeared into the lift.

Afterward, I went back inside, glad none of the neighbors had come out of their flats. I sat in my drawing room and let melancholy thoughts wash over me. Before, after Adam left, my father always took me out to Sunday lunch. I hadn't heard anything, so I knew Father hadn't been released yet.

And I knew he wouldn't be if I didn't find the killer.

When the phone rang, I jumped up to answer. Instead of my father's public-school vowels that I longed to hear, Sir Henry's Newcastle accent came out of the receiver. "Are you free to go to Berlin in the morning?"

"Yes. Adam has returned to the army and my father is now in the hands of Scotland Yard and our solicitor. I'm free to travel anywhere." The sarcasm was unmistakable.

"Berlin would be fine. I want you to help Ruth get

herself and her mother to the train station and off to England as quickly as possible."

"What? Have you heard something?" It had been little more than a month since Chamberlain declared "Peace in our time." And now Adam was off to someplace dangerous.

"Nothing more than the usual rumblings. No, Mrs. Neugard is proving hard to move, even though she's now a widow and not against coming to where her children and grandchildren are. She wants to move the entire flat, and you and Ruth are going to have to separate her from her possessions to get her out of the country. The faster you move, the less time she'll have to find reasons to stay."

"Fly in, train out?" That had been our usual pattern.

"Yes. I have your reservations for the trip in. I'll let you decide when to come back. I know Mrs. Neugard doesn't like to fly. There's no sense battling that when she's going to give you trouble on so many other fronts. And Ruth won't leave without her, no matter how much she wants to get out of that insanity."

"Where do you want me to stay?"

"In one of the big international hotels with a nice dining room. No sense missing out on a chance to pick up some news while you're there. A hint that we can follow and steal a march on our rival papers."

I wanted to tell him what I'd signed, but I couldn't. "Do you have an assignment for me to cover the reason I'm there, or do I admit I'm traveling back with a friend's grandmother?"

"Add in some sightseeing. Perhaps you can find a concert or opera to attend. And try to get out of there as quickly as possible. I have a bad feeling about this," Sir Henry said.

"Oh, thanks. Throw me to the wolves." Sir Henry seldom seemed to worry about the dangers his employees might be facing. He said he couldn't risk letting us do our jobs if he paid attention to every warning.

"We're not at war with them. You speak excellent German. And you're obviously an Aryan. Don't do anything stupid and you'll be fine." He made it sound so easy. He wasn't going.

And then to make it worse, I called Sir Malcolm.

* * *

I was at the airport the next morning in time to catch the first leg of my trip to Berlin. I'd left a note on my kitchen table in case my father, or Adam, returned before I did. I dressed warmly in a heavy blue woolen suit under my wool-lined coat. Travel, and Berlin, in November were normally cold and damp.

It was late afternoon before I finally landed in Berlin and went through customs and questioning by a uniformed border guard. He frowned at all my answers after his surprise at my fluent German, but he finally relented and stamped my papers.

Berlin looked even more grim and determined under the weight of more swastika banners than it had the year before when I'd first visited the Neugard flat. I took a taxi into the center of the city to the large Hotel Adlon on Unter den Linden and checked in.

I took a chance telephoning Mrs. Neugard, since I assumed all the telephone lines were tapped. A woman's voice answered the phone, too youthful to be Mrs. Neugard.

"You must be Aunt Ruth," I said in German. "I'm Olivia Denis, a friend of your niece. Sir Henry has sent me to give you a hand."

"Good. I need help with this project."

I noticed she didn't say anything specific. "I'll be over tomorrow morning, if that is all right?"

"Perfectly." We both rang off.

I sent a telegram to Sir Henry saying I'd arrived. Then, famished, I went up to my room to dress for dinner.

A string quartet played in the hotel dining room when I entered. I told the headwaiter I would be dining alone. He took my name and room number and then with a smile led me to an immaculate table for four. I could have used the plate or silverware as a mirror. I began to protest that I was alone, but he simply pulled my chair out for me.

I was not given a menu. I suspected I was in trouble far from home. And liable to stay hungry.

Before I had a chance to rise and leave the restaurant, two men in full dress uniforms and a lady with sparkling jewels joined me. Shocked, it took a moment for my voice to work. In that moment, I saw humor in the eyes of one of the officers, Oberst Wilhelm Bernhard.

"Oberst. What are you doing here?" I asked in English.

My smile must have lit up my face. I wasn't in trouble. Not with the kindly and clever oberst present.

"I could ask the same thing." Then he switched to German. "Frau Denis, may I introduce Hauptmann and Frau von Hartmann." As soon as we murmured our greetings, he continued. "Von Hartmann told me you were in Berlin and arranged this dinner. Otherwise, I would have had no idea you were here."

I suspected he was warning me to watch what I said in front of the other couple. I noticed differences in their uniforms. I knew the oberst was part of their regular army. The young hauptmann in his dark uniform must be part of the security services or the Gestapo.

Putting on a warm, false smile, I said, "I had no idea you were here, either. What a lucky coincidence."

"Yes. May I say you look lovely in black. Very striking with your auburn hair. I hope you haven't dressed for some other man." Oberst Bernhard was pushing. Did they suspect I was meeting with someone politically untrustworthy?

"No." I gave him a flirty smile. "I like this gown so I chose to bring it with me. I'm glad you approve."

His smile didn't reach his eyes.

Frau von Hartmann said, "Are you here for the jewelry sales? You can pick up some wonderful bargains. That's how I could afford these." She gestured toward her magnificent emerald-and-diamond-encrusted necklace and matching dangling earrings.

"They are spectacular. Where would I find such stunning jewelry for sale?"

Frau spoke with an offhand gesture. "There are notices of auctions in the newspapers all the time."

As if I couldn't guess the source of these auctions, von Hartmann said, "There are Jews leaving all the time. They understand the importance of selling their goods to

Aryans if they want to leave."

His smile reminded me of a snake.

I was glad I hadn't started eating yet. I think I would have been sick, thinking of these forced sales.

"We've been able to furnish and decorate our flat cheaply, and in a grander style, than we could have ordinarily. Of course, you can't transport anything heavy out of the country without paying exorbitant bills, which is a shame for you since I imagine you'll soon be returning to England," Frau von Hartmann said. Then her face brightened. "But beautiful jewelry is so easy to carry with you."

"Yes, it is," I said, trying to sound noncommittal.

"Perhaps Frau Denis has a source of her own," Oberst Bernhard said.

I turned to face him. There was a questioning look in his eyes. He knew about the family I'd visited when I'd been to Berlin the year before. What dangerous game was he playing?

Or was he warning me of a trap ready to spring?

CHAPTER EIGHT

"Perhaps," I told Oberst Bernhard, trying to look mysterious and probably failing miserably. I was out of my depth, and the oberst was sending me vague signals that this was important.

"How did you two meet?" Frau von Hartmann asked.

A safer topic. I took a deep breath. "At a party in London while the oberst was posted to the German embassy," I told her. "How did you two meet?"

I'd hit on the right question. Apparently, the von Hartmanns were newlyweds who never tired of talking about their courtship. They appeared to consider themselves to be the most important people they would ever meet.

By the time Frau von Hartmann finished describing their wedding, we'd finished our soup and our roast courses. I glanced at Oberst Bernhard, wondering when he'd tell me what this dinner was in aid of.

Before either of us thought of something to say, Hauptmann von Hartmann said, "I understand King George isn't as popular as King Edward."

"On the contrary, King George is more popular. And his daughter, Princess Elizabeth, who we believe will one day be queen, is the darling of the entire country."

"Even if he leads you into war?"

Oh, wonderful. I was being sounded out to play a minor role in whatever game Hitler, or more likely, minions such as the hauptmann, had in mind. I needed to stop this now. "I would think Herr Hitler and King George could avoid war if they wanted to."

"So, all you are interested in is picking up jewelry at cheap prices from the Jews?" Frau von Hartmann asked.

Taking advantage of people who had no other option than to sell out and flee their country. As much as it sickened me, I knew I had to play along. I was a long way from London. "That and listening to music. Are there any good concerts scheduled?" I asked Oberst Bernhard.

"I am off duty tomorrow evening, Frau. Would you enjoy hearing the Berlin Opera perform?" he asked.

"I'd love to." The eagerness in my voice wasn't feigned.

"Wear that gown again. It flatters you."

It came to a low vee in the front and back. I was startled for an instant before he turned his head so the other two couldn't see and winked at me.

I guessed the von Hartmanns were supposed to think we were a bit closer than friends. "I can't believe my good fortune in meeting up with you again," I told the oberst with enthusiasm. I lay my hand on his sleeve in what I hope appeared to be a sign of intimacy.

"You must feel safe in our city," the hauptmann said.

"Why?" I asked, puzzled by his words.

"In Paris today, a Jew walked into our embassy, met with one of our officials, and shot him multiple times. Jews can't get away with that here. Can they in London?"

"Even our bobbies aren't armed. No one goes around shooting anybody in London." I sounded as indignant as I felt.

"I understood your husband was shot to death on a London street." The hauptmann gave me a slimy smile.

"By an agent of the German government," I snapped at the well-informed creep. My gaze threw daggers at him.

Von Hartmann reddened. "I beg your pardon, that someone who professed to follow the Führer could act so cruelly. Your husband wasn't Jewish, was he?"

"Of course not. And don't try to make excuses for his killer." Now I was really disgusted. That was hardly an excuse. I was ready to leave the table and walk away.

"Perhaps we should order coffee and discuss our beautiful autumn weather," the oberst said. The look he gave me said he wanted to kick my foot under the table.

"The weather has been delightful, so sunny," Frau von Hartmann said. "Have you ever been in Berlin in the autumn?"

"Just last year, but that visit was less than a day. My boss sent me to discover the favorite meal of the mayor of Berlin."

Frau von Hartmann burst into a tinkling laugh. "Why would he do that?"

"The newspaper I work for was running a series in the women's section on famous men and their favorite meals. I'm the only one on staff who speaks German, so I made the trip. The mayor was very kind. He even gave me a potato salad recipe of his mother's."

"You have an interesting job," she told me.

"I have nothing to do with the news, so it could be more exciting. But I have the opportunity to attend art exhibits and concerts free when I am assigned to write an article about them for the newspaper. That makes work fun." I hoped I was wiping away their suspicions.

"That is fortunate," she replied. Her tone was less enthusiastic than it had been. Maybe I'd convinced her, and her husband, that I would have no value as a German operative.

We had our dessert and coffee while we talked of ordinary things. The von Hartmanns could be charming when they chose. Then we said good night, and after the von Hartmanns left the hotel, Oberst Bernhard asked if I would like to take a stroll.

Hoping I'd learn what was going on, I said yes.

We walked closely together down the windswept street as if we were lovers. Unter den Linden was lovely even at the edge of winter and a popular spot for a stroll. It wasn't until we reached an empty stretch of pavement that Bernhard said, "You handled them very well. Thank you."

"I take it dinner wasn't your idea."

"I didn't know you were in town until von Hartmann came into my office holding the list of the day's arrivals. He had already made the dinner arrangements. I didn't intend to frighten you."

"You didn't." Then with more honesty, I said, "Not really."

He took one of my hands and continued walking. "Are

you here about your boss's relatives?"

He knew so much, there was no point in lying. I hoped he hadn't changed or I was in trouble. "His mother-in-law and her widowed daughter. Both of them much older than me."

"What is your cover?"

"I'm here for a holiday and to visit them." I looked up into his face. "They'll travel back with me."

"Tell them not to leave it too long. Things have become more dangerous for them since you were here last."

"In what ways?"

"Attacks on Jews have become more numerous. The lists of places they cannot go and things they cannot do grows by the day. Tell them to hurry and leave while they can."

I had to ask. "Why are you being so kind?"

"I am a loyal German soldier. That doesn't mean I have to agree with the politicians." He gave me a weak smile. One that said his life as an honorable man in this country was difficult.

"I hope there won't be a war," I said as I squeezed his hand.

"It's too late to hope for that." He gazed into my eyes. "And I think you know the war will come."

"Then I hope you and your children remain safe. How are they?"

"Safe." His smile reached his eyes for a moment. Then sorrow crossed his face. "I miss them. They are growing up without me, but my sister is very good to them. I hope your life is good in England."

My smile told my story before I said, "I'm engaged. To a soldier. A captain in the British Army."

"Are you happy?"

"Very much so." I hoped Adam was as happy as I was. I'd been tired, worried, and disagreeable when we were last together, and I felt guilty.

If the oberst sensed my concern, he didn't indicate that he noticed. "Then I hope I don't meet him until this is over."

I didn't have to ask what "this" was.

* * *

The next morning after breakfast, I took a tram to the Neugard flat. Even though they knew I was coming, Ruth seemed hesitant to open the door. Once she did, she shut it again quickly.

I stopped her in the hallway inside the flat before we went in to see Mrs. Neugard. "Things are worse?"

"In every way. The Nazis make our lives impossible and my mother doesn't want to leave my father." She kept her voice very low.

"But he's dead," burst out before I stopped and thought.

"His body is here where she can visit him. Leaving here feels as if she is abandoning him to the Nazis."

"Is that Frau Denis? Did she bring me a newspaper as I asked?" said the tremulous voice of an old lady.

"Come along," Ruth said with a sigh.

"Yes, Mrs. Neugard. Here they are," I said as I walked into the drawing room. The room seemed barer. I could see where a few paintings were missing from the walls, and there didn't seem to be as many knickknacks.

The tiny, white-haired woman seated in an overstuffed chair held out a blue-veined hand and clutched the three newspapers I put before her. Quickly scanning the front pages, she said, "Ach, always bad news. A diplomat gets shot in Paris yesterday and somehow it is our fault? Did you know they've put a big 'J' on the front page of our passports so other countries can see we are Jewish? I am a little old lady. How can I be such a danger to the world?"

If she didn't know there had been a conference in France the preceding summer where all of the countries attending refused to take in large numbers of German Jewish refugees, I wasn't going to tell her.

"When you finish with the papers, Mama, we need to continue with our packing," Ruth said.

"Your packing. I'm not going anywhere." Mrs. Neugard turned her attention to the newspapers, tucking the duvet closer around her.

Now I understood why Sir Henry was so insistent that I travel to Berlin. Despite the danger and the cold, Mrs. Neugard was putting herself and Ruth in greater jeopardy. "Esther needs you. That's why she sent me over. To travel back with you and carry your suitcase," I said.

"Esther is your friend?"

"Yes."

The old woman nodded. "You are a good friend to her to come all this way, but I don't want to leave my Simon."

"Esther needs you right now. More than she needs me," I told her.

"I'm an old lady. What can I do?"

"With the baby coming, Esther needs her mother. That's not going to happen, so you're going to have to step in. You can come back to Simon once the baby is here and Esther is on her feet again." I saw Ruth make a movement out of the corner of my eye, but I ignored her. I knew once we moved Mrs. Neugard to the safety of England, there was no way she'd be able to return to Berlin.

This was one time I didn't mind lying if it would get them out of Berlin faster.

"How is Esther?" her grandmother asked.

Ruth made us tea and I gave her all the family news from London. Once we finished, Ruth and I went into her room while she packed.

"Mother wants to take everything."

"We can only take what the three of us can carry. I have room in my suitcase, and from what I heard last night, it might be safer if I carry any jewelry or valuables you plan to take with you. With a bill of sale."

"Do you think they won't allow us to travel with anything of worth?" Ruth asked.

"Yes. But you're the one living here. What do you think?"

She nodded. "Every day in the newspapers, we see listings for auctions of furniture, businesses, all sorts of goods that belong to acquaintances. Jewish acquaintances. Everyone is trying to get out."

"As are you."

"Yes, but not my mother. She doesn't see how tense things are. How frightening. I want to go to England and not be frightened any longer." And then the tension slipped off her face, making her years younger. Her pride was evident as she said, "And I want to see my son again. He is studying advanced mathematics at Oxford."

"Why is it so cold in here?" I hadn't taken off my coat.

"The heat is on in the building, but for some reason it doesn't work in our flat. I've talked to the porter, but he says there is nothing he can do. We've been so cold at night. Mother will soon freeze to death if we stay." Ruth shook her head. "One more cruelty on top of the others."

I patted her shoulder. "Let's get you and your mother packed. Set aside the valuables and anything else you want me to carry, so I can slip them into my case when we leave."

"I will. Thank you, Olivia. Although I don't know how we'll be able to convince my mother."

"She's afraid, isn't she?"

"She only leaves here to go to the synagogue or the cemetery. She's terrified of the violence springing up in the streets."

"Is there much violence?"

"There are small groups that strike out and then disappear. And the police harass us." She shrugged. "I'm frightened to go to the shops, and a lot of the shops won't serve us anymore. I don't know how much worse it could be."

"We'll help your mother. And once we're on the train and it's moving, she'll be all right."

"She won't have any choice," Ruth said with a rueful smile.

I did the shopping for Ruth while she packed. I had no

problem getting decent meat and produce, something Ruth thanked me for when I returned. Frau Neugard commented on how much Ruth's cooking had improved when we sat down to eat.

"No, I think it was because Olivia did the shopping," Ruth said.

"Why? Is she that good at choosing produce?"

"No. It's because I'm a Christian," I told the old lady. "And now my German is good enough for me to blend in." From a practical standpoint, blending in was useful, but it felt very wrong.

Ruth set down her fork. "We need to leave, Mother."

The old woman was silent for a long time. "You are right, but it is so very difficult to leave everything behind. My whole life." She appeared near tears.

"You've lived here all your life?" I asked.

"In this neighborhood. *Ja*."

We ate in silence for a while until I remembered the concert that night. "I think I have a way to get something else out that won't be questioned. Do you have a fancy stole?" I asked.

CHAPTER NINE

Oberst Bernhard was again in full dress uniform when he came to the hotel that night to take me to the concert. Not only did I meet him in my dramatic black evening frock, but over it I now wore a silvery fur stole, actually a short cape, that belonged to Sarah Neugard.

His face lit up when he saw me. "You look beautiful," he said, kissing me on both cheeks. As he reached my other cheek, he murmured, "We're being watched."

"You look very handsome," I replied as I gazed at him.

"It's a pretty night and the concert hall isn't far. It's down Unter den Linden, which is always a lovely stroll. Shall we walk?"

"I'd love to." It might be our only chance to talk in private.

It was truly a lovely night, not as cold as I expected, and many people, dressed up for the evening, were also walking along the boulevard. When he judged we were far enough away from other pedestrians, Bernhard said, "Where did you get the fur?"

"As I told Frau von Hartmann, I'm here for the sales."

"And you wore it tonight. It lends credence to your story. Clever."

"Why are we being followed?"

"They are still suspicious of you from last autumn, and I'm believed to be unreliable. Being an officer isn't enough anymore. Make sure when you leave, you don't take even a newspaper or notes for a story with you. And leave nothing behind. Anything can be a pretext for the Gestapo to arrest you if they want."

"Because there won't be another chance to retrieve anything, or anyone, left behind?" I whispered. What would I do about the newspaper Sir Malcolm wanted me to return with? I had to bring it with me.

The oberst was watching someone out of the corner of his eye. He grunted his agreement.

I waited until his posture told me it was safe to ask, "The old lady I'm going to be traveling with. She's going to want to take newspapers and old family photographs."

"Then don't appear to be traveling with them. The Gestapo check everything."

Not the answer I wanted to hear.

As a couple approached us, he gestured at the buildings around us. "Isn't that a beautiful prospect?"

"Yes. This certainly is a beautiful city. Do you live here year-round?"

"No. Soldiers are nomads." He looked around for a minute, standing still on the pavement. "But I enjoy any time I can spend here."

I watched his face in the light of a nearby streetlamp, drinking in the view. "Berlin is to you what London is to me."

Confusion was written on his features. "I thought London was your home."

"It is. I grew up there."

"I grew up in the south. In the hills." He gave me a smile. Then he put an arm on my back and said, "Let's hurry, or we'll be late."

Now that we were walking so closely together, I murmured, "Is there anything I can do to appear less suspicious?"

"When you leave, buy the train tickets for your friends, and buy first-class seats. You'll be less likely to be detained."

"Will you be all right?" He'd been so helpful to me every time I'd been in Nazi-held territory, I didn't want him to suffer because of me or my friends.

"Don't worry, *Liebchen*, I am a very good officer. And I know to always curb my tongue."

The concert hall was majestic and the audience was glittering. I was surprised at how many of the men were in officers' uniforms and how many of the women were in dazzling displays of jewelry.

The concert was wonderful, but any chance I had of finding out more from Oberst Bernhard was ruined after the performance by the appearance of Hauptmann and Frau von Hartmann. "The concert sounded so good, we decided to attend as well," they told us.

Any doubts I had about Bernhard and me being followed were crushed.

They invited us to a club for an after-concert drink in

such a way that we couldn't refuse. We shared a cab, crowded in together. After a drink and a little dancing that proved conclusively that Oberst Bernhard could march but he couldn't waltz, we all took a taxi to my hotel, where they dropped me off.

"Thank you for the lovely evening," I told the oberst as he stepped out of the cab behind me. "I hope I see you again soon."

I heard the hauptmann tell the driver to wait. They didn't want us to have a moment alone.

"So do I." The oberst kissed me on both cheeks again and whispered, "Be careful." Then he climbed back into the taxi and they drove off.

The next morning after breakfast, I took the tram to the Neugard flat. Once again, Ruth pulled me in and shut the door quickly behind me.

"There was no one behind me."

"There are Nazi Party members in our building now, since two Jewish families have fled. Even our Christian neighbors are afraid to be out in the hall."

"We need to get you out of here."

She gave me a wan smile. "My mother has packed three suitcases. She's packed silverware, paintings, old photographs, school report cards, anything and everything."

"I'll try talking to her." I walked into the drawing room and found Mrs. Neugard in her favorite chair. "*Guten morgen.*"

"Good morning to you."

It suddenly struck me that I'd never asked if either

woman spoke English. That would make life even harder for Mrs. Neugard, although I felt confident Ruth would adjust. "Three suitcases? How will you manage?"

"I'll find a porter."

I hated being honest to the old lady, but not countering her memories of yesteryear would have been crueler. "You know no porter will assist you. You can only take one suitcase, although I will carry a few things for you in mine."

"How can I get by with only one suitcase? The Nazis will rob us and take everything else when we leave."

"They'll take everything whether you stay or go." It was brutal, but I suspected it was the truth after meeting the von Hartmanns.

"They wouldn't dare. Not while I'm here." She glared at me.

"I wish that were true, Frau Neugard. But we both know it isn't. Please, pack one suitcase and let's go to see Esther. She needs you."

"She doesn't need me." Her glare only intensified.

"Yes, she does. You have experience and wisdom to pass down to her. And not having her mother, you can help her the way you did your daughter when Esther was born."

"I'm too old."

"Now you're talking rot."

Despite her intension to look stern, her lips quivered as she fought a smile. "I know what you want. It's the same thing Esther and Ruth want. How can I win against such stubborn women? They get it from Simon, God rest his soul."

I grinned. "Get packed while I go to the market for

you."

"And bring me newspapers. I need to know what I'm going to face out there."

I went to the market and the newsstand, returning to help Mrs. Neugard pack while Ruth fixed lunch. The old lady spent more time reading than packing, or rather, unpacking, but we made some progress.

After lunch, I told them to keep packing. I had an errand to run.

An errand for Sir Malcolm. I went to a newsstand near the bahnhof and looked over the bald, wiry man behind the counter. He matched the description I was given. When I asked for a copy of the *Daily Premier,* he looked me over in silence for what felt like ages. Did I go to the wrong newsstand or was he not my contact?

Finally, he glanced around and said in a deep voice, "I don't get requests for that paper very often."

I replied, "There's nothing like it when I feel homesick." That was nonsense, but those were the words Sir Malcolm told me to say.

His eyes moved right and left while his head remained stationary. "You might prefer this."

"This" was a copy of today's edition of the popular *German Leader* he pulled from under the counter.

"Thank you." I paid him and turned to leave. Standing directly behind me was Oberst Bernhard. "Oberst. So nice to see you again." The newspaper burned in my hand.

"When do you leave Berlin?" he asked using the tone of an acquaintance.

"Hopefully in the next few days."

He lowered his voice as he reached past me to pick up the newspaper farthest from him. I was sure no one else could hear him. Only the shopkeeper might have been close enough, but he had stepped back at his first view of the uniform. "All troops are ordered to leave the cities immediately. Get on the next train out. You must leave today."

"War?" I whispered. It was the only thing I could think of.

"I don't know. I'm not a field marshal yet." He gave me a grim smile.

"Do we have enough time to get out?"

"Tomorrow will be too late." Louder he said, "Goodbye, Frau. I hope our paths cross again soon."

"So do I, Oberst." We shook hands, and he flipped a coin to the man behind the counter before he walked off toward the train station.

I knew Oberst Bernhard wouldn't frighten me with a warning such as this without a good reason. A cold shiver ran down my neck that had nothing to do with the cool breeze along the pavement.

I followed him at a distance and bought three first-class tickets to Paris on the night train, leaving Berlin in a few hours. When I looked around again, I could no longer see the oberst in the cavernous station.

Fear sped my actions as I packed and checked out of the hotel before I traveled to the Neugard flat. I couldn't help wondering if I was being followed. Would we be stopped by the Gestapo? Prevented from boarding the train?

Coming into their building, I met two young men coming down the stairs. One of them carried a crate of mismatched bottles full of liquid. They were muscular and blond. My mind immediately dismissed them as thugs. No wonder Ruth was nervous.

I knocked on the door and she called out, "Who's there?"

"It's me, Livvy."

As soon as she opened the door, I burst in and shut it behind me. "I have three tickets on the overnight train tonight. We need to go."

"Why? What has happened?" Ruth asked as she led me into the drawing room.

We gathered in front of Mrs. Neugard's chair. "I met with a—an acquaintance of mine, German Army Oberst-"

"What? A German army colonel?" Ruth exclaimed.

I nodded. "And he told me to get out of Germany tonight. The army has been ordered to leave the cities today. Something bad, war maybe, is going to happen, and we need to get on the train and escape."

"No. I'd rather be killed in my flat than miles from home on a train." Mrs. Neugard shook her head.

"He wouldn't have told me to leave tonight if he thought I'd get killed if I traveled. He thinks tomorrow it will be more difficult to cross the border, and he's never been wrong. I have tickets for us on tonight's train to Paris."

"Will they let us go?" Ruth asked.

"Now, yes. Tomorrow? Who knows. They may be planning to close the border. I have the tickets. Let's finish packing and leave."

Easier said than done. Ruth was already packed and she gave me all the jewelry they had left plus a large gold case, which I packed in my suitcase. I clung to the newspaper I'd bought, keeping it with my handbag.

The only person who needed to get ready was Mrs. Neugard. She and Ruth battled over every item in her suitcase. Finally, we had her down to one suitcase. It was too stuffed to close, and so the process began again.

When we had the suitcase whittled down to a relatively movable object, I thought we'd conquered our biggest hurdle. But Mrs. Neugard now needed to dress for the journey. She couldn't decide if she should dress in her very best or wear something more comfortable.

And the clock kept ticking.

"Wear something nice, but something you don't mind wearing all night," I told her. "I got us first-class tickets, but I couldn't get us into the sleeper car. It was booked up. Still, we'll keep each other company."

"How can it be first class if we have to sit up all night?" Mrs. Neugard asked.

It was a good question, but I knew no answer I gave would be satisfactory.

"Mama, we need to leave soon to get to the bahnhof," Ruth said. "This is our last chance to get out, and I'm going."

"You'd leave your mama?" Mrs. Neugard sobbed.

"It's a matter of life or death," I told her. "We need to leave if we want to live."

"Very well. I'll wear this." She headed toward the front door. "What is keeping you, if it is so important?"

Ruth gave a small shriek as she grabbed up their passports and travel documents. I picked up Mrs. Neugard's suitcase as well as my own.

Once we were out of the flat with our suitcases, money, passports, tickets, exit visas, and in my case, a fortune in jewelry, Ruth locked the door. If there was a war starting, I wondered if a lock would make any difference.

Mrs. Neugard patted the door and whispered, "Good-bye."

I flagged down a taxi and we rode to the bahnhof faster than I would have expected. The cabbie's speeding silenced Mrs. Neugard. I was glad of the quiet, since I was worried about what she might say that would complicate our exit.

And after speaking to the oberst, I was thinking of our journey as an escape.

We arrived and went into the massive train station. After what appeared to be a long walk for Mrs. Neugard, which she made in silence with her eyes down, we reached our platform. And here we found the border officials waiting for us.

Ruth went first, displaying her passport and her documents showing she paid her exit visa. She was allowed through. Mrs. Neugard went next. The guard looked at her paperwork and said, "Where is your husband? This exit visa is for two."

"He is dead."

"You cannot travel without him on this visa."

"You want me to bring his body on the train?" Mrs. Neugard said, aghast.

Before she could say another word, I said, "He's right here." I had my suitcase open for inspection, so I pulled out the large gold box.

The guard blinked. "How—?"

"Cremation."

A shudder ran through the man. "You burned him?"

"I doubt it hurt," I countered.

I thought I heard a snort from Ruth, but I ignored her.

"Now can she go through?" I asked the official.

He checked her address and stamped her passport. "You'll enjoy Paris. Your people shot one of our diplomats there. He died earlier today."

I showed him my British passport. "I'm sorry to hear that."

"Don't worry. We'll get our own back." He spoke with such venom that it was all I could do not to run to the train in a panic.

"What is that?" the guard snapped at me as he looked at the newspaper. Sir Malcolm's newspaper.

"A newspaper. The *German Leader*." My knees began to shake.

"Give it to me."

The moment I had dreaded. I handed it over and waited to be arrested. This wouldn't help my father. Or Sir Malcolm. Or me.

He gave the front page a cursory glance and handed the newspaper back. He didn't open it up.

I felt hot and faint.

"Are you all right, Frau?" the guard asked.

"I'm a little faint. Too much exercise." I'd hoped he'd

offer me a chair.

He turned his attention back to our paperwork. "You English are weaklings."

CHAPTER TEN

After another tense few minutes that dragged on for ages while all three of us kept silent, our papers were stamped, our bags searched, and we were on our way to the train.

I was again carrying my bag and Mrs. Neugard's. Hers was so heavy I was having trouble keeping up with the old woman. When we arrived at the correct first-class carriage, the train staff checked our tickets and helped us get our luggage aboard with blank expressions. I suspected they had seen too much to be interested or surprised.

A porter put our luggage in an empty compartment and took our reservations for dinner and breakfast. He helped me wrestle the suitcases onto the rack above and into the space under the seats. Mrs. Neugard wanted to sit by the window. Ruth sat across from her and I sat between the old lady and the door. I hoped we made her feel safer by surrounding her with familiar faces.

For myself, I wanted the train to start moving.

Mrs. Neugard must have sensed my worry and said, "When will we leave?"

I smiled at her. "Soon."

"I'll never see my home again, will I?" she asked me.

"I don't know," was my honest reply.

She patted my hand, as if comforting me.

"You are very brave," I told her.

Mrs. Neugard gave me a soft smile. "No, Livvy. I have my friends, my family, and my memories. What else does one need?"

I kept waiting for others to claim seats in our compartment, but no one did. All three of us breathed sighs of relief when we felt the train jerk and then slowly begin a rhythmic motion. We were alone and relatively safe. I wished the train would speed up. I wanted this trip finished.

I slipped the copy of the *German Leader* between the seat and the wall of the compartment, where I hoped it wouldn't be noticed.

The lights came on as the sun went down. While we clicked off the miles until the French border, Mrs. Neugard knitted and Ruth and I read.

About the time we should have left for the dining carriage for our reservations, the porter opened the door to our compartment and said, "Please excuse me, but we have overbooked the dining car. You will have to wait for the last seating."

"Why did you choose us?" I asked him, keeping my tone and my gaze level.

The man shrugged. "I don't know. They just told me, and now I am telling you." He gave me the time for the last seating and left.

"Well, it'll give us something to look forward to," Mrs.

Neugard said.

"I'm sorry," I told Ruth, hoping her angry expression wasn't aimed at me.

"You have nothing to be sorry for. You're not German. You are not even our family, but you've come to see us to safety. Without you, we wouldn't be eating at all."

"Still, he shouldn't have—" I began.

"We're still in Germany, Livvy. Relax." Ruth gave me a smile.

I had the feeling things would get worse before they improved.

The train slowed to a halt and my heartbeat sped. We sat for a moment and then a train passed us.

When we continued to remain unmoving, Mrs. Neugard put down her knitting and looked at me with big eyes. "The other train is gone. Why are we not moving now?"

"I don't know. We're waiting for something, perhaps?"

After minutes that felt like hours, another train flew by. Moments later, we began to move again, and Mrs. Neugard returned to her knitting. I found I could breathe normally again.

The last seating was at half ten, and when we reached the dining room, some of the tablecloths were stained, silverware hadn't been replaced, and we were crowded in with three other people at our table. From the conversation, I could tell Ruth quickly discovered all the passengers at this seating were Jews heading out of Germany. Except me.

It felt strange to be the only Christian in the dirty

dining carriage.

The waiters came around and set burned sausages and cold potato salad at every place. "Excuse me, what kind of meat is this?" someone at the next table asked.

"Sausage," the waiter replied.

"Could we have some silverware over here," someone at another table said.

A waiter set a handful of silverware in the center of the table and walked away.

"It is pork. We can't eat this," a woman at our table whispered.

I cut a little off of mine and tasted it. "I'm not sure, it's so burned, but I think it's chicken."

"She's Christian. She can tell the difference," Mrs. Neugard said and cut off a slice of hers to eat.

Ruth stared at me until I said, "I think so."

She nodded and gave it a try. "I'm sure it is chicken. I just found a feather."

The people around us chuckled at this and began to eat their dinner. We stopped at a small German city, Weimar or Gotha, I thought, for a few minutes, before the train began to move again.

It was then I remembered the newspaper I'd hidden between the seat and the wall of our compartment. I'd left it behind where anyone could find and take it while I was eating. While we were stopped in a station. They could be waiting in our compartment to take us away with the evidence of my espionage. Suddenly, the food stuck in my throat.

Conversation began to spread in the carriage of where

people were planning to resettle, but I couldn't listen. I'd left the one thing alone in our compartment that Sir Malcolm told me to bring back. That he expected me to guard. If it fell into the wrong hands, what would happen to me?

The coffee brought around by the waiters was lukewarm at best and sludgy. There was no milk, although after the chicken sausages, I suspected no one here would put milk in their coffee. I wasn't sure if the menu was designed for ridicule or kindness, but it had amounted to the same thing.

Finally, we rose and went back through the swaying corridors to our compartment. It was all I could do to keep from running. I arrived first and my eyes immediately went to the newspaper. It was still there. Looking around, I could tell no one had been in here searching or pretending to clean.

With a sigh of relief, I collapsed into my seat.

Mrs. Neugard did the same thing a moment later. "I don't like walking in a train when it is moving."

"I'm very glad it's moving," was all I could think to reply.

It was after midnight before we reached Frankfurt. As we reached the outskirts of the city, I noticed a glow in the distance. It took me a minute to realize something was on fire.

The train was moving more slowly now as we approached the station, waking Ruth and Mrs. Neugard. Ruth looked out the window and said, "What is going on?"

I noticed then it wasn't one building on fire, but many.

"It looks as though half the city is on fire."

"There are many Jews in Frankfurt, and the Nazis have been very harsh with them. I suspect it's a pogrom," Mrs. Neugard said, restarting her knitting. I noticed her hands shook a little.

"I wonder if it is going on in Berlin," Ruth said.

If it was, I was glad the oberst had warned me to get us on the train and out of Germany.

"We didn't have time to say good-bye to our friends. And now they may be in danger," Mrs. Neugard said, looking at me accusingly.

We sat in Frankfurt station for thirty minutes, long enough for smoke to get inside the train. With the engine quiet, we could hear shouting voices at a distance. At least they didn't seem to be coming closer to the station.

I saw Ruth tremble. "We should be safe here on the train," I told her.

"I'm sure we will be. It's the thought of what's happening outside that frightens me."

Mrs. Neugard looked from Ruth to me. "They will take everything Simon and I spent fifty-six years collecting. All the time we spent building our life together. They are horrible people."

"But Mama, we are getting out alive," Ruth replied.

The two women clasped hands.

By the time our train began to leave the station, the acrid taste of fire was in my mouth. There was a haze in the air and all three of us were coughing. Ruth and Mrs. Neugard looked out into the night and shook their heads at the view, where a dozen fires seemed to melt into one smoky hell.

We continued on our way, the train picking up speed. I knew the worst was yet to come. We had to cross the border into France.

The next time our train pulled onto a siding to let another train pass, both Mrs. Neugard and Ruth were asleep. Sleep was a marvelous defense against the fear that had followed us from Berlin, but I couldn't drift off. I sat and worried alone until the other train finally passed us and we were on our way again.

I had finally dozed off when the train began to slow down and the porter came along the corridor calling, "Passports. Everyone awake."

"What time is it?" Ruth groaned, blinking her eyes as more lights came on inside the compartment and the corridor.

I looked at my watch. "Three a.m." The train was running on time.

In a few minutes, the porter came along, followed by an officer in the same style uniform worn by Hauptmann von Hartmann and two rifle-bearing soldiers in regular army uniforms. As the officer requested our passports, I studied his pale face and blond hair and wondered why all the SS officers I met looked so young.

I reached over, took Ruth's and Mrs. Neugard's passports and handed them over with my own.

He flipped through all three sets of documents. "You are traveling with Jews, Frau."

"Yes."

"Are you also Jewish?"

"No."

"Racially Jewish?"

I looked at him in feigned amazement. "Whatever does that mean?"

"Did you have a Jewish parent or grandparent?"

"No."

"Then you are mixing with other races," he announced in a stern voice.

"We're not having sex," I told him in a reasonable tone.

Ruth's snicker was covered by the officer's choking sound and the guffaw of one of the soldiers. One look from the officer quieted the soldier.

"The term you are thinking of is 'racial defilement,'" the officer told me.

"No, I don't think that's the term I'm thinking of," I replied.

"Where are you going?" he said in an angry tone.

"Britain. All three of us are going to Britain," I told him. I thought I'd better stop teasing him, because his reddened face told me he was furious. He had the power to throw us into prison, and while the British consul would get me out of jail, he couldn't do the same for Ruth and Mrs. Neugard. Two women I belatedly remembered I was responsible for.

He glared at me for a minute while I faced him, trying to keep my expression polite, before he said, "Good. Go to Britain. We don't want you here." He handed back our papers and marched on.

The officer hadn't seen the newspaper pressed against the wall of the compartment. We'd passed the final barrier, and I felt as if I could relax.

Mrs. Neugard slumped in the seat next to me. "When will we get there?"

"Late tonight. Tomorrow you can rest as long as you need to at Esther's."

"Good."

In a few minutes the train moved about one hundred yards. I thought we had crossed a bridge over a river, but the view out the window was hidden in darkness. When we stopped again, I whispered, "France."

After a wait, two French border guards came along the corridor. They looked at our papers and I told them in French that we were in transit to Britain. They handed back our papers with a complete lack of interest and moved on.

When the train began to move this time, all three of us collapsed in our seats with relief and fatigue. I crammed the German newspaper under my handbag before I caught a little sleep. The porter came to wake us for our turn in the dining carriage for breakfast. This time the coffee, eggs, and toast were at a level French trains were famous for. I could see Ruth start to look around her, tension lines disappearing from her forehead and mouth. Mrs. Neugard poked and sniffed at her meal, but when finally satisfied that it was safe to eat, she devoured her food.

We reached Paris at late morning and took a taxi the short distance to the Gare du Nord. We were on the way there when I looked out the window as we stopped at a traffic light. I gasped when I saw Adam cross the street in front of us.

"What is it?" Ruth asked as she looked around in fear.

"Someone I know. I didn't realize he was in Paris." And was dressing in civilian clothes while he was here. Why was he here, and who was he reporting to?

I was about to jump out of the taxi when the light changed and we rode on. I lost sight of Adam almost immediately.

I bought our tickets for the next boat train to Calais and then left Ruth and Mrs. Neugard with the suitcases while I went outside to walk around. I wasn't far from where I'd seen Adam. I hoped to catch another glimpse of him, but after half an hour of wandering the dismal streets, filled with soot-stained buildings and shabbily dressed residents, I gave up. I was glad to rejoin my companions.

We made the train in plenty of time and again had a first-class compartment to ourselves. The scenery must have been lovely, but we were all too tired and eager to reach England to notice. Once we boarded the ferry to cross the Channel, we went to the restaurant. It was from there Ruth and Mrs. Neugard had their first glimpse of their new homeland.

Mrs. Neugard stared at the white cliffs for a while before she said, "It is a welcoming sight."

Ruth sighed as she said, "England." She reached out and took my hand as she said, "Thank you." I could barely see the tears in her eyes through the dampness in my own.

After that, the train ride through the Kent countryside to Victoria Station was almost anticlimactic. Ruth fell asleep to the rocking of the train. Mrs. Neugard studied the view out the window in the last light of day as if she were memorizing it. I counted down the minutes until I could get on with other things in my life.

I checked again. The newspaper was still in my handbag.

It was full dark and nearly dinnertime before we ended our journey. We alighted from the train to find Sir Henry, Esther, and Mrs. Neugard's other daughter Judith and her family waiting for us. A babble of German and English arose as we blocked the path for some of our fellow passengers. I found myself in the role of sheepdog, trying to herd them out of the main path of traffic.

I was included in the family hugs, but all I wanted to do was leave them and go home. I'd been traveling for twenty-four hours and I was exhausted. And I hoped to receive news of my father.

"I've heard nothing about your father," Sir Henry told me when I pulled him aside, "but you certainly missed some news, thank goodness. Last night Germany had the worst anti-Jewish riots they've had in memory. Synagogues, businesses, and homes ransacked and burned. Many people died. Our correspondent in Berlin says the streets are now paved in broken glass. Some German diplomat dies and the Nazis use it for an excuse to run crazy."

"We saw fires when we stopped in Frankfurt. That was about midnight. Was that it?" I asked.

"Yes. It was lucky you left when you did."

"Not luck. I received a warning, but I thought he meant the war would start."

"A warning? From whom?" Sir Henry demanded.

I smiled, thinking of how Oberst Bernhard had helped me again. Once more, I owed him for my timely safe departure from Nazi-controlled territories. "A source."

CHAPTER ELEVEN

Sir Henry gave me the next day off before I had a chance to ask for it. I rose earlier than I would have thought possible, given my exhausting travels. I sat in my drawing room as I drank a cup of coffee and looked around at my flat with relief. Then I glared at the newspaper that had given me so many anxious moments in Germany. I couldn't wait to get rid of it. I phoned the number for Sir Malcolm. A man's voice answered and told me to meet him at the Bristol Hotel dining room.

I went out, wearing my rainproof coat and unfurling my umbrella as soon as I left my building. The weather, clear but cool while we traveled, had turned foul. My stockings were splattered by the time I arrived at the Bristol.

I was shown to Sir Malcolm's table and was surprised not to find Mr. Whittier's silent presence.

"Whittier's back at the office," Sir Malcolm answered me as if he'd read my mind. "Have some breakfast. It's quite good here."

Breakfast meetings probably explained his girth. He seemed to have ordered one of everything on the menu, which was now spread before him. I ordered eggs, toast, and tea, and once the waiter had left, asked, "And where is the office?"

"You've already found us. Now I expect that you'll show up at inopportune moments. You're impulsive."

"I do my best," I said and then thanked the waiter who brought my tea. I opened my handbag and slid out the newspaper I'd retrieved for him in Berlin. "No one was suspicious. Of course, the party was planning a major assault at the time."

The newspaper lay on the table, ignored by both of us.

"Have you heard from my father?" I asked.

"No. I've spoken to his solicitor, and apparently he's still being held at Brixton Prison awaiting trial."

"Can't you get him out?" That was why I was assisting Sir Malcolm.

"No. And if he killed Kenseth, I wouldn't want to."

"He didn't," I snapped at him.

I expected him to snap back, but he calmly said, "Then find out who did." He fell silent as my breakfast arrived. Once the waiter left, he added, "I hear you're quite good at that."

"Who told you that?"

"Your father."

That surprised me enough that I fell silent and considered his words while I ate some of my breakfast. I'd heard that the Bristol Hotel had a good kitchen, and I discovered their breakfasts were indeed delicious.

"My father didn't kill Kenseth," I said. "He had no reason to. But John Kenseth was murdered, so someone wanted him out of the way."

"True." He sat there quietly watching me.

"Do you know of any enemies he had?"

"Yes."

"Who?" When he remained silent, I said, "Oh, for pity's sake..."

"You know of a shipping company owner who would want him out of the way and has the resources to hire someone to do the job. Then there is an angry, spurned wife. Someone could have followed him over from France. Someone who was in his life recently. Use your imagination, girl." Sir Malcolm glared at me before spearing a piece of sausage with more force than necessary.

"What about your organization?"

"What about it?"

"Did anyone want John Kenseth out of the way?" I asked.

"He was doing vital work. As an organization, we will miss him. As a person, he was not universally loved."

"Who disliked him the most?"

"I'll look into that, shall I?" He gave me a superior sort of smile. "If anything comes of it, I'll let you know."

I knew I wouldn't get more than that out of Sir Malcolm. "So, you're telling me if I want to free my father, I'll have to find out who killed John Kenseth."

"Or you might find out why your father doesn't have an alibi," Sir Malcolm said, after blotting his lips with his thick white linen napkin.

"Do you know why he doesn't?" I was learning to be very direct when asking Sir Malcolm questions.

"No."

"Really?"

"No," he said with more force. "That was one of the things we asked him repeatedly while he was our guest."

My eyebrows went up at the word "guest," but Sir Malcolm took a sip of his coffee and ignored my skepticism.

"Do you have any influence with the prison governor that would get me in to see my father?" I thought he should. His tentacles appeared to reach everywhere.

"None at all. You could ask his solicitor."

"That was to be my next call," I told him. The German newspaper still lay on the tablecloth. "Will the paper help you?"

He smiled. "You know I won't answer that."

When I finished my breakfast and rose from the table, I said, "Do you know who the woman was who arrived in Etretat the day before John Kenseth departed for England? She left shortly after him."

"No." His expression gave nothing away. For all I knew, he could have been lying.

"Could this woman have been following Mr. Kenseth when he arrived at my father's house?"

"It's possible."

"So, what do you think?" I hoped he'd provide some guidance.

"*Cherchez la femme.*"

When I reached Mr. Peabody's office, I found that he had arrived moments before me. Since he didn't have anyone in with him, his secretary told me he could spare me a few minutes. After I shed my wet outerwear, I walked into his old-fashioned bookshelf-lined and paneled office to find Mr. Peabody rising from behind his desk.

He welcomed me and gestured toward the leather-covered armchair in front of his desk. "This is a terrible business about your father."

"It is," I said, sitting in the chair. "Can I get in to see him?"

"As his only relative, it shouldn't be difficult."

"Has he told you where he was instead of in church that Sunday morning?"

"No. He refuses to say a word about where he was the entire weekend. I rather suspect—no, I shouldn't speculate." Mr. Peabody sat with legal volumes dating back hundreds of years behind him. No wonder he was uncomfortable speculating.

"Please. What were you going to say?"

"This is rather delicate, but I believe a woman is involved."

I nearly burst out laughing before I gave the idea a second thought. There had been times in the last few months when he'd been less interested in my activities than he'd been previously. Less inquisitive. Less nosy, to be more accurate. Could that be because he had a secret of his own?

"And he won't tell you. Good grief. All the more reason for me to see him. If he has a good alibi, the sooner we tell the police, the better."

"That's what I've been telling him," Mr. Peabody said. "He has a trial date set. November 28."

"That's only seventeen days from now." My heart hammered as I jumped out of my seat. I was ready to panic. "We need to do something soon."

"Let me call the governor and see if I can arrange a visit."

He did, and shortly before noon, I found myself entering Brixton Prison's section for those awaiting trial for the most serious offenses. I followed a warder along a maze of cold brick corridors until I was left alone in a small, gloomy room.

When my father arrived, he didn't look as he did normally. It was as if he'd dried up, gone pale, and shrunk several sizes. Since we were in a private interview room, with a table in the middle and a chair on either side, I could see him close at hand. His suit appeared to hang on him, his hair was whiter than I remembered, and new lines had carved maps of worry and stress on his face.

I sat, waiting for my father to join me at the table, but he stood by the door. "Why have you come?" he finally asked.

"I'm your daughter. Wouldn't you visit me if the roles were reversed?"

"I've always imagined they would be some day, the way you run around for Sir Henry. Conducting your own murder investigations. Hmpf."

"Do sit down, Father. I'm getting a pain in my neck looking up."

A bored-looking warder watched from the other side of a window. Presumably, he couldn't hear us.

My father shuffled, rather than strode, over to the

chair and dropped onto it. It was a sturdy wooden chair identical to the one I sat in, with no comfort built in to the design. "It was nice of you to come."

"Of course I came. I know you didn't do this."

He sat slumped forward, looking down at the table. "I checked with Mr. Peabody. My will is in order. There's a little money set aside—"

"Will. You. Stop." If he gave up, how could I save him? "I intend to find out who killed John Kenseth and get you freed. I'd appreciate a little cooperation, a little fight, from you."

"No." He started to rise.

"Who is she, Father?" When he didn't say anything as he turned to the door, I added, "I will find out. And if I don't get any assistance from you, I will make it very public."

He turned to face me and glowered. "Olivia."

"I mean it, Father. Tell me about this woman, or I swear, when I find her, I'll—"

"Olivia." He sat back down and glared at me, the first signs of life I'd seen in him that day.

I decided to take a guess. "She's married, and if her husband finds out, he'll divorce her. Ruin her."

"No. I would be the one whose actions would ruin her." He spoke so quietly I could barely hear his words.

Still, it was a breakthrough. "How long have you been seeing her?"

"A few months."

"What does she think of you protecting her honor with your life?"

"She thinks it's impossibly good of me."

"Of course," I said with sarcasm dripping from every word, "she wouldn't dream of coming forward to clear your good name with the police."

"She has good reason not to."

"I hope you live to tell me what it is someday."

He leaned forward, glaring as he ground out his words. "I will if you use your talent for finding murderers to free me from this wretched place."

I nodded. It was the least I could do, especially since I wanted to. "Down to business. What time did you arrive at the house?"

"A few minutes before twelve."

"Five minutes? Ten?"

"Four or five."

"How did you end up with blood on your hands?"

"John wasn't quite dead when I found him. He was still breathing. I hoped if I could stop the bleeding, you would arrive in time to call for a doctor and we might save him."

"Did he say anything?"

"No. He died about a minute later. He just seemed to collapse in on himself."

I remembered Adam's words. "The autopsy report said he died almost immediately."

"I heard a sound as I came into the house. Afterward, I thought it was the sound of Kenseth falling to the floor. If it was, from the time I heard him fall until he died was only a minute or two."

"Did you see or hear anything else?"

"I didn't realize it at the time, but I may have heard the back door shut." He looked at me steadily. "Or maybe I've just imagined it. I've had plenty of time to imagine things. Trying to make sense of this nightmare."

I sighed and leaned back in my chair. "The idea is logical. If you came in the front door, the killer would go out of the back door so as not to be seen. I need to question the neighbors."

"I'm sure the police already have."

I rolled my eyes at my father's naiveté. "The police have been certain you killed Mr. Kenseth since they arrived at our house and found his blood on your hands and your knife in his chest. I doubt they did a good job of looking for any other suspects."

"You never give the police enough credit." He crossed his arms and shook his head with an expression that said I was lacking in sense.

That expression had always annoyed me. That day, I looked at my father, diminished, graying, and worn down, locked in His Majesty's prison, on trial for his life, and I found I couldn't be angry with him.

I was determined to find John Kenseth's killer.

And the woman my father was protecting.

I tried to gain further information from my father, but he was singularly unhelpful. As I left the room, I looked back to see my father escorted back to his cell. His head was down and his shoulders slumped as he shuffled away.

My heart nearly broke.

* * *

My next stop was my father's house. In the last few years, I hadn't seen much of the family on the left as I viewed the houses from the street, and when I knocked, no one answered. Then I walked to the other side, to a house similar to my father's that was occupied by a retired couple, the Oswalds.

Their house was also brick, with a small front garden, smallish windows on both floors, and a steeply pitched slate roof.

The door was opened to my knock by Mr. Oswald, who greeted me with "Livvy, how is your father faring? We couldn't believe the story the police told us." He had even less hair than the last time I saw him, and his legs were more bowed, but he appeared in good health.

Then I heard Mrs. Oswald's voice from inside the house call out, "Bring her into the kitchen, Bert. I can't leave my baking."

I remembered Mrs. Oswald as a marvelous baker. She didn't have to offer her invitation twice.

I followed Mr. Oswald down the hall and into the kitchen, where he immediately sat at the table. I walked over to collect a hug from the stout, matronly woman, who seemed to have grown shorter since my childhood.

"How is your father, Livvy?"

"Grayer. Shriveled. Keeping silent."

"That's to be expected," she told me. "Do sit down while I put the kettle on and then we can sample this shortbread."

Her shortbread was a treat. "Who are you baking for?" I asked as I sat.

"Patricia is bringing the family over for the oldest boy's birthday tomorrow. I have to do two days' worth of baking for that lot."

Patricia was their daughter, ten years my senior. "Maybe I better not sample if it's meant for your grandson's birthday."

"Nonsense. They expect me to do nothing but bake every time they visit. She has three growing boys. They won't miss a piece or two."

We caught up on their children and grandchildren and my engagement while we waited for the kettle to boil. Once we each had a cup of tea and a plate with a shortbread biscuit, I asked, "Did you see anyone around my father's house the Sunday before last just before noon? The day he found the body in the drawing room?"

"Yes, we did, didn't we, Bert? The man that we guess was killed and the woman who arrived with him. And then we saw your father come home carrying a suitcase."

CHAPTER TWELVE

"My father had a suitcase? Where had he gone?" This didn't sound like my father's normal behavior. Why would he have told me on Thursday that he'd see me in church on Sunday and then take off for the weekend?

"I have no idea. He left by cab Saturday morning and returned the same way Sunday just before noon," Bert Oswald told me. "It's a good thing we go to chapel early or we'd have missed all the comings and goings." He sounded cheery about the excitement.

"And you told all this to the police?"

"A bobby asked what time we'd seen your father leave and return, and after I told him that, he didn't want to hear anything else. And no one's been by since to question us."

"Tell me about what you saw."

"Are you going to find this killer the way you did for poor Reggie?" Mrs. Oswald said, giving me another piece of shortbread.

"I certainly hope so."

Bert nodded sagely. "Your father's life depends on it."

The shortbread no longer looked appealing. I nudged the plate away. "Tell me what you saw that Sunday morning in the order that events happened."

"I was out in the garden turning over an annual border," Mrs. Oswald said, joining us at the table with the teapot she'd refilled. "I heard voices and looked over the fence to see a man and a woman walk along the side of your father's house. 'No problem,' I heard her say, 'I know another way in.' And in the back door they went."

"What did the man look like?"

"Tall and slender, with thinning brownish hair. Late forties, maybe, wouldn't you say, Bert?"

"I'd say so. I was raking in the front garden and saw them pull up in a cab. They knocked and rang the bell before walking to the back. Was he the murdered man?"

"Yes." I needed to keep them on track. "And the woman? What did she look like?"

"Short, black hair, or at least that's how it appeared under her hat. And I think it was dyed. Her hair, I mean." Mrs. Oswald nodded with a serious expression when she finished.

"Why do you say that?"

"It was too dark and all one color. She was average height, but she walked very quickly. She was well-padded, if you get my meaning."

"A fine figure of a woman," her husband put in. "Nice legs, if a little heavy. I think she was maybe forty."

"Did you get a good look at her face?" I asked.

Both shook their heads.

"Did either call the other by a name?"

"No," Mrs. Oswald said.

"They weren't close enough to me to make out anything they said," Mr. Oswald said.

"He's a bit deaf," his wife told me.

"No, I'm not," Mr. Oswald said, sounding annoyed.

I didn't have time for them to argue. "How long were they in the house?"

"Your father arrived about ten minutes after they went around to the back," Mr. Oswald said.

"Did you speak to him?"

"No. He climbed out of the cab and went straight in."

"And then you arrived about ten minutes after that," Mrs. Oswald said. "I'd come in to make tea and was going to tell Bert it was almost ready when you walked into the house. You were certainly in a hurry."

"Yes." I wasn't about to tell them I had been on a mission to tell my father not to invite people to my still-unplanned wedding. Especially now that we'd quarreled over secrets we had to keep for our jobs. Silence demanded by the Official Secrets Act. Secrets that took Adam to Paris. "Did you see the woman leave?"

"No. We thought she stayed inside."

"She wasn't there when I arrived," I told them. "Had you seen anyone around the house after my father left on Saturday morning?"

"No. The house had been quiet," Mr. Oswald said as his wife nodded vigorously.

"And the Abernathys. Are they in residence?" They lived in the house on the other side of my father's.

"They left about a month ago to visit their daughter in America. They'll be shocked to find out what's happened to your father," Mrs. Oswald said.

"The woman would have been able to leave on that

side without being seen," Mr. Oswald said.

"That's what I was thinking," I replied. I had to ask, "Have you see my father's new lady friend?"

The Oswalds exchanged a look. "We thought that might have been where he was going weekends," Mr. Oswald said.

"He's certainly never brought her back here," Mrs. Oswald said.

As close an eye as the Oswalds kept on the neighborhood, my father was smart not to bring her home if he wanted any privacy.

But that didn't help me find the woman.

I was going to need help from my contacts in the Foreign Office.

I thanked the Oswalds and went into my father's house, amazed at the utter silence, as if the residence waited for his return. The first person I called was Mary Babcock, the first friend I had made among the Foreign Office wives after I married Reggie.

When I greeted her, she said, "Livvy, I was so sorry to hear about your father. No one can believe your father killed John Kenseth, or even that Mr. Kenseth was still alive. Have the police released Sir Ronald yet?"

"No, and I need your help."

She didn't hesitate. "Of course."

"Do you keep up with the goings-on of the Foreign Office wives?"

Mary must have heard something in my tone, because she said, "Livvy, what is going on? What does your father's predicament have to do with the wives?"

"I need you to keep a secret."

"Of course. What can I do to help?"

"The reason my father is in this mess is because he won't tell the police where he was before Kenseth was killed. I think he was conducting an affair with one of the Foreign Office wives." I couldn't believe it even as I spoke the words.

"Oh, Livvy, I'm sure..." Her voice slowed until it came to a stop. "Who?"

"I don't know. It's been going on for a few months. He's afraid the husband of the woman would destroy her—my father's words—and so my honorable father won't tell the police who he was with and she won't come forward." My tone said what I thought of my father's delayed attempt at honor.

"She knows about this?"

"According to my father." My foolish, chivalrous father.

"So, it must be at least a section head with a doormat for a wife. Who do we know like that?"

I made two suggestions, both of which elicited peals of laughter from Mary. She told me in one case, the wife was the one with the fortune, and no matter how much her husband might bluster, he always quickly came to heel. In the other, the wife was carrying on an affair with a titled gentleman, and the husband decided to keep quiet and enjoy the perks of friendship with the aristocracy.

"Are you sure she is a Foreign Office wife?" Mary asked when she'd finished laughing.

"My father doesn't socialize with many people outside

of the Foreign Office." And I was certain I could rule out his housekeeper and the neighbors.

"What are you going to do?"

"If you can't think of anyone, my next step is to talk to some of the men in his section."

"And ask if their wives are conducting an affair with your father?" She sounded as if she thought I'd do that very thing.

"And see if any of them have any helpful suggestions as to where my father might have been or who might have seen him. The usual questions. Then perhaps someone will let something slip."

"In the meantime, I'll listen to gossip and see if any of it revolves around your father or affairs of the heart," Mary said. "If any of the wives are straying, someone will know and tongues will wag."

She was now mother to a strapping six-month-old who had stolen her heart. We ended the call with a long chat about George's accomplishments, which seemed to consist of sprouting teeth and sitting up.

After I hung up the telephone, I considered whom to approach while I waited for Mary to listen to gossip. My father reported directly to Lord Leverhill, who was ten or fifteen years my father's junior. I'd never met a man with less humor or warmth. I scratched him off my list.

I looked through my father's diary and found the name Julia Neal, with her address and phone number. Frederick Neal had been a colleague of my father's for many years. I didn't find any other women listed that I couldn't account for.

Was it possible?

Sir Roger Dunwitty was another longtime colleague. He had such a broad sense of humor he probably found my father languishing in jail to be amusing, but otherwise he was easy to talk to. I decided to try him first.

After a few phone calls, I managed to track him down at his club, the Senior Foreign Service on Piccadilly. He suggested we discuss my questions over dinner at the Penworth Hotel. I knew from experience their kitchen was more than adequate and their prices weren't bad. I agreed.

I wore a rust-colored evening gown that was both warm and matronly, hoping I would look sedate enough that he would take my questions seriously. Sutton, our doorman, frowned at my choice of frock, but he went out and whistled for a taxi for me anyway.

Sir Roger was waiting at our table when I arrived. He stood until I was seated, his mouth quivering under his mustache.

When he was seated, I asked, "What is so funny?"

"Your dress matches your hair. Did you mean to do that? I feel as though I'm dining with Lady Godiva."

There was that sense of humor. I decided that two could play that game. "You wish."

He broke out in a lusty guffaw before he ordered for the two of us and settled down to talk. "What did you want to see me about?"

"You know my father's in jail. He didn't kill John Kenseth."

He took a moment to keep from grinning before he sobered and said, "No one who knows him thinks he did."

"But he won't give the police an alibi."

"Why not?"

I shook my head. "I was hoping you might have some idea concerning what he's been doing lately."

"Working too hard, but we all have been, with Herr Hitler stomping across Europe."

"If he had been working, he could have said that and let the upper echelon of Scotland Yard talk to the Foreign Office chiefs. He wouldn't have to endanger any government secrets."

"I don't know what he's been doing outside the office, but I know he's bought flowers regularly." Sir Roger grinned again as we both fell silent while the soup and wine were served.

"Flowers? Who did he buy them for?" I asked once the waiters left. He certainly didn't buy them for me. I felt a little jealous and had to tamp down my hurt feelings.

"I wish I knew. Those flowers were expensive."

"I imagine he took a lot of teasing, walking into the office carrying flowers." I hoped someone had ribbed him enough that he'd responded with some information. Any information that might give me a hint as to the woman's identity.

"No. He had the florist deliver."

Something he seldom did. "Did he? Which florist?"

Sir Roger told me before he added, "I tried to find out where he sent them from the clerks at the florist shop, but they kept silent."

Why had Sir Roger been so determined to find out who was receiving flowers from my father? It would make no difference to him. Or would it? "Why did you question the florists about the flowers?"

Dunwitty was no longer smiling. "At the Foreign Office these days we're all paranoid. Anyone does anything out of the ordinary, and we all turn into Sherlock Holmes."

"Wish me luck, then, Sherlock. I must speak to her. Have her give my father some sort of alibi."

He shook his head. "The police know when your father arrived home, and he had enough time to kill Kenseth before you showed up at the house." When I opened my mouth to speak, he said, "Our department needs to know if this murder has anything to do with government secrets. So, we know an alibi for where he was before he arrived home won't do him any good."

"How did you learn all these details?"

There was that grin again. "The Foreign Office demanded access to all of Scotland Yard's files."

Wonderful. I wished someone in Scotland Yard would keep me informed. "Why would my father have killed him in those few minutes if he didn't know Kenseth was alive before then? They'd have had no time to build a quarrel strong enough to kill over. There was no animosity from before." I stared at Sir Roger. "He didn't know Kenseth was alive, did he?"

"No. No one in the department knew. That was one very well- kept secret."

"You sound upset that you didn't know Kenseth was still alive," I told him.

He shook his head. "I'm not. I wonder if he learned anything that would be useful to my work, that's all."

I leaned forward and lowered my voice. "I'm certain he was away from England investigating the plans of another government. It had to be of use to someone in Whitehall."

"Are you sure that someone wasn't your father?" Sir Roger lifted his eyebrows before he turned his attention to finishing his soup.

"I spoke to him immediately after he found Mr. Kenseth. He was genuinely shocked the man had been alive until that moment."

"Then that someone wasn't Sir Ronald. Finish your soup. The roast will be here in a moment."

Over dinner I learned that Lady Dunwitty was in the country with their younger daughter, who was having her first child. That ruled her out as my father's romantic interest.

As we drank our coffee, I asked if his colleague Frederick Neal might have any useful information that could help my father. I'd seen Julia Neal's name in my father's diary and wondered why it was there.

"Neal? I doubt it. He's on a temporary assignment to Greece that he seems to be dragging out so he can stay in the sunshine."

"On a day such as today, I can hardly blame him." When the rain wasn't pouring down, the wind was turning umbrellas inside out. "Did he take his family with him?"

"No. He's enjoying the life of a bachelor and soaking up the sun. Julia doesn't enjoy traveling."

"Not a good characteristic for a Foreign Office wife." I had been one. I knew how many wives had to travel. And at short notice.

"They aren't the happiest of couples. Neal is a hard man to like, or even get along with." Sir Roger set down his glass and stared at me.

In that moment, I had an idea of who the mystery woman might be. And I thought Sir Roger suspected the same woman.

CHAPTER THIRTEEN

"How long has Frederick Neal been in Greece?" I asked.

"Several months. And between you and me, it will take an Act of Parliament to get him back to London." Dunwitty smiled at me.

I now had some confirmation concerning my thoughts on the identity of the woman in my father's life. It made sense that the woman would be the wife of a colleague. Armed with her name, I went out to my father's house after dinner and walked directly into his study.

I had no problem again finding the name Julia Neal in the leather-bound notebook on his desk, complete with an address and phone number. I don't know what else I expected to find, but I looked through every page, hoping something he'd written would give me some insight into what my father thought about this woman.

I found nothing of any use.

It was too late to contact her that day, but I vowed to pay her a call the following afternoon. After copying her information, I had put on my coat and gloves when I heard a noise upstairs.

"Father?" I raced up the stairs, leaving my handbag on

the desk. How had he managed to be released without anyone telling me?

My smile must have covered my face.

I turned on the light in the hall and headed for his room. As I opened the door, I heard a sound behind me. Swinging around, I caught a glimpse of a woman disappearing down the stairs—a dark-haired woman wearing a green cloche and coat, moving quickly.

I was after her in a flash, down the stairs, through the kitchen, and out of the back door. I flipped on the back-porch light, but the area remained unlit. The bulb must have burned out.

The woman, a blur of forest green in the light, vanished into the dense blackness of the garden. I slammed the back door and turned the useless lock, cursing my bad luck. Was it my father's girlfriend? The woman with John Kenseth the day he died? Someone else I had yet to hear of?

I grabbed my handbag, pinned on my hat, locked the front door, and headed next door to the Oswalds'. When I knocked, the door opened a sliver and I saw Bert's thin nose peeking out at me from behind the chain.

"It's me. Olivia Denis." I was sure he knew that, since his porch light was shining in my face. "Have you seen a woman hanging around my father's house recently?"

He shut the door, opening it wide a moment later. "Come in, Livvy. No, we haven't, but we've seen a car parked on the street late at night."

I followed him into the hall. "Have you seen anyone getting in or out of the car?"

"Maybe. Shadows mostly. I think."

"You think?" Disappointment filled my voice, and I had no desire to hide it. My father's life hung in the balance, and this woman might be the key. She certainly had no business hiding in the house I grew up in.

"It's so dark out there, it's hard to make out anything," Mrs. Oswald said as she joined us.

"What about the car?"

"Just an ordinary car."

"Why didn't you mention this when I was by this afternoon?"

"A strange car parked on the street? Shadows? Hardly of any use, is it?" Mr. Oswald said.

"I just chased a woman out of my father's house."

The couple looked at each other in surprise. I felt certain this was the truth. "A vagrant?" Mrs. Oswald asked.

"No."

"A burglar?"

I shook my head. I was certain she wasn't.

"Oh, dear. Which way did she go?"

"Through the back garden. The porch light doesn't work, so I don't know where she went from there."

"Bert will take care of that light for you in the morning," Mrs. Oswald said, giving her husband a sharp look.

"Yes. I'll be glad to. Neighbors need to look out for each other," Mr. Oswald said. "Your father's done plenty to help me out time and again."

"Please keep an eye on the house. There has to be a reason this woman was inside."

To find this reason, I'd have to ask Esther to keep me company while I took the house apart.

* * *

When I returned home, I decided Sir Henry probably wouldn't have retired for the night. I rang his house and asked the maid who answered the phone if he would take my call.

Sir Henry came to the phone a minute later, and when he heard my voice, said, "Thank goodness. Esther is driving me barmy. Speak to her, would you?"

Esther and her father normally got along quite well. "What's wrong?"

"Her grandmother won't let her lift a finger. Esther is bored and uncomfortable due to a lack of activity."

"Already? Her grandmother's only been here a day."

"You know Mrs. Neugard. She's quite—determined."

Not quite the word I'd use, but I understood what he meant. "Where's Esther's Aunt Ruth?"

"Taking a well-deserved holiday from her mother by visiting her son in Oxford. I suspect it will be a long visit."

I stopped myself from laughing aloud. Ruth had seemed impatient with her mother, but to be fair, if I'd spent any more time with the old lady, I would have started snapping at her. Ruth needed time to spend with her long-absent son and time to adjust to life in a new country. "Mrs. Neugard is best taken in small doses."

"So I've learned," Sir Henry's voice grumbled down the telephone line. "But this isn't why you called."

I smiled as the idea came to me. "I'm going to need some time off to deal with my father's situation. Tonight, I found a woman hiding in his house, possibly searching it, and I want to see if I can find whatever she or Mr. Kenseth might have secreted there. I could ask Esther to help me. Nothing strenuous, but it would get her away from her grandmother for a few hours."

"Don't bother trying to call her tonight. Her grandmother won't let her talk on the phone uninterrupted, and not at all this late." Sir Henry had apparently already been rebuffed. He sounded astonished that anyone would tell him no. "It's the weekend. James will be there, but I could pick her up on Monday and take her to my office. Meet us there, and the two of you can spend the day at Sir Ronald's home seeking whatever anyone might have hidden."

"I'll come straight to your office Monday morning." Avoiding Miss Westcott and her censorious looks.

Once I was off the telephone, I realized I would have no excuse to avoid talking to my father's lover tomorrow. On Monday, with any luck, I'd find something so she wouldn't have to be involved.

No matter what, I wanted to meet the woman who'd supplanted my mother. I didn't want to admit it was about time.

* * *

I decided to show up on her doorstep rather than telephone or send a note first as good manners dictated. I dressed in a severe gray suit with a black blouse and matching black pumps and hat. I wasn't certain if I was mimicking mourning or judicial robes.

The house was one in a row of upper middle-class

homes in a central neighborhood favored by government bureaucrats, barristers, and physicians. I walked up to the shiny blue door and rang the bell.

A young maid in a crisp uniform answered and I gave her my card as I requested an interview. She left me on the doorstep and shut the door.

I was glad it wasn't raining.

I didn't have long to wonder whether the greeting was meant for me personally or if this was a generally unfriendly household. The door opened again and the maid asked if I would follow her to the drawing room.

She led me up one flight to a charming room done in greens and gold and furnished with Queen Anne style tables and chairs. Thick draperies were pulled back to allow what little sun there was into the room through the lace curtains. Some lovely landscapes hung from the walls.

A moment later, I was joined by a middle-aged woman with lovely dark chocolate-colored hair and soft brown eyes. She wore a beige cashmere sweater and a brown tweed skirt that favored her coloring. Walking toward me, she held out her hand. "I'm Julia Neal."

I shook her hand. "I'm Olivia Denis. Sir Ronald Harper's daughter."

She smiled a gentle lifting of the corners of her mouth. "He's spoken often of you."

"Odd. He's never mentioned you."

"I think he's trying to protect me."

"From me?" I couldn't believe my father would think I'd do anything to upset his happiness.

"From everyone."

"Did you paint these landscapes?" I walked over to study one more closely.

"Yes."

"I like them."

"Your father said you'd appreciate them. He said you're quite talented."

I needed to get to the point of my visit. I gave her a hard look as I walked back to rejoin her in the middle of the room. "It is believed his case would be aided if it were known where he'd been that weekend and that he hadn't seen John Kenseth before he found him dying on his drawing room floor."

She straightened and glared at me. "Your father doesn't believe it necessary and neither do I. He's innocent. Now, if there's nothing else?"

"Nothing." I walked toward the door to the hall, noticing she hadn't asked me to sit even though she knew I was my father's daughter.

I stopped in the doorway. "This innocent man is going on trial for his life in sixteen days. If he is found guilty, he will hang. And you'll do nothing?"

"Your father doesn't want me to."

She was the right size and possibly the right hair color to be the mystery woman with John Kenseth and the one who'd made an appearance at my father's house the night before. For my father's sake, I really hoped it wasn't her.

* * *

Sunday was cold and wet. I looked out the windows of my flat and watched the raindrops, mixed with sleet, slide down the panes. All thoughts of getting a start on searching my father's house fled. I read for a long time and then took a nap.

On Monday, I wore a gray rayon dress with a snag in the fabric, since I planned to take the house apart. I was left waiting outside Sir Henry's office for over half an hour. Just as I was about to give up and head out to my father's home, Sir Henry and Esther arrived.

Sir Henry carried a picnic basket I was certain contained delicacies from Fortnum and Mason. It was fortunate Esther had thought about lunch since I hadn't, and I knew my father's larder was empty.

After Sir Henry's words on Friday night, I almost expected to see Mrs. Neugard. When she didn't appear, I let out the breath I discovered I was holding.

"Grandmama is spending the day with Aunt Judith's children," Esther told me. "I feel as though I've been let out of jail."

"She only wants what's best for you," her father said.

"I know that, but being cosseted, not allowed to move, doesn't feel right. My muscles ache and I feel headachy."

I grinned at Esther. "Today you'll have to tell me when you get tired. Otherwise, I'll expect you to keep going. Does that sound fair?"

"More than fair. Let's go."

We said good-bye to Sir Henry and, with me carrying the heavy basket, went downstairs, where Esther insisted on taking a taxi to my father's house. I saw a curtain twitch in a window at the Oswalds' when we arrived. I hoped they were as vigilant at watching for the unknown woman as they were at watching me.

Esther and I went into the house and started on the drawing room where John Kenseth was killed. The back of every painting, space between the arm and the seat cushion of every chair, and inside every lampshade was examined. I raised the edges of the Turkish carpets to look underneath. We unrolled the spills for lighting the fire, but they were only scraps of letters Father had dripped ink on.

We lifted every dish in the china cabinet in the dining room, stuck a spoon in all the canisters in the larder, and examined every book in the study. I lay down on the floor to look under the stove and the cupboards in the kitchen. We even looked through the seldom-used pots and pans and kitchen gadgets in the pantry. I checked around the back porch and cloakroom, where I discovered my father still kept my wellies from childhood, but there were no messages, hidden jewels, or plans for sabotage hidden inside.

There was the old heavy frying pan on the stove, where it sat waiting for my father's next breakfast at home. I didn't have the heart to put it away. My father's gardening gloves, hat and coat forlornly waited for him on their hooks in the cloakroom. I patted them as I walked by-after first checking the pockets of the coat and inside the hat and gloves for anything hidden.

"Kenseth didn't have much time to hide whatever it is we're looking for," I said, standing in the hall and glancing around.

"If it's even here," Esther said. "Maybe he was going to tell your father whatever it was when he saw him."

I shook my head. "Think of all the planning that went

into Kenseth disappearing in the Channel, faking his own death, and then the setup in Etretat. Whatever news he was bringing, it was important enough to send him back across the Channel. He wouldn't have left getting a message to someone about his discovery to chance."

"Perhaps the woman you saw the other night, or the woman who was with him when he arrived here, took it."

"In which case we're wasting our time." I shrugged. "Let's finish searching this floor and then have the delicious lunch you brought."

I faced the closed door to the last room. I had refused to enter my mother's morning room since the last time I needed to sneak out of the house, and my hand shook as I turned the doorknob.

Esther reached out and put her hand over mine. "What's wrong?"

"I haven't entered this room in daylight in twenty years."

Esther pushed the door open and we both peered inside. "Why hadn't you?" she asked as she looked around.

The room had been redecorated and turned into another drawing room. Cold. Anonymous. It was as if my mother had never existed. Had never written letters in this room or read stories to me in the big armchair that was now missing, along with her desk.

"I was afraid of ghosts," I told her. "It turns out there was no reason to be afraid anymore."

Esther had lost her mother at the same age as I had. "This was your mother's room?"

"It was once. Now it's been redecorated and I don't

recognize the furniture or the color of the walls. I wonder when my father did this. This happened since I married Reggie and left home."

"If you hadn't been in here in daylight, why—?"

I walked over to the French doors. "The lock was broken. I could sneak in and out at night without my father being any the wiser. Very handy during and after university." I smiled. "And in the dark, I didn't have to be reminded of what I lost."

Esther shook her head slowly as she walked past me and started checking the sofa for hidden papers.

After I began checking for anything small John Kenseth could have hidden, I ceased to think of this as my mother's room. Now it was just another place that could contain the secret the dark-haired woman was searching for.

The secret I hoped would free my father.

We had no luck on the ground floor. After we finished off the bountiful lunch in the picnic basket with cups of tea and did the washing up, I said, "Do you mind if we do the first floor as well?" I didn't want to wear Esther out.

"Mind? I'm looking forward to it. This is the first time I've had any fun since Grandmama arrived." Esther started climbing the stairs.

I followed her. "She means well."

"So does my father, and even he isn't this obsessive about my health."

"He's more obsessive about your safety when you're with me," I said and we both grinned, remembering childhood misadventures. "We'll have to see about getting you out more often."

"And making my father nervous."

I chuckled at her too-true words. When we reached the top of the stairs, I said, "Let's start with my father's room. To your left."

I was immediately struck by seeing my mother's picture on my father's dresser, and by how much I resembled her. Then I turned and found a framed photograph of the woman I'd recently met on the nightstand by his bed.

Esther was the one to find the love letters. I told her to read them while I searched for the blueprints to the basement of Parliament or some other plan of attack. I was glad she didn't read them aloud.

I admit I was rougher making my search on the items in the room than I needed to be.

When I finished the room without success, I asked, "Do you think they're in code?"

"No, and the letters aren't flowery. They're straightforward and sensible." Esther glanced up at me. "She loves your father very much."

"How does she sign herself?"

"'J' on some, 'Julia' on others. Who is she, Livvy?"

I held up the photo by his pillow. It had to be a current picture, since the woman looked like the woman I'd met on Saturday, and she wore the same hairstyle. In the photo, her dark brown hair looked black. "The wife of a colleague of my father's."

"I'm sorry." Esther said the words as if she really meant them.

I was still too angry about my father's misplaced chivalry to feel any sympathy. "I'll start on my old room next."

My father had redecorated my childhood room so that any hint of my existence was erased. I often thought that was how he felt about me.

"This was the room you had as a girl?" Esther asked from the doorway. The room was now done in greens and cream and lace. Not the bright colors or sturdy fabrics favored when I was a child. My books and bookcase were gone. My childish paintings had been removed from the walls. The room was now sterile. Anonymous. Just like my mother's morning room. My father had removed every trace that either mother or I had lived there.

"Yes," I muttered as I lifted the mattress to look underneath. Nothing. The mystery woman had been up here for some reason, and I hoped I had interrupted her before she could retrieve her prize.

"Didn't your father save any of your exercise books or dolls or anything?" Esther sounded slightly horrified.

"When I married Reggie, I was told to take what I wanted. The rest would go in the dust bin."

"But he wouldn't—"

"Yes, he would. Check those drawers, will you? They should be empty." I dropped the mattress back in place and checked the cubbyhole under the eaves. There was nothing in this cold space, and nothing in my childhood hiding place under the boards.

"Not quite empty," Esther said.

I spun around to find her holding up two dolls, Annie

and Emma, my two favorite dolls throughout my childhood. My very lonely childhood. I'd been too embarrassed to take them with me to Reggie's flat.

Of all the things my father could have saved when I moved out, he chose the two things that had meant the most to me. Red-haired Emma wore a blue Victorian-style gown with a white collar and apron. Dark-haired Annie was dressed nearly identically, but in red. John Kenseth had helped me draw their likenesses one day.

I walked over and gave the dolls a hug. "Maybe he knew me better than I thought he did. Too bad they can't tell us the secret that woman broke in here to find."

"Wouldn't it be wonderful if they did," Esther said. "Those dolls look well loved."

Both dolls and their clothes were dirty, scratched, and missing a stitch or two.

I gave them another tight hug and something stiff crinkled in Emma's apron pocket. I reached in and found a piece of paper that hadn't been there before. Wide-eyed, I stared at Esther. My heart raced as I unfolded the note.

CHAPTER FOURTEEN

I smoothed out the paper from the doll's pocket and read,

> *R H-*
> *The German woman is staying at Little Hedges, Kent.*
> *I know who she really is, but I'm afraid she knows*
> *who I work for. She is dangerous. Be careful.*
> *J K*

Esther read by craning her neck past my shoulder. "I wonder what's at Little Hedges."

"I was once invited to dinner there. I had hoped never to return." It appeared I wasn't to be that lucky.

Esther and I returned to the *Daily Premier* and Sir Henry's office, the note held close in my handbag and my other hand clutching the picnic basket. Once Esther and I were seated in Sir Henry's office, I told him I would need more time off.

"Will it make a good story?" was his first question. Not *Where are you going?* Not *What have you discovered?*

I knew what was important to him. "Yes, but I don't know if you'll be allowed to print this news."

"We found a note from the murdered man to Livvy's father," Esther said in a tone that told me she was enjoying the intrigue.

"I need to follow up on the information in the message," I told him.

"And this will concern General Alford?" Sir Henry asked.

I wasn't certain how much I could tell him, but I answered, "Yes."

He steepled his short, chubby fingers. "I'm in a position to know how close we are drifting toward war. Take what time you need, but please keep us informed on how you are doing." He glanced at Esther and said grudgingly, "We want to know you're safe."

"Could you do one more thing for me? Could you send a message to Lady Abby Summersby if there's any change in my father's legal position?"

"Reggie's cousin?" Esther asked. "Isn't she the one who lives in Sussex?"

"Yes," I said. "I'll be staying with her."

"You were with her when you worked out the identity of the French assassin, weren't you? The woman who sent Mr. Churchill those exploding cigars," Sir Henry said.

When I looked horrified at how much he knew, he said "After you told me the French assassin was Fleur Bettenard, I spoke to General Alford. We had to decide just how much I could print."

"There's a mystery woman in this, too, who's been seen around my father's house."

Sir Henry leaned forward. "Is it the French assassin?"

"I only saw her for an instant. She has dark hair, where Fleur was a blonde."

"That can be changed," Esther pointed out.

"That's why I'm not certain. She didn't try to kill me. She ran. We were the only two in the house—"

"What?" Sir Henry leaned forward in his chair. "This woman broke into your father's house? She actually went inside?" For someone who grew up in poverty in Victorian-era Newcastle, he was surprisingly naïve about the capabilities of women.

"Yes. That's when I realized there was something John Kenseth must have hidden there." When Sir Henry didn't say any more, I continued. "Fleur is furious with me for ruining her hiding place at the fashion salon. She'd have killed me, so I don't think the burglar was her."

"And the note said 'German' woman, not 'French' woman," Esther said.

Looking back, I didn't know if Fleur was French or German. Her French, including her accent, was perfect, but she could have spent a long time studying the language.

I gave Sir Henry a smile. "How would you like a feature article on the painter, Alicia Crawford, for the women's pages? Little Hedges, which was mentioned in the note, is her home."

* * *

I gave Alicia Crawford a telephone call at Little Hedges and learned she was in London, staying with friends in Bloomsbury. I managed to get the name and number of her hostess by saying Alicia was expecting my call. I either have a naturally honest- sounding voice, or I've become adept at lying since I began investigating after Reggie's death.

I placed a call for Alicia at her hostess, Phyllis Waterbury's, telephone number, and learned she wasn't in. A cheerful young female voice invited me to a drinks party after work where I could speak to her.

Next, I took a bus to Mr. Peabody's office to show him the note. I wanted an officer of the court to hold a copy of it in case it might be needed in my father's defense.

Then I telephoned Sir Malcolm Freemantle's office from a red phone box outside Mr. Peabody's office.

After a minute or two, I was connected to Sir Malcolm. "Yes?" he asked in a suspicious tone.

I identified myself again and said, "I found a note from John Kenseth hidden at my father's house."

"Don't say any more. Come over here and bring the note." He gave me an address and then the line went dead.

I did as he asked, taking the bus to the same central London address that Elise Telfor had given me for the office of John Kenseth's contact. This time, I was on the list, checked by the uniformed guard at the door and escorted to a room on the third floor.

Sir Malcolm sat at his desk, his back to the windows and a spectacular bird's-eye view of bare branches and roofs outside. "Let me see this message," he said without so much as a "hello."

I handed the note to him and his eyes roamed over it slowly. "Are you familiar with this Little Hedges?"

"I had dinner there once." Then I added, "It was a large gathering. All of the neighbors plus some friends from

London."

"Then you've met the Palmers." He made his words a statement.

"Yes. And I've been invited to a drinks party in Bloomsbury that Mrs. Palmer, known as the painter Alicia Crawford, is attending. I'm going to try to find out when she's returning home and then set up a series of interviews with her at Little Hedges. Hopefully, the German woman will be there."

"You did this on your own initiative?" He sounded surprised.

"Of course." I'd smuggled valuables out of Nazi-held territory, unmasked killers, and identified the French assassin. I had to show resourcefulness to work on those tasks, and I was proud of my success.

"Good. Keep in touch. I want to know when you travel to Sussex for these interviews, and you need to tell me about anyone you find suspicious."

"Does that include Mr. Palmer?"

Sir Malcolm straightened his back and glared at me. "Edmund Palmer may be one of the most dangerous men in England."

I didn't like the man, but I hadn't thought of him that way. Maybe going to Little Hedges wasn't such a great idea. "What do you mean?"

"He owns a shipping company and he holds pro-Nazi sympathies. We believe he is smuggling spies, weapons, and explosives into this country. He may be carrying plans of our power plants, maps of our cities, and train schedules to Germany."

"But you can't catch him at any of it?" I was surprised to learn sir Malcolm's officers were incapable of stopping someone that dangerous.

Sir Malcolm looked down and muttered, "No. It's hard to find something small in a huge freighter, especially when we can't find a legal reason to board and search his ships."

So that was why Sir Malcolm hadn't been successful. "Instead, you had John Kenseth listening in on the shortwave radio communications from Palmer's ships as they traveled along the Channel. He was searching for which ones carried contraband." Now I knew who Kenseth had been working for, and why.

"Much of their communications are in code, but not all. We were lucky enough to overhear plans to drop off a spy from Palmer's freighter, *The Phoenix*."

"Plans Kenseth was lucky enough to overhear," I corrected him.

He gave me an infinitesimal nod. "We caught the man shortly after he came ashore. Too little time for him to do any damage, but he gave us some information on Palmer's activities. This proved what we believed. Palmer is smuggling things from his freighters to our shores."

"What is it you want me to find at Little Hedges?" I didn't have any arrest powers, or any skill at capturing enemy agents.

"It's vitally important that we know the identity of the German woman and if she had anything to do with Kenseth's murder." He paused.

"Is that all?" I asked. It appeared that I'd have to do the

government's job if I was to clear my father's name.

"Not in the least. We'd also like to know if Palmer knew someone was listening in on his ships and if he knew who it was. Oh, and if you find written evidence of Palmer's involvement with Germany, steal it and bring it back here."

I stared at him, stunned. Who did he think I was? All I wanted to do was free my father from prison and the noose.

When I reached for the note, Sir Malcolm said, "I'll keep this."

* * *

At seven o'clock that night, I presented myself at a top-floor flat in Bloomsbury. I had considered the artistic talents of the group I'd be meeting and decided on a long, slinky black gown with a flaming red silk shawl. For a change, I wore all black accessories, even my costume jewelry.

The door was opened by a maid who took my cape and handed me over to Phyllis Waterbury, my hostess. We had only met a few times, but she had a formidable reputation in women's rights and artistic circles. Phyllis looked like the elderly bluestocking she was, with a head of gray hair done up in a sloppy bun and a long-sleeved blue gown that covered her from neck to ankle.

I held out my hand. "Miss Waterbury, thank you so much for inviting me."

"Phyllis, please. I followed your articles on Nazi Austria. Most enlightening to learn what the women are thinking."

I loved to hear praise of my work for the *Daily Premier.*

So little of it was worthy of notice. "Please call me Livvy. Is Alicia here for another show?"

"No. She just needs to escape to the city and her friends from time to time. Her husband keeps her locked up in that provincial retreat of his far too much."

"They live in a beautiful area. I wonder if she finds the landscape inspiring."

"Ask her yourself. She's in the drawing room." Phyllis made a sweeping gesture toward the open doorway.

I walked in and gasped. The room was huge and high-ceilinged, with paintings and sculptures of varying sizes and styles spread around the room. I recognized one painting on the far wall as an Alicia Crawford. Stained-glass works hung in front of two of the windows. The effect was overwhelming, but this was still clearly a living space and not a museum.

The room was filled with guests, all female, and from their dress I would guess they could be divided into two groups- academic types such as Phyllis, their gowns older and shapeless, and artistic types such as Alicia, dressed in newer, brighter styles.

"You like my drawing room?" Phyllis asked, standing next to me as she surveyed her guests.

"It's breathtaking."

"When you catch your breath, I'll introduce you to the other guests," she said in a dry voice. She walked forward with all the pomp and grace of her eminent status and I dutifully followed.

She stopped by the drinks table. I recognized the label on the red wine as being a good vintage and said so. "Help yourself to a glass," Phyllis told me, "and then join me."

I learned the stained-glass pieces had been made by a stunning woman called Hama, who was dressed in a sari. She was talking to a painter named Celestine, who was known for creating large, rather shocking modern works. That night, Celestine was remarkable for wearing what appeared to be a man's evening jacket and white tie over an ugly orange evening gown.

The four of us were joined by another academic, judging from her formless gown. She introduced herself as Dr. Warren and then said, "Do you do anything creative?"

Surprised, all I could think to respond was, "Yes. I sketch fashions when I cover teas for the newspaper."

"Oh." She walked off, obviously unimpressed.

Phyllis raised her eyebrows, then wandered away. I followed her over to where Alicia was listening to two women argue about the relative merits of a painting technique.

Alicia excused herself and stepped away to where I stood. "It's nice to see you again, Mrs. Denis."

"Livvy, please. I suppose Phyllis told you I hope to interview you at home in your studio for the *Daily Premier*. I'm sure the view is as outstanding as that from your dining room."

"Yes, Phyllis told me," was said in the most neutral tone possible.

This didn't sound promising. "The scheduling is up to you, of course."

"Yes, well, I don't know when I'll be home and available."

I gave her a big smile. "Are we talking a week? A month? Never?"

She looked either angry or frantic for an instant. "I won't be cornered into making a decision at this time."

"I didn't mean to—" I took half a step back.

Alicia turned and stalked off through a doorway across the room. Every head swiveled from the doorway to me.

"Oh, dear. I must have been too pushy. I'm sorry," I said to Phyllis. "But oh, her art..."

"You couldn't have known. She can't decide whether to go back to Little Hedges. You know what men are." Phyllis shook her head with a gloomy expression.

"There's another woman in the picture?" I asked, wondering if I was right. Could the German woman be Edmund Palmer's lover?

"That's none of our business," Phyllis said.

"That is everyone's guess, and Alicia is furious with us. She denies it, of course," said a voice from behind me.

I swung around to glaze at Celestine's pale face, looking like a cat with a bowl of cream. "Then why does she say she can't decide whether to return home?" I felt she must be giving her friends some reason.

"She says there's no other woman," Celestine said with a shrug and a knowing smile. "She says she just prefers life in big cities."

"Is there anyone in particular you suspect for the role as homewrecker?" I asked.

"Of course not. None of us spend any time in her husband's company. We can't stand him." Celestine lit a cigarette at the end of a long ebony holder. "Edmund has always run his company his way. He's never had a business partner. Can't stand not to be in charge of everything. In control."

"Perhaps Alicia enjoys having him run the house so she can concentrate on her art," I suggested.

"Whose side are you on?" Phyllis said, one eyebrow raised.

"I wasn't aware I needed to take a side. I don't know either of them well. I was merely suggesting a possibility. And if there isn't anything going on now, leaving the field open might allow all sorts of unintended consequences." I tried to sound sympathetic.

Phyllis smiled. "You're in the 'fight for him' camp."

"I didn't know there were camps." Getting mixed up in gossip wouldn't help me free my father. Or get me into Little Hedges on the pretext of interviewing Alicia so I could look around.

When Celestine finished blowing smoke rings, she said, "Half the women here think Alicia should go back and take control of her home and her husband. The other half think if she stays here, he'll come to her on bended knee."

"Where do you stand?" I asked Celestine. From what I'd seen of Edmund Palmer at the dinner party, "bended knee" didn't seem likely.

"She's been here a week licking her wounds. I think it high time she goes back and reclaims her place in his life. Or at least puts a claim on the house. I hear it's spectacular," Celestine said.

I remembered the view from the dining room. "It is."

"Edmund discourages Alicia from inviting her friends down to Little Hedges," Phyllis said.

"Little wonder, with the company he keeps," Celestine said, blowing another smoke ring.

"Whose company?" I asked. Here was some information that might prove useful.

"I think she needs to spend more time here and decide what she really wants," Phyllis said over my question.

"But for how long? Eventually she has to choose," I said. I needed her to return to Little Hedges before my father's trial.

"There's no rush. My home will always be open for her. By the way, how did you get invited to the house?" Phyllis sounded a little envious. Surely she'd been invited to Alicia's home.

"They had a dinner party for the neighbors, some aristocrats, and her agent. I was staying with one of the neighbors at the time and was invited along."

"You've met her agent?" Celestine said with a snicker.

"Oh, yes." Remembering him caused a small shudder.

"Yes. Paul is a horror," Phyllis added.

"Paul?" I didn't remember his name.

"Paul Bigby. Her agent. He leers and leans into you. Even me, and I'm nobody's prize." Phyllis looked down for a moment at her shapeless gown and then peered into my face before looking past me.

I turned my head and found Alicia Crawford standing next to me.

"Please forgive me, Mrs. Denis."

"Livvy, please. And I overstepped my bounds. I

apologize."

"No. It's just—everyone has an opinion on when I should return home. Whether I should return home."

"That's up to you. When and if you do, I'd like to do a photo essay for the *Daily Premier* about you working in your studio in the gorgeous countryside."

"I know my agent would appreciate that. Let's leave it there for the moment, shall we?" She smiled for an instant, shook her shoulders, and lifted her chin. "Golly, I need a drink."

I mentally crossed my fingers that I'd hear from her soon. My father's trial would start in two weeks, and I needed an excuse to spend time around Little Hedges searching for the German woman. I needed to do something to save him from the gallows.

CHAPTER FIFTEEN

The next morning, I called on Mr. Peabody, and by noon I had gained permission to visit my father again. Once again, I presented myself at the entrance to Brixton Prison. I was shown into the same small room as before. A bored warder looked out on us from the window. The only change I could see from the one before was this warder's young age.

My father came in, looking thinner, wearier, and angrier than before. He sat down across from me and crossed his arms in silence.

"John Kenseth left you a message at your house," I blurted out.

He sat bolt upright and said, "Do you have it?"

"I gave it to Sir Malcolm."

"What?" Father shouted loud enough the warder heard him through the glass and half rose from his chair.

"Don't worry. I showed it to Mr. Peabody, who made a copy he can testify to. Who's the German woman?"

"I don't know."

"Have you heard of her?"

"Yes. We don't have a good description of her. She seems to come and go from England at will. We believe she has a network of sources backing her." He shrugged, and I noticed how thin his shoulders had become.

"Kenseth said in his note that she was at Little Hedges and he feared that she was on to him. He was with a dark-haired woman when he came to your house the day he died, and I saw a dark-haired woman in your house the other night when…" I didn't want to say I was looking for evidence of Father's lover.

"A woman burgled my house?" I couldn't tell which shocked him more, that he was burgled or that a woman had done it.

"Yes. Since I disturbed her, I took the house apart looking for what she was searching for. I found the note. It was addressed to you and signed by John Kenseth, using only your initials and his."

"The German woman was at Little Hedges," Father said to himself as he drummed his fingers on the table. He appeared to be making mental calculations.

"But you just said no one knows what she looks like. So how did Kenseth know she's the German woman? I wish someone would please tell me her identity."

He leaned forward and lowered his voice. "I suspect he knew from something he overheard on the shortwave radio. He'd been listening to traffic between Little Hedges and Palmer's ships. Had been for two years."

"How do you know that?" I murmured.

"How does anyone know anything?" Then he gave me a dry look. "Sir Malcolm, while I was in his custody."

"What is her name?"

"No one has told me."

I wondered if no one had said because no one knew, or because Sir Malcolm was keeping that information to himself. "Does anyone have a photograph of her?"

"Not that I'm aware of."

"But how could he have known it was her, and who she was?"

My father tapped the table. "Kenseth always had an eye for detail. He was an artist at heart. He may have recognized her from somewhere else."

"How would that have told him this woman is the German you've been looking for?"

"Some clue he picked up from the shortwave traffic he listened to. This woman was in a certain place carrying a certain book. Something such as that. Perhaps he'd seen her before in a different context." He made a sweeping gesture. "Oh, I don't know."

Guessing didn't get us any closer to her identity. Meanwhile, I couldn't resist the urge any longer. "I found something else. A photograph. On your nightstand. Not of Mother."

"No." He shook his head and looked down. "Not your mother."

"She's married. How could you?"

His head jerked up and he glared at me. "Why are you here? To tell me how superior you are?" Now he was practically shouting.

I glared back. "I'm here because I'm trying to save you from the gallows. What you do with your life is your business."

All the air seemed to leave his body. In a sad voice he

told me, "I loved your mother very much. When she died, it just about destroyed me. But that was twenty years ago. Twenty years of lonely nights. Of emptiness. And then Julia came along. I never expected to fall for her."

I saw something in his eyes I never expected to see. A sorrow so deep that just to glimpse it was painful. "I'm sorry you're going through this," I managed to get out around the lump in my throat.

"I want to get out of here. I want to follow up on John's note." He banged his fists on the table.

"You can't, but I can."

"Olivia, no. It's out of the question. It's dangerous."

"I've already put a plan in motion."

"They killed John, and he was trained. I don't want them to kill you, too." A note of desperation sounded in my father's voice.

"I don't want them to hang you knowing I haven't done everything I can to free you. You're my father. And you go on trial for your life in less than two weeks." We might not get along, but he was my nearest relative and I felt determined to protect him.

"Thank you for reminding me." He glared at me as if this were all my fault.

My shoulders slumped. "Sorry. That wasn't very tactful. But please, try to eat. You're looking so thin."

"They don't serve anything worth eating south of the river." He gave me a weak smile.

I tried to put on an encouraging expression. "I'll try to find the German woman, or whoever's been burgling your house. I think capturing her will be your best hope."

"At least take Adam along. He knows what he's doing."

"I can't. Currently, I can't reach him. Army business." At least I hoped it was an army assignment. But what was he doing in Paris?

"I'm sorry, Olivia. That must be difficult. I know our separations during the Great War were hard on your mother and me. Too bad he's not here to help you."

"You don't think I'm capable of looking out for myself." My father couldn't have made it clearer. At that moment, I was torn between saving him and strangling him.

"No, I don't. I lost your mother. I don't want to lose you, too." He reached out and clutched my fingers with one hand.

The warder knocked on the glass and shook his head. My father dropped my hand.

Breaking that skin-on-skin contact hurt. After my father proclaimed he didn't want to lose me, I felt a heartbreak at the loss of his touch.

"Is there anything you can tell me about the German woman? Any rumors? Gossip? Anything Sir Malcolm let slip and told you not to repeat?" Sir Malcolm seemed the type not to share knowledge that came his way. I needed every scrap of information I could get if I was to succeed.

And I was the only one looking for the truth.

My father leaned forward, and after glancing at the window said in a quiet tone, "There was one thing I heard. I don't know how useful it will be. Palmer has a cottage in the seaside town of Hastings. We believe sailors row onto the beach from his ships and drop off and pick up spies, weapons, explosives, whatever. We believe the German woman may travel this way from England to the continent. The cottage and the shingle beach have been watched by Sir Malcolm's men. Nothing. So far, this information has been useless."

"Who might know what the German woman looks like or anything about her?" I was practically whispering.

"I have no idea. This wasn't one of my projects."

"Whose was it?"

"Apparently Kenseth's, but that's just a guess."

I made up my mind. "I'm going to stay with Abby for a little while."

"You plan to involve Abby in your hunt for this unknown woman?" He shook his head. "No. I won't allow it."

"That's the good thing about having you locked up. You can't stop me. Especially since it's in your best interest that I succeed."

"Olivia—"

"Don't worry, Father. I have to wait for one more thing before I can leave town."

"Sir Henry's blessing, I suppose." Now he sounded grumpy.

I rose from my chair. "I already have that. Sir Henry wants me to get you released. He considers you a man of honor."

I left my father with a surprised look on his face.

* * *

A day later, I received a telephone call from Alicia Crawford inviting me to luncheon the next day at her club. I had never been to the Women's Artists and Poets Club and looked forward to the lunch almost as much as following a path toward freeing my father.

I wasn't disappointed. While most clubs' interiors were bland, gray, and dreary, at this club there were yellow and pink accents to every sofa, and avant-garde artwork hung from the walls. The dining room, where I met Alicia, featured art deco flourishes.

We kept up small talk through the soup and halfway through the main course, which I recognized from my visit to Greece with my father as a spicy mutton stew. The stew in this case was mostly potatoes and hot spices.

"I've made up my mind. I will head back to Little Hedges in a day or two and we can meet for an article on my studio."

"Thank you. Do you mind going back to Little Hedges?"

She studied my face. "Why would I mind?"

"Women don't leave their homes and their artist's studios for prolonged periods of time without a good reason. I hope that reason isn't discord at home."

"You've been listening to the crows. That's what I call them. All the gloomy women around Phyllis. If he's a man, he must be a dog. There are many men I like and admire. My husband is one. And you, Olivia? Are there men you admire?"

I thought of Adam, Sir Henry, James Powell, General Alford. "Yes, several, including my fiancé."

Alicia nodded at my response and promised to call Sir Henry's secretary when she knew what day she'd return to Little Hedges. I hoped I'd have good luck finding the German woman without paying with my life.

As soon as I returned home, I telephoned my late husband's cousin and my friend, Lady Abigail Summersby.

While Abby was welcoming, she asked a lot of questions over the phone. I put her off until I saw her at the station. I packed for a week's stay and left a note on the kitchen table in case Adam was given leave. Or at least returned from Paris. What was going on there that he couldn't receive letters at the embassy?

Adam had a key to my flat so he had a place to land in London whenever he received some time off. He wanted to make our relationship permanent immediately, but since he was out of town with the army so much, I wanted to stay single so I could keep my job with all its challenges.

If I hadn't married Reggie so young, I wouldn't have known how much I'd have to give up to marry Adam. Especially with all his travel for the army.

When I arrived at the station two hours later, Abby was waiting. The porter piled up my luggage on a trolley and rolled it out to the car while Abby gushed about not seeing me in ages and how glad she was I had come for a visit.

I'd visited Abby only a month before. Her voice carried a note of strain even as she appeared too cheerful.

Once the car was loaded and we were on the country road toward Summersby House, Abby began her interrogation. "You should be at work, or breaking your father out of jail, or petitioning Parliament. Anything other than visiting me. So, why are you here?"

"Once again, you need to keep this secret, even from Sir John."

"That's not fair, Livvy. He's my husband and your host." Her response was as aggravated as I expected.

"I've had to sign the Official Secrets Act to help my father, and the less I have to break it, the better off we'll be."

"Why would General Alford—?"

"Not General Alford. A civilian in charge of hunting Nazis. Part of the Foreign Office. My father was working for this man."

Abby pursed her lips and blew out, her focus on the road ahead. After a minute of silence, she said, "Whatever you are here for, will it help prove your father's innocence?"

I told Abby about the female with Kenseth in my father's house, the break-in, the note, and the rumors about the German woman.

When I finished, Abby said, "So we're going to Hastings?"

We? I decided, on balance, that was fair. "Yes."

"It'll be cold and windy on the beach this time of year. We'll stand out among the fishermen."

"Then we'll need to find a way to watch the beach from somewhere warm."

There was silence in the auto for a few minutes. We were almost to Summersby House when Abby said, "Mrs. Miller's."

"Who?"

"She's the wife of a soldier who served under John in the war. He was killed. John looked her up after the armistice and we stay at her lodgings a couple of times a year in the winter to help tide her over. Her house overlooks the part of the beach where the fishing boats rest."

The location sounded ideal. "Terrific. Get packed and we can head down there immediately."

I was wrong about immediately. Sir John was waiting for us when we arrived. When Abby told him that she and I were going to Hastings for a couple of days, he said, "Good. That will give me a chance to catch up with Mrs. Miller. It's halfway through November. She shouldn't be busy this time of year."

I was surprised. I hadn't considered that Sir John would want to join us. Before I could say anything, Abby said, "Then we better get ready. Mary, will you take Mrs. Denis's luggage to her room so she can decide what she wants to take with her?"

I was halfway up the stairs when she warned me, "Make sure you take warm clothes. It's always frigid and windy this time of year."

While I repacked, I could hear the rumble of Sir John's voice. I was certain he was discussing the reasons for our trip with Abby. I had no idea what she would tell him.

I prepared for three days, covering every contingency, and carried my bag downstairs to the drawing room to the sound of Sir John and Abby's voices.

They came in a few minutes later. Abby said, "John is going with us. I haven't told him why we're going to Hastings, and he promises not to interfere, but he is traveling and staying with us on this trip."

Her expression told me not to argue. Sir Malcolm

might not approve, but I didn't care. Sir John knew lots of people along the south coast, he was pleasant company, and he wanted my father freed from prison almost as much as I did. "Good. Abby tells me you know a landlady with a house facing the beach."

Sir John told me a little about Mrs. Miller and the late Sergeant Miller while we carried our suitcases out. We appeared to not have a care in the world. Abby followed, a surprised look on her face.

Sir John drove, Abby rode in the front seat with him, and I sat in the back, waiting for the inquisition.

It didn't take long. We chatted for a few minutes before Sir John said, "Abby said you signed the Official Secrets Act."

"She shouldn't have told you that."

"You shouldn't have told *her* that."

"True." I didn't say another word, waiting to see how much Sir John wanted to know about our trip to Hastings.

"I don't know what your assignment is, and I don't want to know, but you should never have mixed Abby up in this mess."

"I'm after the person who killed John Kenseth. I want to see my father freed." My tone should have told him how serious I was about this investigation.

"And if the Official Secrets Act is involved, you are working for the government," Sir John continued.

"Sort of."

He gave me a quick glance. "What do you mean, sort of?"

"They're using me as part of their investigation, but

they aren't paying me."

"Livvy, if you are part of their investigation, you can't just do as you want. There are rules to be followed. You can't act on every little whim that strikes your fancy. There are orders. Procedures. A task you are expected to complete."

I'd never heard Sir John sound more condescending. Through gritted teeth, I said, "My task is to find the person who killed John Kenseth. To do that, I need to take the investigation to Hastings."

"What do you hope to find there?" he finally asked.

"A woman coming or going by boat in secret from one of Mr. Palmer's freighters. A woman who was seen entering my father's house with John Kenseth the day he was murdered and has since burgled the house."

"All this by one woman?" Sir John glanced at Abby, skepticism written on his face.

"I don't know. I hope so. And if it's all the same person, no one knows her name or has a photograph of her," I answered.

"Anonymous as the French assassin was until you caught up with her," Abby said.

"It might be Fleur Bettenard, the French assassin, but this person is referred to as the German woman. And she has dark hair."

"She's an assassin, Livvy. What are you going to do if you catch her?" Sir John asked.

"I don't plan to catch her. Only follow her and call Sir Malcolm."

"Sir Malcolm Freemantle?" Sir John nearly lost control

of his auto and had to struggle some moments to keep the car out of a ditch.

"Yes," I said when I caught my breath and was sure we wouldn't crash. Why would Sir John know Sir Malcolm, who was a civilian? Sir John's service was with the army.

"You do realize he's England's spymaster. Half of the Foreign Office report to him."

CHAPTER SIXTEEN

I spent the rest of the ride to Hastings considering Sir John's announcement. If he was right, everything John Kenseth had been doing, everything my father was involved with, went through Sir Malcolm's hands.

When we arrived at Mrs. Miller's guesthouse, I was pleased to see there were several windows facing the beach. We carried in our suitcases from the car and found Mrs. Miller, a short, thin, worried-looking woman, waiting for us. Her pinched expression disappeared as she greeted Sir John and Abby, assuring us she had room.

"Facing the water?" I asked.

Her worried expression returned. "This time of year, those rooms can be a mite drafty. Are you sure you want to face the Channel?"

"I do. Abby, which would you prefer?" I glanced at Abby and Sir John.

"It's only for a few days, and the weather has been bright. The Channel it is," Abby said with a smile.

We signed the guest register and Mrs. Miller led us up one flight to our rooms. I looked out the window in my room to find a wonderful view across the street to the net huts on the beach and beyond them to the glistening waters of the Channel. The view of the beach itself was blocked by the tall, narrow huts.

When I slipped off my coat, the chill in the air struck me. The curtains shifted in the breeze coming in through the window frame, warning me there would be no warmth at night. I pulled on a thick woolen sweater and walked to Abby and Sir John's room next door.

Mrs. Miller was with them, talking about the others staying in the house. "There are two fishermen down from London enjoying a seaside holiday. They're on the top floor, one flight up, so I'm sure they won't bother you."

"We'll no doubt meet them at breakfast," Abby said.

"They go out early and never take their breakfast here," Mrs. Miller told her. "And I don't think they're having much luck, since they never bring any fish back here. I told them they could store their catch in the chiller in the cellar, but they haven't."

Sir John looked at me and nodded. I had the impression he was already suspicious of these two men. Then again, so was I. Sir John must have read my questions on my face.

"At least we won't be too much bother, just the five of us," Abby said. "How are your children doing?"

I heard more about the Miller children than I wanted to, especially since I wanted to go down to the beach before it grew dark. Finally, I broke in. "I'm going to look at the boats. Wait for me for dinner, please."

"Do you want me to come with you?" Sir John said.

"Only if you want to get out and stretch your legs and listen to the gulls."

"Just return before it's too dark out," Abby said.

I went back to my room and put on heavy socks and flat-soled shoes. Then I bundled up, adding a woolly hat and gloves to my heavy coat.

The moment I stepped outside of Mrs. Miller's, I was glad of my warmest clothes. The sun lied as it shone brightly in the wide blue sky, pretending to be the same sun that made the water a refuge when people traveled here in the heat of the summer.

A fierce wind stung my cheeks as I crossed the road, until I was in the shelter of the net huts built closely together on the beach. However, even without the wind it was still cold as I cut through a pathway between the tall, narrow, dark-stained huts, while the gulls cried as they circled above me, looking for discards from cleaning the catch.

Once on the far side of the huts, the wind struck me hard unless I was directly behind a boat. The wooden fishing boats, their traps and lines piled up to dry on the sand, sat waiting to be pushed off the shore and into the water. Beyond the boats, there was a narrow strip of shingle beach with waves crashing against the shoreline, while in the distance, freighters passed by.

I walked a short distance in one direction and then in the other on the shingle beach. The wind blew in my face no matter which way I went. If I'd hoped to see a rowboat coming in to the beach from one of the oceangoing ships passing us out in the Channel, I was disappointed.

Any rowboat would have a hard time making its way to shore. The waves appeared to be as tall as I was. Would these waves keep any of Palmer's freighters from sending spies or supplies to shore?

There was no sign of lights around the boats or the huts. It would be dark out there at night, and all I had was my pocket torch. I thought of my visit to Etretat across the Channel. Then I'd had Adam for company. Despite the presence of Sir John and Abby, I missed him.

I was sorry I'd quarreled with him, but I kept coming back to wondering what he could be doing in Paris that was so secret.

Once I pulled my attention back to the task at hand, I took in the details of the beach and how a person might escape detection while coming ashore. I walked back across the road in the direction of town. Sir Malcolm had given me the address of Palmer's house in Hastings and I went to study it.

The area around Mrs. Miller's was an old and shabby section of town. I guessed some of these houses had been in fishermen's families for generations, and they rarely had the time or money to invest in upkeep. The house I was looking for was a weathered gray a short walk from the net huts, and appeared to only be large enough for four rooms, two up and two down. It was also next to an alley, or twittern, that ran between the street the house faced and the next road, as I found out when I walked the length of the alley. A tall board fence with a wide gate blocked my view of the backyard, so I couldn't tell if there were other ways to escape the property.

It would be easy to approach the house from different directions. Was this why no one had caught most of the people being smuggled in and out by boat?

I returned to Mrs. Miller's house to find Abby in a nice, long-sleeved evening gown. "Hurry up and dress. We're going to dinner at the Royal Victoria Hotel in St. Leonard's," she told me.

Sir John then appeared in a white waistcoat and black tie. "Could you fix my cufflinks, my dear?"

I hurried into my room to change. Over my elegant blue gown, I wore my heaviest coat with a wool cloche and thick gloves.

We drove along the shore road to St. Leonard's with its impressive hotel, where the dining room was less than half full. We may have been the youngest customers there. I wondered where the young people of Hastings went for dinner and a good time.

Somehow, I couldn't see Sir John being comfortable in a dance hall. Better we stick to hotel dining rooms.

Once the waiter had taken our order, Abby said in a low voice, "What did you learn on the beach?"

"It would be very easy for any number of people to hide around the net huts or the boats at night, either to land or take off. There's no light. And the house belonging to Palmer is convenient to the fishing beach and easy to reach from different directions by using the alleyways."

"The government has people who are already staking out the beach to catch this woman. I'm certain of it," Sir John said.

"Probably," I agreed, "but from what I learned I wanted to give it a try. And since you know people here, I thought you could help me. Help my father prove his innocence by catching this woman."

"For once, Livvy, I applaud you involving yourself where you shouldn't." He nodded to me.

"And I thank you for getting involved, too." I gave him a bright smile.

"So, what is our next step?" Abby asked. I suspected she was more practical than Sir John and me combined.

"I'm going to look out my window tonight and see if I can spot a boat coming in to shore. Then I'll run down and see what I can find out. I brought warm dark clothing for this purpose."

"You shouldn't have any trouble spotting a boat coming into shore tonight. It's close to a full moon," Abby said.

I looked out the large windows, but compared to the light in the dining room with its massive chandeliers, the area outside was unlit. "It looks terribly dark out."

"The moon doesn't rise until ten." Abby smiled at me. "I can tell you're not a farmer or a gardener."

"See how useful she is," I told Sir John. "With you two here, we should be able to find something to ensure my father's release."

"Was any of this Sir Malcolm's idea?" Sir John asked.

"In a way." I didn't want to reveal too much.

He glowered at me. "In what way?"

I won a reprieve when the waiter came with our soup and poured the wine. Once we'd finished that course, Abby said, "Do you think I'm right in guessing nothing will happen until at least ten?"

I looked at Sir John. He had experience from the Great

War. I was using guesswork.

"I think you're right, my dear. We have plenty of time for dinner before we need to go back and change into very warm clothes." He turned to me then and held up a hand. "I'm going with you. Do not argue with me."

"You and Abby are both welcome to come along. Between the three of us, we may be successful."

Now that we had a plan, even if it was "don't begin a watch until the moon rises," I felt as though we were doing something useful. Something toward catching the German woman and getting my father out of jail.

* * *

I'd have been happy if we spotted a boat coming into shore as the moon rose over St. Leonard's. As it turned out, I didn't see any boat come into shore until nearly midnight, with the moon well up in the sky. I might have missed it, since I was drawn in to the Agatha Christie mystery I was reading. As soon as I saw the boat cutting through the waves toward the shore, I slipped the book I was reading into my inner coat pocket and hurried to Sir John and Abby's room. I banged on the door.

Abby opened the door rubbing her eyes. "Shush, you'll wake John."

"I'm awake," came from the still figure on the bed. "Old soldiers learn to wake on an instant's notice." He rose fully clothed and pulled on his coat.

We were ready in our heavy dark clothing in a minute and hurried downstairs. Sir John had obtained a front door key from Mrs. Miller, which he carried in his trouser pocket. While he locked the door, Abby and I trotted across the empty road and moved between the net huts, the moon guiding our path and a few startled gulls serenading us.

Sir John came up behind us and whispered, "I'll go this way and patrol the perimeter. Remember, follow. Don't try to be brave." He went off to the right.

Abby and I stuck together as we wove our way between the huts. The boat came ashore, but instead of being dragged onto the beach as the fishing boats were, we could see two figures head in our direction while the others fought against the surf to push the boat back into the water.

I moved forward and then realized someone, not Sir John, was walking down the beach toward the two arrivals.

I stopped and Abby bumped into me. "Where's John?" she whispered.

I shook my head.

She dashed around a boat, staying low, in the direction where we had last seen Sir John. I moved forward between the boats, keeping the figure who'd come from the town in sight.

Staying in the shadow of one of the fishing boats, I saw the figure from the town greet the two from the boat. I could hear them speak, but I only caught about every fourth word on the breeze.

Why couldn't the wind blow toward me when I wanted to hear something?

One of the words I did hear clearly was "Palmer." Another was "ship."

Then I heard a shout and an oath and looked toward the water's edge, where the boat had capsized. The men were struggling with it, but in the process, they were battered by the waves and the wooden hull. The boat rose on a wave and plowed into someone, sending him under the water. Then the boat seemed to sink.

The trio stopped and looked at the men trying to float the boat, who were now shouting and cursing loudly in German and English. Then the couple and their guide from the town hurried up the beach, moving closer and then nearly beside me as they followed a path through the boats.

I started to follow them, having seen them clearly for a moment in the moonlight. One was male, one was female, and one, oh, dear Heavens, was Fleur Bettenard, the French assassin. I felt a shiver run through me that had nothing to do with the wind.

I couldn't tell who had come off the boat and who had come from town. Fleur's presence did make me wonder if the German woman and the French assassin were one and the same.

Hopefully, Sir John and Abby would catch the other two, or at least be able to identify them again. I was going to stop Fleur.

Keeping to the shadows, I followed the group to the first net huts when a searchlight blinded me. A whistle blew twice. A voice called out, "Police. Halt."

The trio darted in different directions. In the dark and cold, police seemed to pour out of boats and huts, colliding with other figures. Some raced after the three who had come ashore. Some went to the aid of the boatmen still fighting the surf.

With my dazzled eyes I tried to keep track of the French assassin. I saw Fleur dash between some net huts and I followed her at top speed, turning on my torch.

I caught up to her and grabbed at her jacket. I managed to get a fistful of material and yanked, turning her around. We stared at each other for what was probably an instant, but felt like an hour. We were only a few inches apart. Close enough even in the light of my small torch and the moon to recognize each other. I kept my clutch on her jacket and glared at her.

She snapped, "You," and then I saw her hand reach into her pocket. The flash of what must have been a knife blade glittered. She struck out at me.

I let her go as I jumped back. My feet caught in some nets and I fell backward. The back of my head struck the side of a hut as I went down.

I lay there, listening to shouts and running footsteps for a moment before the blinding stars in front of my eyes stopped. I rubbed my aching head and felt a bump begin to rise. Angry at losing Fleur once again, I dashed off in the direction I thought she had gone, turning off my torch to make myself harder to find. She wouldn't get away again. She couldn't. My father's life might depend on it.

I'd passed two huts, running in the shadows, before I tripped over something large and solid on the path and went flying, landing sprawled in the sand.

I turned on my torch again and shone it around me. When the light fell on the slack face and unseeing eyes of Mr. Whittier, sprawled behind me on the blood-soaked rough sand where my feet were still tangled up with him, I let out a shriek. Then I saw blood on my leg and my sock and the shock made me begin to scream.

CHAPTER SEVENTEEN

Men dressed in both police uniforms and civilian dress sprang out of the dark from all directions. They lifted me into a standing position and out of the way as they attempted to render aid to Mr. Whittier. I looked at the poor man and saw a bloody wound sliced across his neck.

Abby appeared out of the crowd and put an arm around me to pull me aside. "Are you all right, Livvy?"

"Yes." I clutched Abby's arm and pointed between two huts. "Did you see her? Fleur ran that way toward the road."

"No, I didn't. Are you sure?"

"Yes. Well, I think so." I looked around at the trench coat- and bowler-wearing men who appeared to run hither and fro and the uniformed constables who were closely examining the area around Mr. Whittier's body. I should tell the man in charge. But which one was he?

"Ah, Mrs. Denis. You certainly stir things up, don't you?"

I whirled around to find Sir Malcolm Freemantle staring down on me. "I saw—"

"A great many things, I'm sure. Let's move you out of everyone's way, shall we?"

"Mr. Whittier—" I looked over and swallowed as I saw someone had covered the poor man's face with a coat. I started to shiver.

"Yes, I know. A terrible shame. He was a good man. Someone will answer for this." In the tricky light of competing torches, his face took on a sinister expression. Hateful. Evil.

My shivers changed to shudders.

"You're not going to fall apart on me, are you, Mrs. Denis?"

I fought the tremors running through my body, making it hard to breathe. "Of course not," came out as a gasp.

Abby saw the blood on my leg and my sock and said, "Let's get you back to the house and clean you up."

"Not just yet, Lady Summersby," Sir Malcolm said. "Let's join Sir John and go back to my lodgings."

He gathered us up with a man in a trench coat and another dressed as a sailor, both appearing half-drowned, and headed toward the town. At least the wind didn't seem so fierce here.

The house he led us to, half a block up a main street from the beach, was as large as Mrs. Miller's and apparently had been taken over by Sir Malcolm and his staff. The drawing room contained a pair of desks where men were typing and a table and chairs, which was where Sir Malcolm led us. He sat down first.

"Get Wilby and Littleshaw some dry clothes and something hot to drink," Sir Malcolm barked. "Did the local police take the other two sailors to their lockup?"

"Yes. We told the locals we'd interrogate this one. Welcome back, Littleshaw," one of the men said.

Sir John held Abby's chair for her as he murmured, "Sorry I lost you, old girl."

I faced Sir Malcolm. "Is that Michael Littleshaw?"

"Yes, but keep it to yourself. He was working as a deckhand on one of Palmer's freighters. I think his cover's blown now." He stared at me and scowled. "Where do you know him from?"

"You recruited him from the news section of the *Daily Premier*. He disappeared, and they think you killed him."

"Nonsense. I don't kill people on our side." He appeared annoyed as he pursed his lips. "Littleshaw's a willing member of our team. We'll be sending him on another assignment soon. After we learn about the cargo his boat was carrying." Sir Malcolm waved me into a seat.

I sat down and felt the weight of the book in my pocket. I unbuttoned my coat and reached for it to get it out of my way without looking at the volume.

Abby let out a gasp. "Livvy! You've been stabbed."

My heart skipped at her words. I looked down to see a slit in my coat. Then I noticed a hole had been sliced into my book. I examined my clothes while Sir Malcolm took the mystery from me. No blood. "No, I haven't been," I said with a relieved sigh.

"You can thank Mrs. Christie for that," Sir Malcolm said. He held up the book to show us the path of a knife through most of the pages.

"It was Fleur. The French assassin. I saw her up close when I grabbed her. I let her go when I saw her knife. She stabbed at me, but I thought she had missed when I tripped and fell against a hut." I was still upset I had let her get away again.

"I heard about her when General Alford filled me in on your investigation into the dressmaker's shop."

"It was a haute couture salon of Mimi Mareau's, now closed," I said. Why did men never understand the difference between buying designer gowns and cheap frocks unless they were personally responsible for the bill?

Sir Malcolm smirked at my words before he turned serious. "You're certain it was the French assassin."

"Very. We were only inches apart. And she recognized me, too."

"You had a lucky escape, then. Which way did she go?"

"Toward the road. Toward Mr. Whittier."

"We need to find that woman." Sir Malcolm's voice was cold with menace.

* * *

We were late rising and going down to breakfast the next morning. With hindsight, I was more shaken by my close call than I had been the night before, and at odd moments I caught myself trembling.

In contrast, Sir John appeared quite placid and Abby admitted she would have been thrilled by the adventure if no one had died. They had a good appetite and polished off eggs, bacon, mushrooms, tomatoes, toast, and coffee with enthusiasm.

I had tea and toast and a poached egg, and even that made my stomach queasy.

Then Sir Malcolm and two other men arrived.

"Fishing not good today?" Mrs. Miller asked them as they walked into the dining room.

I realized with a start that the fishermen had wanted the upper rooms for their vantage point, not for the view. Of course, they never caught any fish. They had no interest in fish. They were Sir Malcolm's men.

The three of us set down our forks in unison and watched the new arrivals. Sir Malcolm approached our table and said, "You've done well, Mrs. Denis, but I think it's time for you to go home now."

"Did you catch the French assassin?"

"No." The planes of his face shifted as if he was clenching his teeth. "When we arrived, Palmer's house was empty. One of our cars spotted an auto driving away from the area near the house and gave chase, but they lost sight of it in the dark."

"Where?"

"On the road to Royal Tunbridge Wells. Why?" Sir Malcolm glowered at me.

"That would be in the direction of Little Hedges. You think they went there," Abby said to me.

I nodded. "That would be the best place for them to go to ground."

"All the more reason for you to go home. Go back to your daily lives and forget all about this," Sir Malcolm said.

"The French assassin tried to stab me and hit my book instead. She also stabbed Mr. Whittier, who was in the path she was taking after she left me. I think you'll be able to prove a charge of murder against her if you can catch her," I told him.

"I know," Sir Malcolm snarled. "Ladies. Sir John." With a sharp nod, he stalked out of the room. The two fishermen followed.

"I think we've been warned," Sir John said.

"I doubt there will be anything else happening here," Abby said. She sounded disappointed.

"Do you mind if I come visit you?" I asked. "Sir Henry has given me a few days off to try to help my father's defense, and I need to think of what else I can do."

"Of course you may. I'm sure John will be able to think of something, won't you, dear?" Abby gave her husband an adoring smile.

"I don't know what we can do, but you are certainly welcome to visit." Sir John finished his coffee and rose. "I'd better make our farewells to Mrs. Miller. We'll come down in the new year, don't you think, old girl?"

"Of course." Abby rose from the table. "I'd better go and pack."

We went back to our rooms and were ready, suitcases in hand, half an hour later. As we piled them into the boot of the car, Sir Malcolm, trailed by the two supposed fishermen, walked up to us. "I want to remind you once again never to mention what happened last night."

"We know what the Official Secrets Act demands," Sir John said, sounding insulted.

"I know that you know, Colonel. But your wife has never signed, and Mrs. Denis seems to live by her own rules."

"I'm sure I know when a topic is out of bounds," Abby said, sounding more insulted than her husband.

I glared at Sir Malcolm. "I'm not stupid."

"No one has ever accused you of not being bright," Sir Malcolm replied. "Just willful."

"Since you didn't capture the French assassin or the other woman, if there is another woman involved, it won't do my father's defense any good. There's no reason for me to mention the melee on the beach." I folded my arms over my chest.

Sir Malcolm growled deep in his throat. "Make sure you don't," he finally managed and stomped off, the other two silently following.

"Well, let's be off. I want to arrive home in time for lunch," Sir John said. Then he looked at me and winked.

While no one had taken the woman who'd been in my father's house into custody, I was certain she still must be in England. From Sir John's wink and Abby's confident smile, I felt sure they believed we'd catch the killer.

* * *

In the afternoon, Abby went to work on her rose bushes while she had me rake leaves out of the flower beds. The heavy, repetitive job worked its magic on me as I began to feel more energetic and less fearful. However, while it gave me time to think, it didn't give me any insights on how to free my father and capture the dark-haired woman I believed killed John Kenseth.

I had cleaned up and dressed for dinner when the maid called me to the telephone. When I answered, Sir Henry's voice boomed out at me. "Livvy, how is your hunt coming along?"

I thought about the activity on the beach the night

before and how I couldn't tell Sir Henry. "Nothing concrete, so far. What can I do for you, sir?"

"I know that tone. Something is happening." He paused, suspicion dripping from his words. When I didn't reply, he continued, "However, we'll set that aside for the moment. Alicia Crawford has called for you. She's at Phyllis Waterbury's, and she said she has finally settled her plans. She intends to return to Little Hedges tomorrow. She'd like you to call her tonight."

"Good. Maybe something will turn up to finally prove my father's innocence." And I would have my excuse to go to Little Hedges and hopefully find the spies who had landed on shore in the rowboat the night before.

Sir Henry gave me the numbers, wished me good hunting, and rang off.

I dialed Phyllis Waterbury's number. A female answered in a voice too young and high-pitched to be Phyllis. I shouted my request for Alicia Crawford over the background noise.

"Who? Wait, I can't hear you. Somebody turn down the music, will you?"

The jazz blaring out of the telephone lessened to a murmur. Then I asked for Alicia Crawford again.

When she came to the phone, I identified myself and said, "I understand you now plan to return to Little Hedges tomorrow. Are you still willing for me to do a profile on you and your studio for the *Daily Premier*?"

"Yes. I look forward to your arrival at my home." She sounded determined, but she didn't sound happy about the interview.

"I'm in the area now. At Summersby House."

"Could you come to Little Hedges at three tomorrow afternoon?"

"I'd be glad to." So glad I was nearly jumping up and down in Abby's hallway.

She dropped her voice. "And if anyone tells you no or that I'm not home, don't believe them."

Is Alicia Crawford afraid? I swallowed. "I won't. Don't worry. I'll be there at three."

"And park the car in front."

"I'll come by bicycle. That will make it harder for anyone to track me down." I tried to sound jovial and failed miserably.

"Bicycle?" Now she sounded confused.

"That's how people get around in the country. That and by horseback. Don't worry. I'll arrive looking presentable."

"I haven't ridden a bicycle since I was a girl. Edmund doesn't approve."

"You don't have bicycles at Little Hedges?" Edmund Palmer must run his house with a fiercer grip than I imagined.

"No." She sounded wistful.

Odd. "You may have the only house in the area that doesn't. If you ever want to ride, I'm sure I can find someone to lend you a bicycle."

"I may take you up on your offer."

We chatted thirty seconds longer and then Alicia excused herself, saying she needed to get back to her farewell party.

I hung up and walked away to locate Abby. I found her and Sir John in front of the fire in the small drawing room. "Abby, may I borrow your bicycle tomorrow afternoon?"

"Of course, but would you rather I drove you? I don't mind."

"I may take you up on the offer, but not the first time I go to Little Hedges."

"Livvy," Sir John said, setting down his drink, "it's too dangerous. While we were in Hastings I learned they suspect Palmer is involved with this group of Nazi infiltrators."

"I'm doing a story on his wife as Alicia Crawford, the painter, for the *Daily Premier.* My only official interest is Alicia's studio, but this will give me a chance to keep my eyes open and see if Fleur or anyone else under suspicion is staying at the house."

"Livvy, she'll recognize you," Abby said, reaching out a hand to me.

"I plan to avoid her if she's there." I squeezed Abby's hand. There was no point in disguising myself. Fleur was better at that than I was.

"And if you don't?"

"You'll know where I am. If I'm late returning home, come looking for me. And tomorrow morning, we'll both go out on bicycles and find all the lanes between here and Little Hedges. Fair enough?" I gave her a smile.

"I'm not happy about this, Livvy. And I know your father wouldn't want you to take chances," Sir John said.

"His trial is in ten days. If we don't start taking chances now, it will be too late and my father will hang. We have to prevent that. And the only way to do that is to find the woman who was in my father's house with John Kenseth and hand her over to the police."

"But why do you think you'll find her at Little Hedges now? It's been weeks since Kenseth died." Sir John went about the business of relighting his pipe.

"We have no reason to believe her mission is complete, and Little Hedges would be a safe, comfortable place to hide. The police can't look for her there." And we were going to have to force her out into the open if we were to have any chance to save my father before his trial.

CHAPTER EIGHTEEN

When I set off for Little Hedges the following afternoon, I was already sore from my bike ride with Abby in the morning. Fortunately, Abby knew all the lanes through and around her property, and she showed me every shortcut to Little Hedges. It took me less than half an hour of easy pedaling to arrive at Alicia Crawford's front door.

I rested my bike against a tree and stepped onto the stoop to knock. A man in an old-fashioned evening coat answered and looked down his nose at me before I opened my mouth. Annoyed, I said, "Alicia Crawford is expecting me."

"She is not here."

I heard his foreign accent, but I couldn't immediately place where he was from. "She said you'd say that. Please tell her I'm here for our interview."

The word "interview" appeared to startle him and he backed up. I stepped into the house before he could stop me. "She is not here," he repeated as he stood with his head up and his shoulders back.

"Yes, she is. Now go and get her."

"You're here for Alicia?" Edmund Palmer said as he

came out from around a corner into the hallway. "You're Mrs. Denis, aren't you? Alicia's in her studio. Helene, take Mrs. Denis out to Mrs. Palmer."

A platinum blonde in a black maid's outfit came into view, gave a bobbed curtsy, and headed toward the back of the house.

"Thank you," I called to Mr. Palmer as I hurried after the maid. I was surprised. I hadn't expected him to be helpful.

I followed the maid out of the back door and around to what must have been a barn at one time. Now the interior was finished with a skylight, and a series of large glass doors replaced what must have been an entrance for farm equipment. Alicia sat facing a half-finished painting on an easel in the center of the room.

"This is lovely. I'll have to get a photographer to take pictures to go with the article," I said.

Alicia turned around and looked past me at the maid. "Thank you, Helene."

"Mr. Palmer wanted me to ask if there was anything you need." The maid had the same accent as the butler, which I still couldn't place. Not quite German. Not quite Swiss. Not quite Austrian. She was probably from a rural area near the border between all three.

"Nothing."

"Some tea, perhaps?"

"I don't want anything. Thank you." Alicia nearly spat out her words.

"Perhaps your guest...?"

"Nothing for me, thanks." I turned to look at the maid.

She seemed older than I was, but what struck me was her fair coloring. Pale eyes. Pale eyebrows. Pale skin. So why did she evidently bleach her probably blonde hair?

At least I didn't have Fleur staring back at me from under those pale brows. I realized I still both feared and desired meeting her again.

The maid looked away from me. "Very good, ma'am." She was gone in a second.

I turned back to Alicia in time to see her relax as she let out her breath. I walked over to the easel and asked, "What's wrong?"

"My husband has the servants watching me."

"Have you ever given him a reason not to trust you?"

"No." She sounded startled by the question.

"You're sure?" I thought there might be skeletons in her past.

"Of course I'm sure." She sounded indignant.

"Maybe he feels uneasy since you spent time with your London friends without him," I suggested.

"Then why did he not object to you interviewing me? He doesn't trust you."

I shrugged. "Maybe he thinks I'm part of Miss Waterbury's circle."

"Where do you know her from?"

"I don't, really. I should say, just in passing." I'd only met her once or twice. "She thought I was a friend of yours."

"I thought you were a friend of hers. Otherwise, I'd never have agreed to this interview."

We stared at each other for a moment. I smiled,

knowing I'd have to convince her. "I have friends in the area, and I'm staying at Summersby House. My late husband was Lady Abigail Summersby's cousin. I'm really quite trustworthy."

Alicia studied me a little longer before she finally smiled. "All right. Let's do this interview."

"I will want to get a photographer out here before we finish."

"Only the studio. Edmund doesn't want anything else photographed. Especially the outbuildings."

"The only old barn I have any interest in is your studio. It is quite magnificent. The stonework in the walls is quite lovely." I suddenly had a strong desire to see inside the other buildings, but I couldn't admit that. It wouldn't be safe. "Are the other buildings as impressive as this?"

"No. They're just old farm sheds. He uses them for storage."

I pulled my notebook out of my handbag. "I'll need to start with some background. How long have you been painting?"

"Since I was a girl. I had a great-aunt who introduced me to oil painting, and then I went to art school."

"Where?"

"It doesn't matter. It was provincial. I wasn't there long before I began to study in Paris and then at the National Gallery of Art."

When she didn't continue, I asked, "What can you tell me about turning an old barn into an artist's studio?"

"We only bought the property a year or two ago. This—"

"You want to know about Alicia's studio," Edmund Palmer said as he walked in.

I wondered how long he'd been listening outside. "It would make a great story for our readers."

He proceeded to plant himself in the studio and tell me, with only few additional comments from Alicia, about the remodeling efforts. It was growing dark by the time he finished with, "You'd better be getting back. It's not safe to ride a bicycle in the dark on these country roads."

"Thank you for your directions on how to turn a barn into an artist's studio. I'll see you tomorrow, Alicia?"

"I'm sure she'll be painting. Won't you, darling?" Palmer said with false-sounding cheer.

"Come around whenever you want, and come straight back here. That way we won't interrupt you, dear," Alicia said. Her helpfulness sounded equally fake.

Edmund Palmer left without another word.

Alicia gave me a relieved smile. "I'll see you tomorrow?"

"Directly after luncheon." I went out, collected my bike, and began to ride home. I'd only gone about fifty feet when I heard an automobile engine rumbling behind me. The road was straight there, but I didn't see the light of any headlamps shining from behind me in the dark.

The hairs on the back of my neck stood on end as I heard this phantom grew closer. I began to pump the pedals harder. When I glanced back, I could barely make out the gleaming chrome and shiny surface as the auto raced toward me under a cloud-obscured moon. A Wolseley Saloon, maybe, or an Austin 18? I sped up and turned onto a farm track just before I felt, as much as saw, the car fly past me.

The car was so close the bicycle shook from the air rushing past. I nearly fell. When I could look away, I saw a large shadow disappear at a bend in the road, its lights still off.

I continued to bounce along the narrow track to the next lane and made my way to Summersby House. I'd never pumped the pedals as hard and fast as I did that night. I entered through the kitchen garden gate, still glancing over my shoulder.

Abby was in the hallway when I reached the back door. She looked me over and said, "What happened?"

"What makes you think anything happened?" My gasping breaths and shaky legs ruined my attempt to act nonchalant.

She examined me closely. "The straw blown onto your jacket and skirt tells me you cut through a field in the dark. That isn't something you'd normally do."

"Someone drove by without his lights on and frightened me." Honesty made me add, "I suppose I scared him, too."

"You think it was a foolish driver?"

"Or a stolen car. Or a drunk." I wouldn't admit I thought the car might have come from Little Hedges determined to cause me harm. Abby would drive me there if she thought I was in danger, and I didn't want to mix her up in anything dangerous.

I headed for the stairs, my leg muscles throbbing. "Let me get cleaned up and changed and I'll be down for dinner shortly."

* * *

No more was said about my wild bike ride until Abby and I left church the next morning. "Are you planning to go to Little Hedges today?" she asked after we shook hands with the vicar.

I glanced back and saw Sir John deep in conversation with one of the villagers. "Yes. Straight after luncheon."

She stopped and introduced me to some neighbors who were chatting in the churchyard. When we walked on, she said, "So, you'll be back before it gets dark."

"I certainly plan to."

"I could drive you."

"No." My answer was more abrupt than I intended. "It's kind enough of you and Sir John to provide food and lodging whenever I take it into my head to come down here. I can't expect you to rearrange your schedule around my work for the newspaper."

"Livvy, at least be honest. You're down here trying to find a spy at the behest of Sir Malcolm in an attempt to save your father."

I stopped before I opened the car door. "I'm trapped between two spies, Sir Malcolm and whoever, probably Edmund Palmer, is running this German ring. Either, or both, could hold the key to freeing my father, and no one is telling me anything. Worse, I've dragged you and Sir John into this mess. I'm sorry, Abby."

"You know we'll do anything we can to help free your father."

"I know. You wouldn't have gone to Hastings with me

if you weren't. But I'd like to keep you in the shadows in case I need you to rescue me. Or rather, to call in the rescuers. But you'll probably do something clever and save everyone." I grinned at her.

She laughed. "I doubt it. Do try to be careful, Livvy."

I remembered her words when I arrived at Little Hedges shortly after luncheon and rolled my bicycle past the cottage. I admired how it had been restored in such beautiful style with half my mind while the other half wondered where everyone was. No one was in sight. I couldn't hear the sounds of human voices or machinery running. I didn't even hear the sound of birds singing.

I went past the side of the restored farmhouse and the kitchen garden into what had been the stable yard. Behind the cottage was a two-story barn on the right that appeared to be used now as a garage. To the left was the former barn that was now Alicia's studio.

I continued to the side of the studio, noticing for the first time how spectacular the view was with the barns in the foreground and the fields, empty at this time of year, behind. I knocked on the door and waited.

Knocking for the third time convinced me either Alicia wasn't in the studio or something was wrong. Still pushing my bike, I went around to the back of the building where the magnificent glass doors were and looked inside.

Nothing moved.

I could see Alicia's easel, illuminated by the skylight, in the center of the room where it sat, unused. Finished paintings and empty canvases leaned against the walls. All the tubes of paint lay unopened on the table. Brushes were lined up. Everything lay in wait for the return of the artist.

We had agreed to meet just after luncheon. Alicia must be nearby. Leaning my bike on the wall near the glass doors into the studio, I walked off toward the nearest barn. The day was sunny. Perhaps she was painting outdoors in the back of the property.

I walked as far as the short hedge that separated Little Hedges from a local farmer's field. No one was there.

It was beginning to seem eerie.

Had John Kenseth come here after leaving France? What had led him here, and what had he discovered? Certainly, he'd found *something* or he wouldn't have been murdered.

Curious, I stepped as quietly as I could to the nearest barn, hardly more than a shed, and pulled the door open a couple of inches. It was dark and quiet inside. I opened the door fully and saw farm equipment, barrels, and coils of rope. Dust and cobwebs showed none of this had been used recently.

I shut the door and went on to the next outbuilding. As soon as I opened the door, I saw they were indeed using this for a garage. There were two recent model automobiles inside, a gray Rolls and a black Rover 12 Saloon, with space for a third. A space with some recent-looking oil drips showed another vehicle normally belonged here. Two bicycles, new but muddy, leaned against one wall. Shelves along another wall held tools of every description.

Noises above me from the huge loft propelled me further into the barn. How many people were up there?

Two? Three?

Then a noise behind me made me turn. Edmund Palmer stood inches away as he placed one hand on the railing of the stair leading up to the loft, trapping me with his body and blocking my path to the door.

"Where's Alicia? I didn't see her in her studio," I asked, looking past him.

"She's not here." His smile was menacing.

I could feel an icy wind slide down my spine. I was sure there were at least two people upstairs in the barn, but they were no longer moving around or whispering. I was trapped between them and Palmer. Would they rescue me or support Palmer with his threatening plan? "I imagine she'll return soon. She knew I'd be here now."

I took a step toward Palmer on shaky legs. Toward the only way out that didn't involve opening the heavy massive garage doors.

"Who knows where the artistic temperament will take her or when she'll return?" He stepped back and gestured for me to precede him out of the garage. As soon as I moved past him, he followed on my heels. Once we were out, he shut and locked the door. "Is there anything I can help you with in the meantime?"

"No. Our readers want to learn about the artist. There's such mystery and romance about painting and painters, especially one with a studio similar to the one you've created."

He seemed to relax as he walked beside me toward the studio. I hoped that meant he'd bought my story. I must be lying with more finesse if Edmund Palmer believed me, because I had the impression he would be hard to fool.

I decided to press further. "Any idea where Alicia has gone?"

"None at all. Too bad you made a trip over here for nothing."

We were in front of the studio where I'd left my bicycle. "I'll wait here. With any luck she'll be home soon."

He was on me quickly and silently as a cat, his lips locked on mine as he held me in his powerful grip. A moment later, I heard a gasp that I feared came from Alicia.

Why did he want to ruin any chance of the *Daily Premier* publishing a story about his talented wife? Or was it the writer—me—that he was trying to sabotage?

He let me go, a smug smile on his face. His smile made me think he was trying to destroy my chance to get this story.

I looked past him into the angry, reddened face of his wife. I was sure he had heard her gasp. The bounder.

An instant later, I connected the palm of my hand with his cheekbone.

CHAPTER NINETEEN

My hand hurt before the sound of the smack against his face reached my ears. I wanted to clutch my stinging fingers, but I refused to show any emotion other than fury.

I heard feminine laughter before Alicia walked up to us and said, "Someone who doesn't melt at your feet? You must be losing your touch, darling. Come inside, Livvy."

She walked off with a light step, swinging her arms, but as I reached her, I could see her hands shaking so badly she could barely unlock the door.

As soon as we walked inside, out of sight of Edmund, Alicia leaned against the wall. Her shoulders trembled and her breathing was ragged.

"Are you all right?"

Her laugh sounded bitter. "Just fine. I should never have come back here."

"You can always leave again."

"I can't." She gave a deep sigh and turned her moist eyes on me. "I know too much. He'll kill me if I try to leave. And if he doesn't, she will."

I lowered my voice to match hers. "Know too much about what? And who is *she*?"

She shook her head and walked to the stool in front of

the canvas she was working on. With her chin up and a pleasant expression, she asked, "Would you care to talk about my painting technique?"

No longer did she tremble or sound upset. I was surprised at how fast her demeanor changed. She must have become a great actress living with Edmund Palmer, needing to hide her feelings all the time. "What about your inspiration?" I asked her. "I can see some of your paintings are influenced by the fields around here, but I don't see where you find your subjects. Your human models."

"Photos in magazines, people I meet, strangers on the train. There are always fascinating people around, don't you think? Each one has their own flaw, their own distinct feature."

"Do you see these individual traits as flaws?" I'd never heard the details that made us unique called flaws before.

"Perhaps that was the wrong word." She gave me a smile and began talking about painting techniques, using the canvas in front of her to show me what she meant. We had a lively talk and I learned a great deal.

"I've done a little painting. I prefer sketching fashions, but nothing compared to what you can do with a brush. This has been a most enlightening afternoon," I told her.

"You think of yourself as an artist?"

"I dabble. I've not had any formal training. Not such as you have."

She looked out the wide glass doors, a look of disgust crossing her features for a moment. Did she feel she was wasting her time talking to me? "I hate to be rude, but I'd prefer to get some work done before it grows dark."

"Of course. Shall we continue tomorrow?"

"Yes. Perhaps at ten?"

"That would be wonderful. Thank you." I turned toward the glass doors to see a couple of hours had passed and the sun was much lower in the horizon.

I hurried toward the doors, saying good-bye as I went, only to collide with Helene, Alicia's maid, in the doorway.

She said "excuse me" in her unplaceable accent and faced Alicia.

I lingered by the doorway to hear Alicia say, "What do you want?" in an annoyed tone.

"Mr. Palmer wants to know what time you would like dinner served."

"Oh, for...Tell him eight o'clock. Run my bath at seven, will you?"

Alicia glanced at me. I smiled and hurried to my bicycle.

I rode back to Summersby House, wondering why Alicia didn't like her maid. Presumably she had hired her. Perhaps Edmund Palmer had hired the German woman to act as his wife's maid. No one ever noticed servants. That would be the perfect disguise in the perfect hideaway.

But then why would Alicia, with money of her own from selling her paintings, put up with a servant chosen by her husband?

Why did Alicia say they didn't have any bicycles? And who was the "she" Alicia was afraid would kill her if she left?

The questions continued in my head until I reached Abby's back door.

* * *

The next morning, I started out early to Little Hedges, hoping to see something of the servants or guests or anyone else who might be staying there. Cycling down a farm lane near the property, I found a good spot for observing the house and outbuildings from the side of Little Hedges. I could hide behind a dilapidated hut, lay my bike on the ground, and never be seen. Overgrowth around the short hedge along a drainage ditch on the property line made for a partial screen.

Unfortunately, there was nothing to see. No one entered or left the house or any of the barns.

I was bored within fifteen minutes. My mind and my eyes started to wander. It was then I spotted the pipe tobacco packet. It was a French brand, expensive, and foul smelling. The only person I knew who smoked that brand, at least while living in England, was John Kenseth.

I'd found the place where he'd watched Little Hedges and spotted the German woman. I wanted to tell Sir Malcolm right away, but I didn't have enough time to leave my spot and return for my ten a.m. appointment. I'd have to wait until I returned to Summersby House.

I was about to leave to cycle over to meet Alicia when I saw a flash of sunlight in an upstairs window of the garage barn. I lingered to see if anyone would leave the garage. I didn't see anyone leave, but I didn't wait long before Helene the maid came up the field, her route hidden from Little Hedges by a section of hedgerow.

"Who are you and what are you doing here?" she demanded.

"Where are you from?" I wasn't on Little Hedges property. I could be as rude as she was, asking questions I had no right to ask.

"Are you one of them? One of the spies?"

That stopped me for an instant. "I'm not a spy. I'm a newspaper reporter. Where are you from?"

"None of your business. Are you one of Mrs. Palmer's friends?" she asked in German.

The change in language surprised me for a moment. "You mean her artistic friends? No, although I've met them," I continued in English.

"Not them. I thought you were..." She switched back to English, her voice trailing off. Shaking her head, she hurried back the way she came.

"Wait," I called out.

She glanced back and then moved even faster away from me.

Shaking my head, I pushed my bicycle along the track. Glancing back, I saw the flash in the upstairs window again. Too soon for Helene to have reached there. I walked on to the road and then pedaled to Little Hedges. I went past the house to the studio and saw Alicia inside, hard at work on the canvas in the center of the room. Propping my bicycle on the wall out of the way, I knocked on the glass doors.

She looked up and waved for me to enter before turning back to her painting.

I went in quietly and stood a distance behind her, studying the canvas. Alicia was working with bright red paint, and I suddenly realized it was a mouth. The way she was painting it meant I could see smiling lips with lipstick applied or someone, or something, enjoying a bloody meal.

"What do you think?" she asked, pausing.

"I think it will be a powerful portrait."

"Powerful is so much more effective than pretty, don't you think?"

Coming from a woman I had previously thought of as decorative and under her husband's thumb, I was surprised. "It can be more useful," I answered cautiously.

"I'm painting this in the modern style. All feelings and emotions right on the canvas for the viewer to interpret."

"Do you think that is what draws people to your paintings? The emotions your work elicits?" I had slid my notebook and pencil out to begin the day's interview.

She looked over her shoulder and smiled. "Don't you?"

"It doesn't matter what I think. I'm interviewing you."

She laughed. "All right, I think people relate to my work because of the strong emotions my paintings create in the viewer. People should not stare at my paintings, they should experience them. Let them into their soul."

I scribbled down her words before I said, "You hope to reach people's souls with your work. Why? What do you want to make them feel?"

"I want them to feel whatever it is that my painting says to them."

"What does it make you feel?"

She stared at the canvas for a minute, and I thought she had forgotten I had asked a question. I had to strain to hear her murmur, "We can make the world better if we have the strength to force past all difficulties in our way."

I jotted her words down as I asked, "How do you want to improve the world?"

She gave me a bright smile. "Oh, I'd like to see everyone get along." Her jubilant tone was at odds with the murmured words I'd heard just a moment before.

I had expected her answer to touch on the gloomy state of European politics or women's rights. Whatever Alicia Crawford might think, she wasn't going to share it with me or our newspaper readers.

She faced me and said with her head tilted, "Would you care to join me for some lunch? You've been so nice to ride over here to interview me for your newspaper, I think I should bribe you to write a flattering piece."

"Do all journalists look hungry?" I asked.

"You're the only one I've met, and you look hungry."

I made up my mind. "I'd love to have some luncheon."

I took notes on how she cleaned her brushes and on her favorite spot to paint under the skylight, with the view of the fields out the glass doors. When she was ready, we walked back to the house.

"Why don't you wait here, Livvy?" she said, pointing toward her dining room with its magnificent view. "I'll go find out what the cook has planned to serve us." She walked off to where I suspected her servants or her kitchen was.

I waited a minute or two, the need to use the facilities growing until I was forced to call out, "Alicia? I need to powder my nose."

My request, even when repeated, was met with silence. Where was her kitchen? In another building? And where were the servants?

I had no other choice. I began to search the ground floor for the room I needed, but I'd had no luck when I found the door to the stairway leading up. I hoped there was a loo upstairs and climbed the steep, dark, narrow staircase.

At the top of the stairs I found the room I needed and used it. I washed my hands and slipped out. Curiosity made me move down the hall and open the door. It was a sparely furnished bedroom with a thick carpet and a sloping ceiling. I walked to the small window and looked out, discovering it was barred. Why would anyone bar the inside of an upstairs window?

I was about to leave when I heard footsteps on the stairs. I thought about apologizing for wandering around the cottage when I heard a key in a lock. Then a weak voice called out, "Untie me, please."

My hand froze on the handle. There didn't seem to be enough air in the small room to draw breath. My knees knocked together and my insides shook.

I stayed still as a female voice said in German, "I'll untie your hands only so you may eat."

"Please, let me go. I mean you no harm." This voice, also female, had the same distinctive accent as the lady's maid, Helene. Was it her? I wasn't sure.

"So you can report to your bosses? No."

"Please. I have no bosses but the Palmers. I'm just a servant."

"A servant of your English masters," the German speaker sneered. "We know all about you."

"May I at least go to the loo?"

I didn't wait to learn if the prisoner was given the privilege she requested. I opened the door and rushed down the hall and the stairs on tiptoe. There was no way I wanted to end up a prisoner in the upper level of the renovated farmhouse. When they renovated, maybe they not only created the large dining room with spectacular views, but also built cells with iron bars and chains. Who would have known or guessed?

I reached the bottom of the flight of stairs and threw open the door, only to find Alicia was waiting for me in the hallway. I let out a gasp, feeling guilty as my face heated.

"How did you enjoy your tour of my home?" she asked in a dry voice.

"I found the one thing I needed to find. The loo. I do beg your pardon, but I called out and asked. I know you didn't want me to ruin your lovely carpets." I spoke with my hand on my stomach below my belt. I didn't want to reclimb those steps for anything.

"Well, I'm glad you were successful. Come along." She turned on her heel and walked away, certain I would follow. "Do you think you'll be able to eat soup and bread without difficulty?"

"Yes. I'm quite recovered now." Except for hearing the words of a woman who was bound inside an attic room. How could I ask Alicia why her husband was turning their home into a prison?

Two places had been set at one end of the table, and I was directed to the seat with the best view out the windows. Another blonde maid silently served us and left the room.

We ate in silence for a few minutes before Alicia said, "Do you have any other questions for me?"

Besides why was there a prisoner in her house? "Do you ever get tired of this magnificent view?"

"I am at heart a city person. I draw my inspiration most often from people. This is beautiful," she said as she swept her hand in the direction of the windows, "but barren. Particularly in the winter."

I had pulled out my notebook while she spoke, my soup forgotten as I hurried to capture every word. "Your husband apparently loves the emptiness of the countryside, since he's made this his base of operations."

"Not at all. He carries on his business dealings in London. This is his sanctuary."

"Would it be safe to say your sanctuary is London?"

She shook her head. "No. This is my sanctuary, while London is my stimulant. Similar to coffee. I need it to be fully awake. Here I feel half asleep."

I finished jotting this down and put my pencil aside. "How does your husband feel about having a half-sleeping wife?"

"My husband is happy with the bargain he's struck."

"And you? Are you happy?"

She gave me a sharp look, telling me I'd crossed a boundary. "Of course."

I decided to press her. "You're always happy about your husband's decisions and his friends?"

"Of course." Her tone seemed to dare me to say another word.

I ate a spoonful of my cooling soup. It was clear I couldn't ask about the prisoner in their house. What could I do about this secret?

CHAPTER TWENTY

Afterward, I rode to Abby's and found her sitting with Sir John planning what part they would play in the Christmas celebrations in the village and when the boys would return from school. Instead of paying attention to their conversation, I was focused on what I would tell Sir Malcolm when I reached him. I excused myself to go to the phone in the front hall and hoped neither Abby nor Sir John would listen in.

When I reached Sir Malcolm, I told him about finding the tobacco pouch that had probably belonged to John Kenseth and how Helene came out to question me. "She has a peculiar accent, too. I can't place it."

"You don't need to worry about the lady's maid. You need to find the German woman."

"How do you know Helene isn't the German woman?"

"Because she isn't."

"How do you know?" I was getting frustrated.

"I know and that's all you need to know," boomed out of the phone at me.

"Well, Helene, or another woman with her accent, is a prisoner in the attic level of the Palmers' cottage."

"How did you discover that?" Sir Malcolm's tone

demanded an answer.

"By needing to go to the loo. Sir. I overheard the woman asking to be untied. To be released."

"Did you see her?"

Maybe Sir Malcolm was that brave, but I wasn't. "No. I was hiding in the other upstairs bedroom when I heard two women talking. One spoke German and was only going to untie the other woman's hands so she could eat."

"How many women have you seen at Little Hedges?"

"The only other women I've seen at Little Hedges beside Helene are Alicia Palmer and the maid who served us luncheon."

"Are you sure?"

"Yes. I've only seen three women there. There could be others." I hadn't checked the entire house yet, and I didn't expect to be able to carry out a search. Not now that I'd gone upstairs. The Palmers both probably knew I had been up there by then and had guessed what I had discovered.

"Go back tonight to the place where you think Kenseth was watching the house," Sir Malcolm told me. "Keep Little Hedges under observation all night. We've received intelligence that Palmer will be receiving something tonight. They called it a 'package' over the shortwave radio. See what arrives."

My mind went in a different direction. "You now have someone else listening in to Palmer's ships' transmissions the way John Kenseth did?"

"Of course. And you need to find out what the package contains."

"Do you know how cold that is going to be? There's no

shelter there but a falling-down hut." I couldn't imagine spending the night in a frigid field. And I certainly didn't see it as my job. I didn't work for the Foreign Office. I wouldn't be paid.

"Surely you're more resourceful than that."

"You don't pay me to be resourceful. At least, not yet." Sir Malcolm was starting to annoy me.

"Very well. I'll send someone down to watch. He'll come to Summersby House and then you can show him the way to the field." He was sounding huffy, but I didn't care as long as it wasn't me in the field with the mice and the foxes. "He'll be there about five."

The line went dead.

I still had no idea what Sir Malcolm would do about the woman I'd heard in the attic.

* * *

I had warned Abby that someone from the Foreign Office would arrive at five and I was to take him over to a spot I'd found near Little Hedges, but neither of us were prepared for the Adonis that knocked on her door.

I was right behind the maid who opened the door, so I spotted the town's one and only taxi riding away beyond the wide shoulders and youthful grin of Sir Malcolm's agent. I supposed he was my age, but just looking at his innocent face made me feel a hundred years old.

"Mrs. Denis?" he asked, dropping his stuffed knapsack and holding out his hand. "I'm Tom Cunningham."

I shook his hand. "Livvy Denis. Come in, and set your pack in the hall. We're about to have tea."

He left his satchel behind and I walked him into the

small drawing room where Abby and Sir John were just sitting down to tea. The maid watched us the whole way down the hall with an amazed expression, the front door still wide open.

Abby's jaw dropped when we walked in, but Sir John, untroubled by the man's handsome face and well-developed physique, rose and walked over to shake hands, introducing himself.

Abby finally found her voice. "You must stay and have tea with us. Afterward, you can borrow a bicycle and ride over to Little Hedges with Livvy."

"That's very kind, Lady Summersby," Tom told her.

"Please call me Abby."

"And I'm Tom."

After we got through pouring tea and helping ourselves to sandwiches, Sir John said, "How long have you worked for Sir Malcolm?"

The young man gulped his tea and stared at Sir John with wide eyes.

"It's all right. We're all part of Sir Malcolm's network, although Livvy is more involved in this than Abby or I are."

Tom glanced at Abby and me before stammering, "I—I've worked for him for two months."

I guessed experience wasn't necessary to watch a location and decided to fill him in on the details. I suspected Sir Malcolm wouldn't. "I'll show you the spot I found where I believe John Kenseth watched Little Hedges. So far, I've not seen any possibilities for the German woman. I have heard a woman claiming to be a prisoner in the attic of the cottage, but I didn't see her. Behind the cottage you'll see the barns. One of them is Mrs. Palmer's studio, and I'm doing a feature on her and her painting for the *Daily Premier*. Another is the garage. I heard people in the loft the day I slipped in there, but again, I didn't see anyone. Now, what do you know about the German woman?"

Tom looked slightly stunned. "Only that if I find her, I'm to get a good description. What does your husband say about you running all over the neighborhood?"

"I'm a widow, so he says nothing at all." I gave him a superior smile.

He grinned back, and I wondered if I'd given away more information than I should have. Oh well, if he gave me any trouble, I could leave him in the dark in unfamiliar fields.

After tea, after Tom put away several sandwiches, I put on woolen stockings and walking shoes and led Tom to the barn to our bicycles. Even carrying his knapsack on his back, he was a decent rider and kept up with me along the country lanes. Despite the dark, we arrived at the lookout point by seven.

We leaned our bicycles on the shed and sat on a rise behind it on a woolen blanket Tom brought with him. From there we could see anyone coming or going from Little Hedges in the light pouring out when the doors were opened and the bright light from the still nearly full moon.

Thank goodness it was a clear night. Sitting in a field in the rain would have been unbearable.

Of course, nothing happened and I got bored. I think Tom did, too, because he started looking around and studying the stars in the sky.

"That's the Big Dipper up there," he said as he pointed.

"Aren't you going to get tired of watching the house? Won't you get cold?"

"I won't get cold because I packed my rucksack for just that eventuality. However, I'm already tired of watching for activity. Nothing seems to be happening." He pulled out a pair of binoculars and surveyed the house.

"Did you volunteer for this?" I swung my arm to encompass the hill we were on and Little Hedges.

"Yes. It's one way to come to Sir Malcolm's notice."

"You want to come to his attention?" I couldn't think of anything I wanted less.

"Of course. There's a war coming and the interesting jobs, the ones that will win you fame and medals, will be handed out by Sir Malcolm."

I didn't think I should point out that ambition such as that would get him killed.

I really hoped Adam didn't think the same way.

Something passed close to us, making the dead grasses rustle. I jumped and Tom grinned at me. "Not a country girl, are you?"

I really didn't want to spend the night with whatever I heard lurking nearby. We sat in silence for some time before I asked, "What time is it?"

He came prepared with a watch and a tiny light. "Just after nine."

I rose, wondering if Abby had saved me any dinner. "I should be getting back."

"I think we should knock on the front door. Shake

things up a bit. What is their name again?"

"Are you nuts?"

He was standing now. "I'll tell them I got lost."

"You'll have to do that on your own. I know my way here."

"You'll miss all the excitement."

"That's fine. I don't want fame and medals." I gave an exasperated sigh. "What will you tell them you're looking for out here in the dark in the middle of fields?"

"Summersby House."

"Why don't you tell them you were headed for the train station and became lost?" Both the Palmers were already suspicious of me. I didn't want this acolyte of Sir Malcolm to make my job more difficult.

"Sit down," he murmured and pulled me to the blanket next to him.

"What—?" I landed with a jolt.

He put his finger to his lips.

I followed his lead and kept silent despite my annoyance. Any lingering temper was erased a minute later with a click from a gun.

"What are you doing here? Spying?" The glare of a torch blinded me, making it impossible to tell the identity of the man speaking.

"No," Tom said. "My friend fell off her bicycle and injured her hip. I've been trying to figure out how to get her home."

"It's late to be cycling through a field." Suspicion dripped from every word.

"This happened earlier when we decided to take a

shortcut." Tom sounded as though he was the jovial Boy Scout I suspected he'd been.

"Providential that you brought a blanket to sit on." The man didn't believe him, and with good reason.

"It was. The ground is pretty cold and I was afraid she'd go into shock."

"Can you put any weight on that leg?" the man asked. He sounded slightly more sympathetic.

"No. I tried. I can't tell if I broke anything," I answered the light. At least with the torch shining in my face, I couldn't see where he aimed the weapon.

The unknown man sighed. "Wait here. I'll get help."

As soon as I felt certain the man was out of hearing range, I struck Tom on the arm and said, "Hip? Really?"

He murmured, "Would you rather I said it was your back?"

It wasn't long before the man with the torch returned with another man, but by then I was chilled to the bone. The second man, the butler with the odd accent, helped Tom get me to a standing position and with their help, I hopped toward Little Hedges.

Tom let his rucksack hang from one shoulder and it bumped against me as we moved along more or less in unison. It was a long way and I had to order them to slow down several times. We became unbalanced once and I started to fall on my "hurt" side. Tom, always a gentleman, dropped me and I landed on the stony ground of the verge along the road.

I let loose a scream and then burst into sobs. I think I was dramatic enough. In truth, the fall hurt, and I wanted to tell Tom off.

They got me up, but my skirt and stockings were ruined. My "good" foot was dragging by the time we hopped to the Palmers' front door. I'd been jarred and pulled until every bone in my body ached.

I didn't see who let us in since I was too busy watching where I was hopping as Tom and the butler jerked me in through the front door and then to a couch in the drawing room. As soon as my backside hit the cushions, I fell over onto my "good" side.

"Your reporter friend has returned," said a man as he walked in. I looked up to see the man suspected of running this spy ring. Edmund Palmer. And he was holding a revolver.

"And appears to be injured," Alicia said as she followed him into the room.

"I hit a hole and flew off my bicycle. It was getting dark and I decided we should use a shortcut. Not one of my better ideas." I glanced over at Alicia and for an instant saw Fleur Bettenard, the French assassin, behind her as Fleur vanished down the hall.

The French assassin and the German woman in the same place at the same time? And I had to pretend to be injured? How could I do anything to help release my father from prison? I couldn't stand on my own two feet without proving we had lied.

CHAPTER TWENTY-ONE

The glimpse was so quick, could my sighting of the French assassin have been a product of my imagination? Of wishful thinking? No, I decided, I had seen her. She was here somewhere.

I hadn't seen this drawing room when I visited for the dinner party. The same as in the dining room, it had an Alicia Crawford painting in pride of place. In this room, it was over the fireplace. The room was done in overstuffed chairs and rustic-looking furniture, all artistically arranged. Cozy without looking lived in. Impersonally cold but trying to be inviting.

The staircase to the attic must have been down the hall and then behind this room. I wondered if the prisoner was still up there. I didn't want to join her.

"Should we call a doctor?" Alicia asked.

"Just call Sir John and Lady Abby to come over and get me. I hate dropping in on you this way, filthy and battered." I looked at the scrapes on my leg. "And bloody."

"It's all right," Alicia said, although her tone told me either I had interrupted something or she was annoyed at me bleeding on her furniture. "What's their number?"

I told her as I thanked her for calling them and

apologized again.

"What about your bicycle?" Tom asked.

This was his idea. Why hadn't he thought of that? "Just leave it there until tomorrow. Someone from Summersby House will fetch it then," I told him.

"Would you care for something to drink?" Edmund asked. He set his pistol on the table within easy reach.

"I think we'd both appreciate a cup of tea," I said.

"Too bad my maid's not here," Alicia said. "I'll see if any of the staff are in the kitchen." She strode from the room.

"This is a lovely room. I'm sorry we've messed it up with our dirt," I said.

Edmund looked over at me as he lit a cigarette and said, "Mmpf."

"I'm sorry. I couldn't move Livvy on my own," Tom said. "Did we interrupt something?"

"Nothing. Just a quiet evening at home," Palmer said.

I didn't believe him. We had arrived in the middle of something. Something to do with German spies and messages sent from his freighters in the Channel. Something Sir Malcolm had learned.

"I wonder if I could possibly use the facilities. I'm awfully dirty and I have a couple of scrapes that need tending," I said.

"You'll live," Palmer said.

"I'm sure I can hop there—"

"No, I don't want you wandering around my house again."

Two thoughts hit me at once. He didn't believe us,

either. Especially since he'd heard about my trip upstairs to the loo. And whatever was going on, his wife had to know what was occurring there. She lived there, as much as she might travel to London. This was her house. And she was here on the night when something or someone was expected to arrive from a Palmer freighter.

Looking over the second thought, I realized how little I knew about Alicia Crawford Palmer. She had to know what was going on, but was she involved? I needed to search for someone who had known her a long time. Phyllis Waterbury, perhaps?

Could Phyllis tell me if Alicia had ever been involved in politics? Although it was a long stretch from being politically active to spying against your country.

"I'm sure Sir John will be here in a hurry and take us off your hands," I said. I hoped Alicia had called him. I wanted out of here.

Tom kept up a conversation by himself while Mr. Palmer and I kept quiet. Finally, he fell silent and all I heard was the ticking of a clock.

Then there was the crunch of tires on gravel in front of the house and a glimmer of light through the draperies. "That must be Sir John," Tom said and rose to go to the door.

Edmund Palmer reached the doorway to the hall first and then swung around to block Tom's path. "Why don't you sit down? We have people to answer the door."

Through a thin gap in the draperies, I could tell when the automobile's headlights were turned off.

Unable to reach the hallway or the front door without

plowing the bigger man over, Tom said, "Certainly." He came over to sit on a chair next to me.

Palmer stayed in the doorway, keeping his watch on us and on the front door as the butler went to answer it. I was aware of the pistol Edmund Palmer had set on the table. He certainly wasn't taking any pains to hide the weapon.

I heard a muffled conversation without making out any of the individual words. Both of the voices were male. Well, they sounded male, their voices deep and rumbly, but even that was difficult to tell since they kept their voices low. Palmer stayed in the doorway and watched the front door area closely, but his expression never changed.

When neither man came down the hall, I knew the new arrival wasn't Sir John.

Alicia came into the room carrying a small tea tray. She poured us each a cup but she said little.

"Thank you. This is refreshing," I told her.

She acknowledged my comment with a brief smile. She glanced at her husband, but she mustn't have been able to read anything in his glacial expression, either.

I heard the front door shut and then Edmund Palmer stepped fully into the room. "Your new lady's maid has arrived."

"I hope she's better than the last one."

Alicia had told me she felt Helene, her former lady's maid, had been spying on her. Was her comment made for her husband's benefit, or mine?

"We'll wait for the household to settle down, and then we'll give you two a ride back to Summersby House,"

Palmer said, a veneer of politeness in his tone.

"I thought you were going to call Sir John to come get us," I said to Alicia. My voice was high-pitched from the fear choking me.

"Why, when it will give me great pleasure to see you off?" Her husband smiled then, his teeth showing in a dangerous display. I suddenly doubted he'd take us home safely.

"I couldn't reach him," Alicia said with a shrug.

I knew that was a lie. Someone would have answered the telephone. A shiver ran down my back. I looked at Tom. One of us was going to have to think of a way to get us out of here, and he was sitting, drinking tea, and acting as if this was normal.

"Alicia, why don't you show Tom your art studio? I've been telling him what a marvel it is." Twisting my head around to see Tom, I added, "Though you need to see it in daylight for the full effect."

"No, I don't think so," Alicia said.

Palmer smiled again. I thought I could feel a winter's gale spring from his expression.

And behind him, I again caught a glimpse of the French assassin hurrying down the hallway. The vehicle I heard must have brought more saboteurs or weapons or explosives to the Palmers. The barns at Little Hedges must be bulging with the people and supplies to cause Britain harm.

"I really would enjoy a tour of your studio sometime," Tom said. I wished he'd spoken up sooner. Sir Malcolm needed to have a talk with this boy.

And he was a boy in a man's body. I wished Adam were here. He was clever. He'd think of something. He knew how to take control of a situation. I'd just have to pretend I was Adam. What would he do?

I hadn't a clue.

Someone down the hallway murmured to Edmund Palmer and he went out of the room. After a brief discussion, he came into the room and said, "Mr. Cunningham, if you and I can get Mrs. Denis out to the car, we can give you a ride now."

A ride to where?

"Hold this." He handed Alicia his pistol.

She held it pointed down with a disinterested look on her face. Still, she held it with the assurance of a countrywoman trained to use firearms.

I wouldn't try to escape. I was certain if it was a choice between her husband or me, she could shoot me dead with the dispassion of putting down vermin. And I wasn't feeling brave.

I made myself a dead weight, but both men were strong and they soon had me on my feet. From there, I either had to hop or be dragged along.

After the long walk to Little Hedges from the field and then the road, every muscle was tired. I could barely make it down the hall. I glanced behind me to see Alicia walk away toward the back of the house. The gun wasn't in her hand.

The front door had presented a narrow challenge to get three people through together, including one who had to hop up each step. I knew going down the steps would be even worse. I decided if I was going to fall, it would be to my left and I would take Edmund Palmer out with me.

Palmer hadn't thought this through, or he didn't realize I could attack. He went through the narrow doorway first. As he turned to face me, I saw a man with a gun silhouetted in the headlights of the auto.

They were planning to kill us. And Alicia wouldn't be there to stop them.

I leaped from the landing onto Palmer's foot and let my motion throw us both off balance. We hit the ground hard, but at least I had Palmer to land on rather than paving stones. His groan turned into a gasp as my knee hit his groin.

I rolled away and looked up. The man with a gun had it pointed at Tom. They were only a few feet apart. While Tom stood just outside the front door, the man with the gun was on the drive facing the house. The front door was wide open, letting light spill out on us and adding to the light from the moon.

There was no way to escape. Slipping away in the darkness was not an option. And Edmund Palmer, when he recovered, was going to want my blood.

And Tom couldn't save himself, much less rescue me.

The crunch of gravel and the sound of a horn made us all turn our heads toward the drive. We must have made an interesting tableau to the driver.

I recognized Sir John's car as it pulled up next to the auto that was to take us away. The headlights shone on the scene with Edmund Palmer and me sprawled on the ground. The unknown man held his revolver behind him, giving Tom a chance to jump off the porch.

Tom came over to me but didn't offer me a hand up.

A figure, hidden behind the bright headlights, climbed out of the driver's seat. Knowing it was Sir John's car, I was elated no matter who was driving.

"Livvy? Tom? Are you ready to come back to Summersby House?" Abby called.

CHAPTER TWENTY-TWO

"Yes," I shouted. I was never so glad to hear Abby's voice. "Tom, give me a hand."

Tom scooped me up and carried me to Abby's car. "Good evening, Lady Summersby." He dropped me on the passenger seat and then climbed in the back.

I straightened myself from the awkward position in which he'd dropped me and called toward the house, "Thank you for your hospitality."

The two men stared into the headlights, their expressions angry.

Abby said, "Well, we'll be going. Thank you for taking care of my wandering bicyclists." I could see Edmund Palmer slowly rising from the ground with the help of the unknown man, who kept one hand out of sight. When no one said a word, she said, "Goodnight" and got back into the car.

We were off in seconds. When we were back on the road, Abby said, "What happened? I thought you would be back for dinner, Livvy. What were you doing at Little Hedges? Weren't you only supposed to observe?" Then she glanced at me and said, "Did you injure yourself?"

I heard Tom in the back seat laughing.

I shot him a glare and said, "We were caught spying on them. Tom said I'd fallen off my bicycle and injured my hip. Didn't Mrs. Palmer tell you I'd been injured when she telephoned?"

"Livvy, no one called."

As I suspected. My eyes must have been huge. "Then why did you come looking for us? Not that I'm not thrilled to see you, you rescued us, but how did you know we needed you to come to Little Hedges?"

Abby glanced at me. "I thought you were joining us for dinner. We'd already eaten, and when you still didn't show up, I began to worry."

"You saved our lives. And after I have dinner, I'd like to make a call to Sir Malcolm. I saw an old friend in the hallway in Little Hedges. I don't think she realized I saw her."

"They weren't planning to kill us," Tom said in a defensive tone, not showing any interest in my words. "I think as long as we acted innocent, they would have given us a ride back to Summersby House."

"There were a lot of guns pointed at us if all they were going to do was go out of their way to give us a ride," I said. Tom was good looking, but good grief, he was gullible. I thought Sir Malcolm trained his agents.

When Tom didn't respond, I added, "What was in the vehicle that they didn't want us to see? That must have been why people were patrolling the area beyond Little Hedges before the vehicle arrived. Didn't Sir Malcolm send you down to watch Little Hedges because he believed a shipment was coming in from one of Palmer's freighters?"

"Are you going to tell Sir Malcolm that I messed up?" Tom sounded miserable.

"I'm just going to tell him the facts. What he makes of our evening is up to him." I didn't think Sir Malcolm was blind to what those facts meant. From the sigh in the back seat, Tom didn't think so either.

We rode in relative silence the rest of the way to Summersby House. On occasion, Tom would let out a sigh to which Abby responded with a growl. I just shook my head. Whatever else happened, I didn't see how this disaster would get my father released from jail.

We returned to find dinner waiting for us on the kitchen stove. "You'll have to serve and clean up after yourselves. I've released Mrs. Goodfellow and Mary for the evening. They have to get up early enough as it is," Abby told us.

Early enough. "Abby, who owns the field that the track goes through?"

"Mr. Nesbitt."

"Would he mind a dawn trip with a horse and wagon through his field?"

"Whatever do you need a wagon for?"

"To retrieve the bicycles without admitting there's nothing wrong with my hip. And to spy on Little Hedges a little more while we're at it."

"Good idea," Tom said around a mouthful of dinner. He'd found a plate and a knife and fork and had helped himself to a liberal helping of chicken stew.

All the women I'd seen at Little Hedges were blonde or had light brown hair. I was still looking for a woman with dyed black hair.

"If you don't mind getting up before dawn and hitching up our little cart to old Mullins, that would be fine. Mr. Nesbitt won't mind. He doesn't like the new people at Little Hedges," Abby said.

"Why is that?" Did Mr. Nesbitt know something about the Palmers that we should find out?

"They're strangers."

I frowned as I looked at Abby. "Then why did they come here?" People seldom moved to the area around a village if they didn't know anyone there.

"Mr. Palmer said he wanted a country retreat and this was as pretty an area of England as he had seen."

"There had to be more to it," I told Abby. His house was close to the coast and in a secluded position with plenty of outbuildings. Perfect for sabotage. Secreting spies. Hiding weapons.

"If there was, I never heard him give any other answer."

We agreed on a time to meet in the morning and Tom headed up to the room Abby had assigned to him. On his way, I heard him stop in the hallway and murmur into the phone.

I picked up the pan with the chicken stew. Tom had practically licked it clean. Grumbling, I put it in the sink to begin scrubbing.

"I saved a couple of rolls and some jam," Abby said.

"You mean he actually left some food in your larder?"

She laughed. "He's no worse than my two when they're home from school."

I looked down the back hall when I heard the door shut. Sir John was just struggling out of his coat and wellies.

"How did it go?" Abby called out.

"Touch and go for a while, but Doc Brown and I pulled Sally through. Matt is watching her now."

"What happened?" This was a side of Sir John I seldom saw.

"A cow fell ill. Didn't think she'd make it. She's a good milker, and I didn't want to lose her. But she's a tough old thing and the vet knows his stuff. All's as well as can be expected." Sir John looked into the pan I was scrubbing. "No stew left?"

"Tom ate it all." I made his name sound as though it were a curse word.

"Oh, well. He's a growing boy." Sir John pulled out his pipe and began the ritual of lighting it.

"I have bread and jam," Abby said.

"No thank you, old girl. Never could abide jam," came out in a cloud of smoke.

"I'll be glad of some as soon as I finish the dishes," I told her. My stomach growled in response.

Abby picked up a dishtowel and dried the dishes as she told her husband what had happened at Little Hedges that evening.

"We'll pick up the bicycles in the horse cart as soon as it's light," I added.

"Hiding the fact that there's nothing wrong with your hip," Sir John said, sending another cloud of smoke into the air. "Do you want me to go along?"

"Yes. It will keep Edmund Palmer from doing anything drastic while we look over his property," I said. "And once I get something to eat, I'd better call Sir Malcolm. I can't imagine what Tom told him."

"I'm sure he was truthful," Abby said.

I gave her a dark look. "And he doesn't know I saw the French assassin twice during the time we were in Little Hedges."

Abby set the silverware down with a *thunk.* "The woman who killed Mr. Whittier?"

"Yes. Sir Malcolm will want to know."

"If she's there, I definitely need to go with you in the morning," Sir John said.

* * *

My alarm woke me early the next day. It was still dark out as I dressed and banged on Tom's door before I headed downstairs.

Sir John was already at the kitchen table drinking a cup of coffee. I helped myself to tea and sat down across from him.

"Any sign of Tom Cunningham?" I asked.

Sir John shook his head. "As soon as I finish this, I'll harness old Mullins. Drink up and see if you can rouse Cunningham. We need to be going soon if you want to catch anyone for Sir Malcolm."

"Sir Malcolm said he would be coming down here this morning."

"Does Cunningham know?" Sir John asked.

I shook my head.

Sir John finished his coffee and headed for the back

hall. "Better get him up then," he called over his shoulder.

I finished my tea and went upstairs to bang on Tom's door again. This time he called out and a moment later opened his door. I was gifted a close-up look at a muscular bare chest, sleepy eyes, and a seductive smile.

If he hadn't eaten all the leftover stew, made me pretend to be injured and hop everywhere, and naïvely believed Palmer wouldn't kill us, I might have fallen for his looks. As it was, I was hungry and annoyed. He was a child pretending to be a man. "Hurry up and get dressed or we'll leave without you."

As I ran back down the stairs, I called out, "Sir Malcolm's on his way."

I had to give him one thing, he could dress quickly. I had barely reached the barn when he raced up behind me. "Ready to go."

"Good," Sir John said. "Open the barn door so I can lead Mullins out. Livvy, hop up and drive. You and I will walk, Cunningham."

"Yes, sir." Tom looked at old Mullins as if he didn't believe the horse would make it that far.

I knew differently. Mullins wasn't pretty, but he was strong. As long as we didn't overload the cart, he'd be fine. If we did overload, Mullins would turn into the grumpiest of grumpy old men and refuse to move.

We started out at a walking pace as the eastern sky lightened, making it easier to see our surroundings. I was glad I wore a hat, coat, and gloves in the early morning chill. Tom didn't have a hat or gloves on, and he frequently blew on his hands.

Mullins made little puffing noises and one of the wheels squeaked. In the hush of the early morning, I was sure everyone at Little Hedges would hear us coming, but when the house and barns were in sight, I didn't see movement or any additional lights suddenly blink on.

I steered the cart toward where we'd left the bicycles, all the time watching Little Hedges. A light shone in the upstairs window of the garage barn, but none in the house. I didn't see any motion on the property or in the fields from anyone walking or riding outside.

Maybe they were all sleeping after the excitement the night before. I'd have loved to know what had been delivered to Little Hedges, but I knew no one would tell me.

As I watched, the door of the barn with a light on inside opened and an auto drove out. "Tom," I called out as quietly as I could, "somebody's leaving."

He dropped the bicycle he'd picked up and ran over to jump onto the cart with me. "And we don't have any way to follow. Too bad we didn't use a truck to pick up the bikes."

"Where would you have found a truck around here?"

"Surely somebody has one."

"The vet, but he might need it for a call."

Tom grumbled as we watched the car pull into the road and head in our direction. I felt an urge to stomp my foot as I watched the car drive past. I couldn't tell if the French assassin was in the vehicle or not.

Suddenly, two other cars pulled out into the road and turned their headlights on, one in front of the Palmers' vehicle and one behind. They blocked the road and came to a stop. The driver of the auto from Little Hedges rolled down his window and gestured to the driver of the front vehicle. I could hear men's voices, but I couldn't make out what they said.

Men wearing trench coats and bowler hats exited both vehicles and surrounded the saloon from Little Hedges. They opened all the doors. Then one of the men reached into the back seat while another called to the car behind them. The unmistakable bulk of Sir Malcolm climbed out of the passenger seat.

Tom jumped down from the wagon and dashed toward Sir Malcolm. Fortunately, it was light enough now to identify people at a distance, or I was sure someone would have handcuffed him.

I was hungry and sore enough from hopping that I would have enjoyed seeing his downfall.

Sir Malcolm said something to him and then they both strode to the auto where a woman was pulled out of the back seat. A half minute later, Tom turned to face me, waved his arm enthusiastically for me to join them, and whistled the way you would call a dog.

Sir John stared up at me, an amazed look on his face. "Did he just whistle for you?"

"Yes, he did." I glared in Tom's direction. "Can you keep old Mullins here, please?"

"Of course."

I jumped down from the cart and stalked to where the group of men were standing along the side of the road, aware that all eyes were on me. When I reached them, I jabbed my forefinger in Tom's chest and said, "I will deal with you later."

Then I turned to Sir Malcolm, putting my back toward Tom. "You wanted me, sir?"

"Yes. I believe you know this woman?"

He stepped back, and I found myself facing a woman I'd never met before. A very blonde woman who bore a superficial similarity to the French assassin I'd seen last night.

CHAPTER TWENTY-THREE

I shook my head and turned away from the woman. "I don't know who this woman is."

"What?" Sir Malcolm looked apoplectic.

"I've never seen her before. She's not Fleur Bettenard."

"Are you certain Fleur Bettenard is the French assassin and killed Whittier?"

"Yes. And this isn't her. She's a decoy."

Sir Malcolm turned to the driver. "Where is Fleur Bettenard?"

"I know no one by that name."

"Or you, madam?"

She shrugged.

"Drive back to Little Hedges and tell them their ruse didn't work," Sir Malcolm said. "And you, madam, get back in the automobile."

The woman sneered at me, but she didn't say a word as she climbed back inside and slammed the door.

Sir Malcolm's men stepped back from the car. The driver stood by the driver's door, protesting in heavily accented English. Then the tall, thin man climbed back into the driver's seat and reversed the vehicle before roaring back to the barn near Alicia's studio.

I had turned back to the horse cart when Sir Malcolm said, "Just a moment." I took a step or two toward the spy and waited. "That should have been a good piece of intelligence. I sent down a carload of agents to keep watch as soon as I received your phone call. Are you certain you saw the French assassin last night?"

"Yes." I held his gaze. "She could still be in there, or she could have left as soon as we did."

"We can't search the place for her." Sir Malcolm grumbled as if he thought that was a terrible limitation on his powers.

"None of this helps my father," I said. "Fleur has bleached blond hair. The woman with Kenseth had black hair."

"Maybe she dyed it previously," Tom said.

"It could be a wig," Sir Malcolm said. "We'll try to trace her movements. Perhaps we'll get lucky."

I trudged back to the horse cart and helped Sir John load the bicycles. Then we rode slowly back to the house. By the time we arrived, Abby told us Tom had already picked up his gear and left in a car with Sir Malcolm.

"Breakfast is ready, and I didn't invite Mr. Cunningham to have any," Abby said. "He didn't even thank us for our hospitality." There was a tone of disgust in her voice.

"He whistled for Livvy as if she were a dog," Sir John told her.

"Where do they find these boys?" Abby sounded aghast.

After a delicious breakfast, improved by a quantity

that made up for the lack the night before, I went into the front hall to make a telephone call. When Little Hedges answered, I said, "Mrs. Palmer, please."

"She's gone to London," a woman's voice said and hung up.

"Wonderful," I muttered. I then made a trunk call to Phyllis Waterbury in London. "Hello. Miss Waterbury, please," I said when a female voice came on the line.

"Just a moment." A minute later, an older woman's voice came on the line. "Hello?"

"Miss Waterbury, this is Olivia Denis. I was told Alicia Crawford has come back up to London. Have you seen her?"

"Yes, she's here now. But she doesn't want to see you."

She must have traveled half the night to arrive in London this early. Why, I wondered. "I'm afraid I tried to take a shortcut and took a tumble off my bicycle last night and ended up in her drawing room."

I could hear a muffled conversation before Miss Waterbury came back on the line. "Alicia says you lied to her."

"Perhaps she was the one who lied to me," came out before I thought about it. Did I have a reason to mistrust Alicia? She might not have had time to call Abby last night while making tea.

No, she would have had time. Unless something else was going on in the house I knew nothing about.

Her husband was considered a danger to the British government for his Nazi sympathies, if not outright assistance to the German government. But Alicia? She claimed her husband's sanctuary stifled her creativity.

If it did, why did he create that magnificent studio for her from a barn?

Their conversation over, Phyllis came back on the line. "She has nothing more to say to you."

"What about the article I'm writing that is to go into the *Daily Premier*? All it needs is some good photos of her studio to be complete. She wouldn't need to talk to me. You could come down and be a buffer, if she finds me so odious."

I heard another muffled conference before Phyllis Waterbury said, "She'll consider it. Good day."

She hung up and I was left wondering what my next step should be. Before I walked away from the phone, it rang. I answered, "Summersby House."

"Sir John, please. This is Mr. Nesbitt."

"Just a moment." I set down the receiver. "Sir John? Telephone."

He came out from his study and picked up the instrument. "Hello? Sir John here."

There was a pause and then, "Have you called the police?"

I lingered in the hall and heard him say, "Yes, of course, I'll be right over."

Sir John hung up as I said, "What's happened?"

"Nesbitt found a dead body in the field where you left our bicycles."

"I'm going with you." I started for the back hall to get my coat.

"No, Livvy. It won't be pretty. Don't get involved."

"I already am. I was in that field last night and this morning. And I may know the person who's died."

Sir John looked heavenward and then said, "All right. Let me tell Abby what's happened."

We drove to the field and parked on the verge near Little Hedges behind an ambulance. With the French assassin present earlier at Little Hedges, I doubted there would be much need of a quick trip to the hospital.

The local constable, the ambulance men, and an older man in farm-stained clothes and wellies stood near the short, overgrown hedgerow along a ditch. Sir John was greeted with a nod as we joined them. I was ignored.

"Any idea who she was?"

Sir John stepped forward to get a closer look at the body. At this angle, looking over the edge of the ditch toward the greenery, I could see bleached blonde hair, a blue dress, and a sensible shoe on one foot.

"No, I've never seen her before," he said.

I moved to Sir John's side. Looking down from this vantage point, I could see the body lay on her back as if she'd been dropped there, her limbs at odd angles. A blue-patterned scarf was pulled tight around her neck, making her swollen face difficult to recognize. Her exposed wrists and ankles showed red abrasions as if she'd been restrained. I quickly looked away. "Her name is Helene. She was, until recently, lady's maid to Mrs. Palmer."

"At Little Hedges?" the constable asked.

"Yes." I looked around. "Has anyone seen her other shoe?"

I was answered with grunts that I took to be "no."

"She may have been working for Sir Malcolm. He'll need to be notified."

Sir John said, "Why don't you go back to the house and do that, Livvy." It was an order, not a request.

I strode back across the field, aware that all eyes were watching me leave. For what reason, I wondered. I doubted any of those men had a hand in her death.

I was most of the way across the field when I heard a car with a siren pull up on the road. The police from the nearest good-sized town had arrived.

I suspected none of the men wanted to talk to officials with a woman present. Especially since a strangled woman was the victim. They would have been concerned about my delicate sensibilities and would have felt constrained to talk in front of me.

When I finally reached Summersby House, I told Abby what I'd seen and then called London. A male voice I didn't recognize answered the telephone. When I asked for Sir Malcolm I was informed he was busy. I gave the voice a message for his boss about Helene and hung up.

Abby came into the hall then and suggested I get cleaned up and into better clothes since we would be invaded soon with all sorts of officials.

She was right. I had no more than bathed and dressed when the maid knocked on the door. The police were there to ask me questions "about the dead woman in the field."

I followed her downstairs and into the drawing room, where Abby was sitting with two men. The younger's clothes looked well pressed and he looked freshly shaved. The older man looked slightly rumpled and weary. Both rose when I walked in.

"Mrs. Denis?" the younger one asked.

"Yes."

The younger one introduced them. He was the detective sergeant and the older man was the detective inspector.

Abby rose. "Just call if you want anything," she told me before she left the room.

The three of us sat.

"I understand you recognized the dead woman in the field," the older man said.

"Yes."

"That must have been difficult for you, seeing someone you knew in that state. Can you tell us how you knew her?"

"I write for the *Daily Premier.* I'm doing an article on Mrs. Palmer, who is the renowned painter Alicia Crawford. I met Helene the first time I went to Little Hedges to work on the story."

"What do you know about her?" the older policeman asked.

"She had a foreign accent. I couldn't place it. She was Mrs. Palmer's lady's maid. Other than that, nothing."

"Would it surprise you to learn Helene Schmidt had been fired as Mrs. Palmer's lady's maid?" he continued.

"No. Mrs. Palmer indicated Mr. Palmer chose Helene and she, Mrs. Palmer, didn't like that or her. She said she was planning to replace her."

"How long had it been since you saw Miss Schmidt?"

"Days. I couldn't tell you how many. Three, perhaps."

Then I took a chance. "She didn't have any apparent rope burns on her wrists or ankles when I last saw her, but she does now."

I heard the phone ring in the hall, but I didn't think anything of it until Abby came in and said, "Excuse me, Inspector, but the call is for you."

Abby, the sergeant, and I sat looking at each other or the floor until the inspector returned. He walked in, his expression grimmer than before, and said, "We'll need to continue this later. Come along, Sergeant."

As they headed down the hall, I said, "What's happened?"

"We'll speak to you later, Mrs. Denis."

Abby and I watched in surprise as the two policemen drove off. "Now, what would have caused them to leave in mid-interview?" she asked me.

I shook my head. I suspected I needed to find out. And Sir Malcolm would be the best source of information. In fact, I wouldn't be surprised if he had stopped their investigation.

Sir Malcolm, Phyllis Waterbury, and Alicia Crawford were all in London. My father was in jail in London. I needed to get back there.

I told Abby my change in plans as I rushed upstairs to pack.

* * *

By the time the train reached London, the evening was cold and rainy. Every street was lit with the paths of automobile lights. Buses glowed. Buildings glimmered. Streets shone. I had missed the constant noise and yellow-tinted fog. Now I wanted the excitement and possibly a surprise or two that I was sure would lead to my father's freedom.

I took a taxi home to my flat. In the post among the bills and circulars I found an invitation to a reception in Bloomsbury for that evening. The party was in honor of a friend of Phyllis Waterbury's. Perhaps Alicia or a longtime friend of hers would attend.

It didn't take me long to unpack and dress for an evening out in my blue satin gown with flared sleeves and an off-center-cut neckline.

There was nothing in the house to eat. I'd have to dine on hors d'oeuvres and hope they were generous. I didn't know the hostess of this reception, Miss Tan. I loved mysteries, but I hoped this reception would help me find answers, not more questions.

When I arrived, I found Miss Tan's Bloomsbury flat was one floor up. The art deco decorated drawing room was crowded with women writers I recognized, artists, and a few radio performers. Rosemary Tan told me she performed various bit parts in several popular radio serials as she welcomed me, pointed out the table with trays of glasses and wine bottles, and went off to speak to another arrival.

I was pouring myself a glass of red wine when I heard Phyllis Waterbury's voice. "Did you come to talk to Alicia again?"

I glanced over to find her at my elbow. "No. I'm going to let her think about my article on her and whether she is in favor of seeing it in print. I hoped to talk to you."

"Me? Whatever for?"

"Alicia won't speak about her past. Do you know why that is?"

"Are you asking if there's some scandal in her past? Or in her parents' lives?" Phyllis Waterbury looked ready to jump in and defend her friend.

"No. I'm just looking for the usual biographical information. Birthplace, schools, parents' names. Do you know any of these things?"

She considered a moment and then shook her head. "No. She just sprang onto the art scene five years ago. She didn't tell us anything about her past. Only that she had just left art school in Paris before coming to London and studying at the National Gallery. She knew Edmund Palmer before I met her, and they married over four years ago."

"Did you attend the wedding, or know anyone who did?"

Phyllis shook her head.

"Where was she born? Are her parents still alive?"

"I don't know." Phyllis gave me an openhanded shrug.

"Who in your circle has known Alicia the longest?"

"Probably me. I met her at the National Gallery and she told me she'd just arrived in town from Paris. She said she didn't know a soul in London, so I let her stay here."

"So, you were the one to introduce her to your friends."

"Of course. She once told me I'm her oldest friend in London." Phyllis sounded proud of the title.

"And you've never met anyone from her past?" This

sounded odd. Why would anyone be that closemouthed about their past?

"No. Why are you asking me these questions?" Phyllis stared at me.

"Background for my story for the *Daily Premier.*" And because nobody else seemed to wonder where Alicia Crawford had come from. Had her path crossed that of the French assassin sometime in the past?

Phyllis waved to someone behind my back and a moment later, Celestine appeared at my elbow, wearing brightly colored silk pajamas and smoking a cigarette in her long, enameled holder.

"Why did you tell me Edmund Palmer discourages Alicia from inviting her friends down because of the company he keeps?" I asked.

"Dear me. Did I say that?" Celestine asked me.

"Yes." I tried to pin her in place with my gaze, but I lost the battle to her smoke rings.

She sighed and nodded. "Are you familiar with the German-English Friendship Society?"

"Englishmen who like Hitler's ideas?"

"Close enough." Celestine took a deep breath, as if gathering her nerve to tell me. "They had a meeting at the Marylebone Hotel. I was there meeting a friend and saw Palmer in a hallway in close discussion with Oswald Mosley. If he invites people such as that to his home, I doubt Alicia would want any of us to visit her and be contaminated."

CHAPTER TWENTY-FOUR

"Do you have any reason to think the Palmers invited Mosley to Little Hedges?" I asked. Meeting Mosley in a London hotel was bad enough.

"No, but if someone like that fascist is a house guest, it stands to reason none of us mere artists would be asked. Especially at the same time." Celestine walked off, arm in arm with Phyllis Waterbury.

I had hoped Celestine had new information, but meeting with Mosley fit Edmund Palmer's reputation. Another possible clue that might help my father went up in smoke.

I glanced up and recognized another painting by Alicia Crawford on the wall behind the drinks table. It was smaller than the works I'd seen of hers elsewhere, and it didn't have the flamboyant brushwork I'd come to expect in Alicia's paintings. Still, there was something that made it definitely hers.

I checked the signature just to be sure. Alicia Crawford.

Mingling with the other guests, I finally reached Rosemary Tan. "I see you have an Alicia Crawford painting."

"Yes, an early one. I was over in Paris, acting in a Shakespearean production, and went to an art show. I fell in love with the image immediately. She had several on exhibit, but this one spoke to me."

Someone who'd known Alicia longer than Phyllis. "Did you meet her that day?"

"No. I didn't like the looks of her friends." I must have had a shocked expression on my face, because Rosemary laughed. "They all looked like members of the master race. Being Chinese and living in the West, I'm sensitive to threats."

"Since we've not met before, I wonder why you invited me to your party."

"I was asked to."

"Who would ask you?"

"Phyllis Waterbury."

I must have worn a stunned expression, because she patted me on the arm and walked off. I stayed another forty-five minutes at the party, but the guests I spoke to didn't know Alicia well. Alicia herself never arrived. I was ready to leave after helping myself to some biscuits and paté that served as my supper when Phyllis walked up to me.

"Why did you ask to have me invited?" came out before she had time to say anything to me.

"I wanted to know why you were keen to speak to Alicia and why she is avoiding you."

"Do you have your answers?" I asked.

"No. Only more questions." She walked off with a puzzled expression.

Phyllis's confusion added to my curiosity.

The next morning, I went to the top floor of the *Daily Premier* building and asked to speak to Sir Henry. I was shown in almost immediately.

"Please sit down, Livvy. I'll be with you in a moment," Sir Henry said. He conferred with Colinswood on the situation in Spain and then as the editor was leaving, asked me, "How is the story on that painter coming?"

"Mr. Colinswood, wait," I asked. "Could you have someone trace Alicia Crawford Palmer's background further than five years ago?"

Both he and Sir Henry narrowed their eyes. "What's going on?"

I told them about the attempt to capture the French assassin when she left Little Hedges and the murder of Helene, Alicia's lady's maid. "Please don't publish anything you don't verify elsewhere. What I want to find out is who Alicia's parents are and where she lived as a child."

"What do you think we're going to find?" Sir Henry asked.

"I don't know. I want to find out if she has any connection to the German woman. It's the German woman, if she's the dark-haired woman, I want to find to clear my father of the murder charge." Then I added, "Phyllis Waterbury met Alicia shortly after she came here from studying art in Paris. That was five years ago. Before that, she doesn't seem to have existed."

"I'll put someone on it," Mr. Colinswood said and, at a nod from Sir Henry, turned to leave the office.

"One more thing. I found Michael Littleshaw."

"What? Where?" Colinswood came back and looked as if he might hug me. "Is he all right?"

"He was working for Sir Malcolm on one of Edmund Palmer's freighters. That assignment ended when he rowed some spies in to shore at Hastings and the boat capsized. He's fine, but his cover story was ruined. Sir Malcolm plans to use him again elsewhere."

"That bounder. Poaching my employees," Sir Henry said with a shake of his head.

"I doubt we'll see him until the end of the war," Mr. Colinswood said as he left, shutting the door behind him.

"When are you coming back to work, Livvy?" Sir Henry asked when we were alone.

"When the trial is over. It starts next Monday." Frustrated, I banged my fist on Sir Henry's desk. "There's a black-haired woman out there who knows what happened to John Kenseth. But every woman involved with the Palmers or the murders of Helene or Mr. Whittier is a blonde or has light brown hair. Where is she? And who is the German woman?"

"I don't know, but if anyone can find out if Mrs. Palmer has any connection to this German woman, it'll be Colinswood. Go home and wait for his call." The finality in Sir Henry's voice told me to get out of his office so he could again focus on the newspaper.

Especially since I wasn't helping with the day-to-day assignments of the *Daily Premier.*

* * *

I stopped at the greengrocer shop on the corner and then lugged my purchases home. At least I wouldn't starve now. I tried calling Esther to see how she was feeling, but there was no answer. I did housework, but my heart wasn't in it. I sat with a pencil and paper, writing down everything I'd learned since my father first discovered John Kenseth's body.

The good news was I'd learned a great deal. The bad news was none of it would help release my father from jail.

The phone rang about midafternoon and I nearly knocked over a table in my dash to the phone in the hall. When I answered, Sir Malcolm's voice came over the phone.

"What are you doing in London?"

"I live here."

"Oh." There was a pause and then, "I called on the off chance you might actually be at home. I need you to come down to Scotland Yard tomorrow and give a statement to the police about how you know the French assassin and what you saw her do."

He gave me the particulars and hung up. I wrote them down and then went into the kitchen to fix a cup of tea. The pot was steeping when the telephone rang again.

I walked in this time and picked up the receiver. "Hello?"

"Livvy, it's Colinswood."

"What have you learned?" I nearly shouted down the telephone line.

"A woman obtained a British passport while in France over five years ago in the name of Alicia Crawford. Before that, she didn't exist."

"She had to. Somewhere, under some name..."

"Relax. We found her. We involved the Sureté. Turns out they'd been watching her. Previously, she was known as Anna-Liese Cradenberg, German national. She'd lived in Paris nearly a year before she changed her name and was found to be in possession of a British passport. She met Edmund Palmer at about the time she changed her name."

"Did she recruit Palmer to help the Nazis, or was it the other way around?" I said more to myself than Mr. Colinswood.

He surprised me with, "That we couldn't find out."

I felt my excitement rise. "With a background such as that, she could be called the German woman."

"But you said that woman has black hair."

I was immediately deflated.

"Who's seen the German woman?" he asked me.

"Kenseth, my father's next-door neighbors—"

"Your father?"

"He said no."

"Do you believe him?"

Did I? "About this? Yes."

"If there's anything else I can do, Livvy, let me know. We miss you at the paper."

"Thank you." Colinswood made me feel better about using the *Daily Premier* to help free my father. "That was a big help. Now if only I can figure out how Alicia Palmer is involved in the murder."

"Good luck." Colinswood hung up.

The Oswalds, my father's next-door neighbors, had seen the mystery woman. Now that I had an idea, I needed to speak to them again.

I rode the bus over to my father's house. By the time I arrived, I was glad I'd brought my umbrella. Rain splashed on my shoes and stockings. But instead of passing them by, I stopped by the Oswalds' house first.

Bert Oswald opened the door to my ring. "Mother, look who's here. Come in. You'll get wet."

Mrs. Oswald came in from the kitchen as I entered the hallway and hung my coat and hat on their coat stand. "Oh, good, I'm glad you came, Livvy. I think someone's been inside your father's house."

"When?"

"Today. Just now." She motioned for me to follow her into the kitchen as if the burglar could hear her speak. She cut off the light and we tiptoed to the side window.

It took my eyes a moment to adjust to the darkness outside and the deeper darkness inside my father's windows. Then I saw it, so quickly I hardly believed I'd seen a torchlight glow somewhere within the house and reflect in the dining room window.

"There, did you see that?" Mrs. Oswald said.

"Yes. Did you see anyone enter the house?"

"No."

"But we were busy watching the Weatherlys across the way get a delivery of new furniture for their bedroom. Tea was late from watching them," Mr. Oswald told me.

"So, anyone could have gone in then."

They both nodded, looking guilty.

I dashed to the coat tree. "Give me two minutes and then call the local police station and report a burglary occurring at this moment. Exactly two minutes."

Quickly, I pulled on my coat and hat. Leaving my umbrella behind, I ran next door, sliding on the wet grass, to the French doors opening to what had been my mother's study.

I hoped when my father had redecorated the room, he hadn't had the door repaired. It had never locked properly, allowing me to come and go undetected at night when I was home from university.

The balustrade was slick, but I hung on and climbed on to the little porch. Then it was only a second of well-practiced maneuvers to get the French doors open and to slip inside silently.

I waited until my eyes adjusted to the blackness and my breathing slowed. I didn't hear any footsteps running away, so I hadn't been heard.

But where was the burglar?

I felt my way to the door of the room and opened it slowly, sticking my head into the hallway to watch for any beams of light. After a moment, the light shone out of my father's study. It was the quick flash, rather than the light itself, that I noticed.

The light must have been aimed toward something that didn't reflect into the hallway.

I slipped into the hall and shut the door behind me. I didn't need a light. I'd grown up in this house and I knew every squeaky board and hiding place.

The door to my father's study was open. I stood in the shadows in the hall and watched. It was a woman, judging by the shape of the clothing. She was searching the bookshelves by pulling out each book and shaking it before dropping it onto a pile. She'd left piles of my father's books everywhere in the room.

I was barely breathing, but she should have heard my heart because of the way it was pounding in my chest.

How long until the constables the Oswalds were to call arrived? I hadn't figured on a delay in the police's arrival.

I stepped forward and flipped on the overhead light switch.

The burglar had the presence of mind to immediately throw a book at me. Then another. As I dodged, she tried to run past me.

I tried to block her and we both fell into the hall. She rolled over on top of me and kneed me in the stomach while I ran my nails down the side of her face. She clambered up, but I grabbed her cloche.

She ran into the kitchen, leaving me with a hat and a fistful of short dark hair. A wig.

I pulled myself up using the wall, and still holding the wig and the hat, I stumbled after her, one arm over my aching stomach.

When I reached the back porch, still gasping from her blow, I flipped the switch for the light. It came on. Thank goodness Bert Oswald had changed the bulb. I could see a figure crouched behind some drooping bushes in the back yard.

With a whoop I went running into the yard toward the woman. She backed up into a hawthorn tree and stopped, jerking away from the needles. Then, in the light from the porch, I saw the gleam of her knife as she pulled it out and came toward me.

Her footsteps were measured. Determined. It was my turn to back up now. And wonder where those constables were.

"You don't look good as a brunette, Alicia," I told her, forcing my tightened throat to allow my voice to carry. I wanted the police, the Oswalds, someone, to hear me. And to hear her.

She didn't say a word. She just kept coming toward me.

"You're not a killer. That's Fleur's job. Anna-Liese, if that is your real name, you were trained to be a painter."

For some reason, she stopped just a few feet away from me. "I was taught to kill, too. To fight for the Fatherland."

"They have a school for that?"

"Of course. Unlike Britain, we've planned for this war for a very long time."

"And Kenseth? What did he do to you?"

"He listened to the transmissions from Edmund's ships. He figured out where we were based and spied on us. Then he realized my real identity. I needed to stop him."

"Wasn't that your husband's job?"

Was it the stress of having to hide her true nature that kept her talking? The need to tell me who she really was after all the acting she'd done in front of me? Whatever it was, I hoped she'd keep talking. And that the police would arrive.

She sneered when she said her husband's name. "Edmund is a weakling. He's English through and through."

I thought I saw her plan. "You wanted someone weak.

Someone you could control. The smuggling and the spying, that's all been under your direction."

She smiled proudly, but she didn't say a word. I wished she'd admit her actions and let me know my guess was right.

"Why the black wig? Why did you need a disguise?"

For a moment, I didn't think she'd answer me. Then her smile grew. "All anyone has described is my black hair. It's the only thing about me that isn't ordinary. Otherwise, the only thing anyone can say is average height, average weight, average clothes. So dull. So boring. And without the wig I can walk around London without anyone growing suspicious."

She was clever. I wanted to learn more about her while my brain screamed for the police. "Have you always been German? At least until you went to Paris."

"I was born in Germany. I lived there until I finished my training. Then I was given an English identity. A cover story that a man like Edmund Palmer, a self-made industrialist, would appreciate." She took two steps toward me.

"So, John Kenseth spied on you. Why kill him?" I retreated onto the back steps, hoping she'd keep talking.

"He recognized me from years ago. From an art show in Germany."

I reached behind me and opened the back door. I slipped in and slammed it in her face. She grabbed the handle and twisted, and the door began to give way. I pushed as hard as I could on the other side.

Through the glass pane in the door, I could see the

strain in her reddened face. Her fury. The knife was pointed down in one fist. I knew I couldn't hold out much longer before she forced the door open enough for her to come in.

At the last second, I jumped out of the way and she slammed the door into the wall. With that split-second advantage, I picked up the frying pan on the stove and swung it, hitting her in the head.

Alicia Crawford Palmer, and the knife, slid to the floor.

CHAPTER TWENTY-FIVE

Then I heard pounding on the front door and Bert Oswald calling, "They're in the back." The police had arrived.

I flipped on the kitchen light before a constable and a sergeant came to the back door, Bert Oswald right behind them. I said, "This is the woman who was burgling my father's house. She was wearing this hat and wig to do it."

"Really. How exciting!" Bert said. "I must tell Mother."

The policemen looked at him, back at me, and then at the woman on the floor, who was holding her head and groaning. The constable pulled out his notebook and pencil. "What's your name, Miss?"

"Mrs. Olivia Denis. This is my father's house. Sir Ronald Harper."

"Is your father here, ma'am?"

I was twenty-six and feeling my age that day. I would have preferred *Miss*. "No. He's being held in your prison for a murder this woman committed. Alicia Crawford Palmer. She's the ringleader of a nest of Nazi spies."

"Oh, for pity's sake. The woman's delusional," Alicia said.

The two policemen looked at each other. The

constable clicked shut his notebook and turned to Mr. Oswald. "May I use your telephone to call the station, sir?"

The two walked off. Alicia sat up, straightened her skirt, and ran a hand over her hair and the rising bump I knew must be there. "I don't know why you decided to attack me. Perhaps because you have no talent as an artist."

"It was because Mr. and Mrs. Oswald saw you searching this house by torchlight before I came over here. And you attacked me with a knife in the backyard. If you search her, you will find a wicked-looking blade on her person," I added for the sergeant.

"Miss?" he asked.

"It's Mrs. Mrs. Palmer. And my husband is an influential man," she said with a sniff. "A wealthy industrialist."

"Who has been under observation by the Foreign Office for some time," I added.

"Did you know it was Mrs. Palmer who was in your father's house?" the sergeant asked, watching us both with suspicion.

"No. Only a figure with a torch."

The sergeant turned to Alicia. "What were you looking for?"

"I wasn't looking for anything. I received a note to come here, and this woman attacked me."

"You came here because you received a note, armed with a torch and a knife? And you were going through the books in my father's study." I'd accuse her of everything I could think of if it convinced the sergeant to arrest Alicia

Palmer.

"May I see the note?" the policeman said.

"I—I didn't bring it with me."

"Let's take a look at the study. Ladies?" He nodded for me to lead the way and then gave Alicia a hand up. The knife, a narrow, sharp blade, slid across the floor as she rose.

I grabbed it off the floor. Watching Alicia carefully, I handed it to the sergeant. "Please keep that safe."

Alicia gave me a look that left me in no doubt about her plans for my demise.

The policeman wordlessly pocketed the knife, eyeing Alicia with more suspicion.

I led the way, turning on the lights as I went. The study was enough of a mess that the sergeant narrowed his eyes as he stared at Alicia.

"What were you looking for, ma'am?"

She sat on a chair, crossed her arms, and refused to say another word.

"If it's here, we'll find it eventually," I told her.

She turned her face away.

The constable returned with Mr. and Mrs. Oswald. "I've contacted the station. They're sending more men," the policeman said.

"And I found her torch out in the backyard," Mr. Oswald said as if he'd found a prize.

He then retrieved the wig and hat and handed them to his wife. She adjusted the hat on the wig that rested on her fist and then turned to Alicia. "I said her hair didn't look right. That's the woman who came here with the man who was murdered."

Alicia jumped up, shoved Mrs. Oswald into the constable and took off for the front door. I chased her down the hall, but the moment she opened the door, she ran headlong into police standing on the front stoop.

"Arrest that woman," the sergeant said.

All the fight seemed to leave her. Her shoulders slumped and she gave the police no resistance. She looked straight ahead, not down the hall where the Oswalds and I stood watching. No matter what the police asked Alicia, she never said a word.

After the police took her away, the sergeant finished his questioning of both the Oswalds and me and then he and the last constable left. Mrs. Oswald invited me to supper, but I told her I needed to make a telephone call first.

"Then we'll see you in a few minutes. Come along, Bert."

I waved to them from the back door, locked up, and went into the hall to call Sir Malcolm. The male voice at the other end of the line said he would contact Sir Malcolm and have him return my call.

A few minutes later, the telephone rang. As soon as I picked it up and said hello, Sir Malcolm's voice boomed out at me. "What is so important?"

"The police just arrested the German woman for breaking into my father's house and trying to kill me."

"Who is she?"

"Alicia Palmer."

"She's not German." His voice grew louder over the

telephone line.

"Yes, she is. She told me Alicia Crawford was her alias in Paris while she tried to recruit her target. Edmund Palmer."

"You mean she was the brains behind the Nazi ring and not him?" Sir Malcolm was silent for a moment. "This explains the note that Kenseth left at your father's house. I wonder how he figured out British citizen Alicia Palmer was the German woman."

"She was a well-known painter," I said as I leaned against the hallway wall. "While Kenseth was still in London living under his real name, he attended art exhibits in Europe, even though his talent was in drawing maps. He had an artist's eye for detail. He must have remembered the woman under her German name at an exhibit a few years before. Later, when he saw Alicia Palmer, he recognized her. From there it was just a short leap to realizing how involved she was in the Nazi cause in Britain."

I remembered my father mentioning that John and Louise Kenseth traveled to the continent for art exhibits. I was at school or university and paid little attention. I wished now that I'd shown more interest, as I might have guessed Alicia's role in the spy ring earlier. However, I would never admit that to Sir Malcolm. "Was that why he came back to London? Supposedly he had some important information to share that he didn't trust to the post."

"It could have been he recognized Alicia Palmer as a German citizen. It could have been someone had found his listening post in Etretat. I suspect we'll never know," Sir

Malcolm told me.

"I think Alicia was the one who started this spy ring," I said. "Still, I don't think she could have used her husband's ships for smuggling without his approval."

"Good work, Mrs. Denis. I'll talk to Scotland Yard and then we'll drop in at Little Hedges. Search for clues. Maybe this time we'll catch the French assassin."

"Do I still need to talk to Scotland Yard?"

"Now you have even more to tell them." Sir Malcolm gave me a name to contact at police headquarters.

"I don't know how much they want to hear." And then I asked the most important question on my mind. "Now will they release my father?"

"I have no idea. Talk to his solicitor." The click reverberated down the line, telling me how little Sir Malcolm was worried about my father's fate.

His trial was scheduled to start the following Monday. I felt panic rise inside me. Would this be enough to save him?

I rang Mr. Peabody at home and told him of the events of the evening. He promised to consult the barrister in the morning. Then I went next door for a delicious dinner of chicken and mushy pea pasties with potatoes and gravy. Mrs. Oswald's cooking made me feel comforted even as it filled me up.

I took a taxi home and from there I called Sir Henry. "Guess what?" I told him as soon as he came to the phone. "I found the German woman with the black hair who was in my father's house with John Kenseth. It was Alicia Crawford Palmer. I'm hoping my father will be released before the trial can start and I can come back to work."

"I was beginning to think you were going to work full time for Sir Malcolm and leave us." Sir Henry sounded both sad and annoyed.

"No, sir. But I'd hoped to get a byline for my article on Alicia Crawford. Since she's now in police custody, hopefully standing trial on the murder charges that have been my father's, that's one article I'm sure will never see the light of day." And with my success at finding a killer, I lost my chance to see my name below the headline on my story. "Unless," I suggested, "you want a story on the talented painter now being questioned for murder."

"No, your article has been scrubbed. But don't worry. You'll get a byline someday." He sounded too cheerful about the demise of my feature article for my liking.

"I needed, well, I still need, to get my father released from prison and the murder charge against him dropped before I can get back to work. It looks as if that will happen, and life can get back to normal. Will Miss Westcott accept me back in the women's pages section?"

"She'll have to. I want you back at work, Livvy. And Esther is looking forward to seeing you again."

"I'm looking forward to seeing her." I felt guilty. It felt ages since I'd spoken to her.

"Come to dinner tomorrow night."

* * *

I traveled to Scotland Yard the next morning and made my statements about the attack on me by Alicia Crawford, what the Oswalds said about her being disguised in a black wig when John Kenseth was murdered, the attack on Mr.

Whittier by the French assassin, and what little I knew about Helene. Everything was neatly typed so I could sign the formal documents and leave.

I called Mr. Peabody and learned an appeal had been made to the trial judge before eleven that morning. The barrister was confident all charges would be dropped against my father. I was free to go back to work after calling Abby and the Oswalds and giving them the good news.

Once in the office, I found writing wedding announcements was as dull as I remembered. However, I soon felt relieved. Relaxed. Thankful that my father would soon be a free man and life could get back to normal.

Unfortunately, my mind tended to wander and my fingers to hit the wrong keys on the typewriter.

Near quitting time, I received a call from Sir Henry. Miss Westcott's face showed her displeasure as she called me up to the phone, but her voice stayed pleasant and cheerful.

When I said hello, Sir Henry's voice boomed out of the receiver. "Dinner will be served at eight. Be sure to arrive at my house by seven-thirty. We want to hear all about your adventures."

Even as I agreed, my mind leaped between not knowing how much I could actually tell them and knowing Miss Westcott would never admit to Sir Henry how much my abandoning my position annoyed her.

I went home and immediately called Mr. Peabody to find out my father's status. The dry solicitor sounded positively jovial as he told me my father would be released shortly.

Relieved at the news, I readied for dinner by wearing my warm gray evening dress with its beaded jacket that covered my bare upper arms and back. I left my building bundled up against the weather. It was cold and windy out, rattling the windows of my flat and sending newspapers flying down the street.

I rode in a taxi to Sir Henry's, where the maid took my evening cape and sent me into the study. Sir Henry, Esther, and her husband, James, all turned to the door as I walked in. Sir Henry offered me a seat by the fire and James handed me a glass of sherry.

"Now, you have to tell us everything. I've been bored out of my wits because my grandmother won't let me lift a finger."

I glanced around. "Where is Mrs. Neugard?"

"At Aunt Judith's. She's watching their children so my aunt and uncle could go out for their anniversary. So, tell me everything. I have to live vicariously through you." Esther's stomach had grown in the past few weeks, but she didn't look too uncomfortable yet.

"I can't tell you much. I've been working for a Foreign Office department head in exchange for his help in getting my father released from jail. Most of what I've done has been down in Sussex while staying with Abby, Reggie's cousin."

"I remember Abby. Her sons were Reggie's godsons, and she lives in that wonderful grand house in the countryside," Esther said.

"Now that things have settled down, maybe we can

slip away from your grandmother and go down there for a day."

"Yes, let's." Esther looked thrilled.

I suspected if I'd suggested disappearing to clean sewers for the day, Esther would have agreed.

"We were finally able to find the woman who'd been with John Kenseth in my father's house that Sunday," I told her. "Scotland Yard can no longer claim my father was the only person who could have killed his old colleague."

"So, they're going to release him?" Sir Henry asked.

"The solicitor says it appears that he'll be released tomorrow morning." I faced the heat from the fire and sighed.

"You must be so relieved," Esther said.

I nodded. Before this happened, if anyone had told me I'd feel this way about getting my father off on a murder charge, I'd never have believed it. I guessed this meant I loved the old stuffed shirt.

"So, who was the killer?" James asked.

"Alicia Crawford, the painter and wife of the shipping line owner, Edmund Palmer."

"Why would a woman with so much to lose kill someone?" Esther asked as she gave me a puzzled frown.

"She's actually German, a spy pretending to be English. She believes in the Nazi cause. John Kenseth found out what she was doing, which was smuggling in spies and armaments. She had to silence him." I shook my head, thinking of her beautiful art studio. And her incredible talent. There was no doubt in my mind that she'd hang. "Such a waste."

Sir Henry was informed that dinner was ready. He urged us all to stop talking shop and go to the dining room, where a warm dumpling soup awaited us. He didn't have to tell me twice. I was hungry.

We followed his rule not to discuss work at the table. Instead, we talked about Esther and James's baby, food, and the BBC concerts.

After dinner, we had coffee in Sir Henry's study. I told them as much as I could without telling them much. James didn't know the people involved, but I noticed Sir Henry was listening very closely as he sat completely still before the fire.

Esther asked all the questions. I could tell this was more from boredom than any desire to solve the country's espionage problems. Once the baby arrived, she would be too busy to worry about my work woes.

And then she asked, "What does Adam think of all this?"

"I wish I knew. We haven't exchanged a single letter in ages, and when we have written we have to be careful not to offend the military censors since his work is hush-hush. I haven't spoken to him in what seems like forever. I have no idea where he is or what he's doing, and he doesn't know what I've been involved with."

"That's a shame."

I thought of Sir Malcolm's warnings. "Neither of us can tell the other what we're doing."

Esther shook her head. "It's going to make dinner a very quiet meal when you two marry."

She then gave a huge yawn. James went to warm up

their auto and the maid came in with our outerwear. I called for a taxi before James could offer to give me a ride. It was too far out of their way and Esther's eyelids were drooping.

They left first, and in a few minutes the taxi arrived. I said good night to Sir Henry and climbed into the back seat, giving the driver my address.

We were nearly to my building when we stopped at a red light and the traffic-side back door opened.

Who would be crazy enough to walk in traffic and yank open car doors? I looked over, about to say that the cab was occupied, and found myself staring into the face of the French assassin.

CHAPTER TWENTY-SIX

I felt the cold ring of the barrel of a small revolver against my side as Fleur reached over. "I thought I'd ride back to your flat with you. Lucky I ran into you."

"Isn't it. Lucky you didn't get struck by a passing auto," I growled. Unlucky for me. I'd rather she was anywhere other than in my taxi pointing a gun at me.

The driver glanced in his rearview mirror and asked in a tone between shock and disgust, "Do you know this lady?"

"Yes." That was the truth. And with a gun pressed to my side, I didn't want to say anything more.

He shook his head and turned his attention back to the road.

"What do you want?" I murmured.

"I want to tie up a few loose ends." She gave me a smile, but her eyes were cold and sharp as diamonds.

She plans to kill me.

When we arrived at my building, I paid the cabbie extra for our unwanted passenger and then hurried toward the entrance. Fleur moved fast and was next to me in a moment, her gun barrel sticking into my back. "One wrong move and your doorman dies. You wouldn't like that, would you? You want to save people, not cause their deaths."

I wasn't going to let her put Sutton, our doorman, in danger. He'd been helpful too many times to risk anything now.

I walked in, my head held high, and headed for the lift. "Good evening, Sutton."

"Evening, Mrs. Denis. You and your friend have a good night."

"We will, Sutton," Fleur said.

I saw a tiny frown on Sutton's face. Had he seen the gun? I gave my head a little shake.

We rode upstairs as the lift rumbled slowly along and walked into my flat without any trouble. I wondered how long that would last. "You always attacked at a distance before. Exploding cigars for Churchill. That sort of thing. So why are you coming after me with a pistol? That's awfully close up for you." I walked into my drawing room.

"With you, it's personal. You're constantly blundering into my hideaways and destroying my supply channels." She stood quite close, her pistol aimed at my chest.

I had just taken off my evening cape, not wanting to get blood on it, when the telephone rang.

"Don't..." Fleur began.

I walked back into the hall. "If I don't answer, someone will be suspicious. Hello?"

"Olivia, it's your father."

"They've released you?" I almost jumped for joy until I felt cold steel through my gown. Then I jumped in shock.

"Yes. The paperwork came through a little while ago.

I'm home now."

"Oh, I am so relieved. You've heard Alicia Crawford is the German woman and she killed John Kenseth? She was in your house searching it again last night. We don't know what she was looking for."

"Who is Alicia Crawford?" My father sounded surprised.

"She's a painter, but that's not her real name. Do you know what her real name is?" I asked, holding the receiver away from my mouth and looking at Fleur.

"How would I know?" she replied.

"You're on the same side," I nearly growled at her.

In my ear, I heard, "Olivia, who's there? Are you all right?"

"No," I said brightly. "She married Edmund Palmer, you've heard of him, and he is British. He owns Little Hedges. We had dinner with them while visiting Abby and Sir John."

"Do you want me to contact someone?" My father was whispering.

"Yes. I've looked around and so has Sir Malcolm, but we can't find what she was looking for in your house."

"You want me to call Sir Malcolm?" He sounded both astonished and worried.

"Yes." I hoped my father would soon catch on to my requests without Fleur getting wise to my efforts. "She seemed to think it was hidden in your study."

Fleur appeared to have had enough of my chattering. She gestured me away from the stand holding the telephone with a wave of her hand holding her gun.

"It's awfully late. I'm afraid I need to get off the phone if I'm going to be worth anything tomorrow, Father."

"Adam isn't there, is he?" He sounded annoyed.

"I haven't heard from Adam in ages." I would have loved for him to be there at this very moment. He'd think of something.

"And you want me to call Sir Malcolm. It's that important." My father sounded as if he wanted to be very sure of what he was doing before he interrupted Sir Malcolm this late in the evening.

"Yes. I love you, too." I don't know why I felt compelled to say those words to him. Maybe because I might not have another chance. And they were true.

"I'll call him immediately." He sounded shocked.

"Good night." I hung up the phone and turned to Fleur. "You don't have to shoot me. You can just escape as you have before."

"I'm tired of having to escape every time you're around." She sounded weary.

"Then you're in the wrong line of work," I replied. "And I'm certain it's not just me who keeps you on the run." I walked into the drawing room and sat down. I slipped off my evening shoes and rubbed my tired feet.

"I'm in the right line of work if it lets me rid the world of troublesome busybodies such as yourself."

"I am not a busybody." How could she say that? "I'm trying to protect my country."

"If you really wanted to help England, you would work with us to align your country with Germany." She sat down in the chair across from me. I noticed beneath her evening gown, she wore brown leather oxfords better suited for rambling.

"Like the Duke of Marshburn?" I was certain he had helped her escape a countrywide search when she left Mimi Mareau's fashion salon a few weeks before.

"He is a loyal friend of both Germany and England." She gave me a brief smile. "And before you ask, he was a Nazi party member before I met him. I didn't have to recruit him. There are many in England who believe in our cause."

As long as I had a chance, I decided to ask some questions. "How did you escape from Little Hedges? Sir Malcolm had the house watched from the time I saw you there."

"Yes, you certainly caused problems." She glared at me. "We went out the back and across the fields. Someone brought a car around to pick us up and then drove us to London."

"We? Us?"

"Alicia Crawford Palmer and me."

"Nothing could be easier," I murmured. "You have friends everywhere."

"Of course. There are people all over England who want to see Germany succeed. Either because they don't want another war with Germany, or they want the prosperity Germany has. From the ruin all around us when I was a child, we've built a massive economy. A prosperous country. And your countrymen want that."

"I thought you were French."

She shook her head. "My family was French, and

Alsace has gone from French to German to French hands many times. I grew up across the river from Strasbourg."

"I don't believe my countrymen want prosperity enough to help an assassin. Most people, well, most Englishmen, don't believe in murder."

She leaned back in her chair and smiled at me. "How do you know I'm an assassin?"

I was told she'd killed several political figures in France, but that was hearsay. "I know you tried to kill Churchill with exploding cigars. We tested the chemicals kept in your trunk at Mimi Mareau's salon. Explosives and poisons, including the explosive used in the cigars."

"But I didn't kill anyone. Do you know of a single person I've killed?"

"Helene Schmidt?"

"I was having a private conversation. A delicate conversation. We caught her spying on us and then she tried to escape."

"So you strangled her." I shook my head.

"No. The other party killed her." She opened her eyes wide. "That person certainly surprised me."

"Who was the other person?"

Fleur shook her head.

"Mr. Whittier, then. On the beach in Hastings."

"That wasn't me."

"One second you were sticking a knife into the book in my pocket, and the next I find Mr. Whittier stabbed dead in your wake."

She smiled as if I'd told a good joke. "So that was how you escaped harm. You had a book in your pocket. Good for you. I hid behind a hut and waited to see where the police were. I watched you get up off the sand and run down a path. You were ahead of me. I couldn't have killed the man I saw you trip over."

I shook my head. I still believed she had killed those people in France. And I suspected what she just told me was a lie. She had killed Mr. Whittier.

She must have seen the skeptical expression on my face. "What I told you is the truth. I didn't kill that Englishman. Aren't you judging me unfairly?"

"You're pointing a gun at me. Aren't you being unfair to me?"

She laughed then. "Touché."

I stared at her. "Why did you become an assassin? Aren't there better ways to serve your country?"

"I was a good gymnast as a child, a fast runner, and curious about everything. I was chosen to go to a special school. And once you are chosen, there is no turning back."

"The Nazis have trained more like you?"

"Yes. There are many of us." She gave me a satisfied smile. "If one of us is killed or captured, another goes in to take over our assignment. The Fatherland always succeeds."

I wasn't sure if I was more horrified or angry. "Why did you stab me on the beach in Hastings? An order from your Führer?" I took that attack very personally.

"Reflexes. I was trained to strike out with lethal force at any challenge. It's ingrained in me now. You grabbed me from the back and I knew you wanted to stop me. I am sorry."

Her tone was sad. Her life sounded sad. I had to ask, "Don't you wish your life was different?"

"It can't be. There is no point in wishing for what cannot be." She stood up and gestured with the pistol for me to stand. "We've given Sir Malcolm enough time to get here. We need to leave."

When I looked surprised and probably embarrassed, she added, "I'm certain that's what you told your father. To contact Sir Malcolm. That wasn't a difficult code to break, hearing half the conversation."

I struggled into my high heels. "What if I don't want to leave?"

"Then I'll shoot you where you sit and escape. Live up to that ridiculous name people have given me."

When she cocked the pistol, I decided she was serious. I rose from my chair, my shoes pinching my feet. "Where are we going?"

"You'll see." She took my house keys and my compact out of my bag, and she left her dark evening wrap on. I left mine off. I hoped we'd be staying inside. It was cold out.

She followed me closely out of the flat, down the hall toward the lift, and stopped at the stairs. First, she tossed my compact a few steps down from the landing for my floor before she directed me up a half flight. Then she said, "That's far enough." She broke the light bulb on the landing with the butt of her gun and then swung it back to aim it at me.

Certain I couldn't escape at that moment, I turned and looked down the staircase, where I could see the hall leading toward my front door. "We're going to watch and see if anyone goes into my flat."

"If you make a sound, I'll shoot you. If you keep quiet, I may allow you to live." She stepped onto the same stair I stood on with her gun poking into my left side. This close, she'd kill me instantly if she fired.

We didn't have long to wait. I heard Sutton's exclamation rise up the staircase, followed by the squeak of the lift going downstairs and running footsteps coming up the stairs. A man's voice exclaimed over finding my compact. Constables rushed past the staircase on my hallway and presumably entered my flat. Next came a few men in trench coats and bowlers.

I sent up a prayer that no one would look up the staircase. Even in the dark, even in my gray gown, I might be noticeable.

A minute or two later, some of the men must have come out of my flat as they walked past and headed down the stairs, one of them saying, "The doorman said they came up in the lift. Check all the lower floors. She must have dropped her compact in an effort to show us which way they went. Keep an eye out for a lipstick or a comb."

I noticed none of my neighbors had set foot in the hall or on the stairs, trying to question the constables. I was grateful they didn't have an ounce of curiosity between them.

I turned my head to look at Fleur, but she was closely watching the hall. *What did she want?* If she wanted to kill me, I'd have been dead half an hour ago. With her gun pressed against my side, I could still end up dead, but I was beginning to doubt I was her target.

She stood very still, watching and waiting.

Meanwhile, my mind raced.

Had she known my father had been released early? If she had, she could have guessed he'd call me. She would know, from my time writing the story on Mimi Mareau, that I was my father's closest relative. And she may have found out that my work for Sir Malcolm was to free my father from a murder charge.

Was my father her intended target? I didn't think he was important enough to assassinate, but in the past few months I'd learned there was much more to my father's work than I'd believed.

He wasn't involved in John Kenseth's work, but Fleur might not know that. Or maybe she did, and she wanted to kill my father for his work involving some other facet of espionage against Germany.

Maybe she was carrying out the orders of some unknown master spy in Berlin. Perhaps she had no say in who she murdered. Perhaps she didn't care. Was one target pretty much like another to her, and was Fleur's passion directed at perfecting the finesse needed to kill someone and escape?

Did the targets not matter, as long as their deaths aided the Nazi cause?

I wanted to ask her, but the gun barrel sticking between my ribs kept me silent.

Fleur and I stood silently watching from the shadows in the stairwell. I was terrified into immobility, and Fleur no doubt had learned to keep still during her training to become the French assassin. Sooner or later, someone would look up here and discover us.

Why had she agreed to become a paid killer? Did she have no choice as a child? What had her training been like? Did she ever want to quit this line of work?

I doubted I'd ever get the answers.

I heard the lift groaning up the shaft. I was certain it would stop on my floor, and when all grew silent followed by the sound of the doors clanking open, I found I was right.

The first voice I heard was my father's.

A sharp pain shot through my stomach. I found I couldn't breathe. I looked down to make sure no blood was seeping through my gown. The gun still poked me in the side and no bang echoed around me.

Fear, not a bullet, had stabbed me.

I forced myself to breathe as I heard my father say, "I can't understand it. She's just a child. You can't use her that way."

Then I heard Sir Malcolm say as the lift door was shoved closed, "She's not a child. She's a very clever, capable young woman. If it hadn't been for her, you'd still be facing a murder trial."

"She does have some talent in that regard. She proved her husband had been murdered and wasn't a suicide. I'm afraid I didn't believe her for the longest time." My father walked past in the hall, looking toward my front door.

Please don't look over here.

My father disappeared down the hall past the opening to the stairwell. "Coming in?"

"Yes. I'd like to see her flat. Maybe there's some clue..."

Sir Malcolm moved into our line of sight in the hall, strolling toward my front door.

In that instant, I felt the gun barrel leave my side. I glanced at Fleur. She aimed her pistol down the short distance toward the hallway and Sir Malcolm. At this range, a trained assassin couldn't miss.

CHAPTER TWENTY-SEVEN

I grabbed her arm with my left hand and pushed down as a deafening bang shook the walls.

She shoved me. I marveled at how strong she was as I reached out but found nothing to hold on to. I fell down the steps, my feet going into the air. When I landed, men stepped over me as they raced up the stairs after Fleur.

My father helped me up. "Are you all right?"

"I am now." I winced at the pains I was sure would be bruises the next day. Then I hugged my father tightly. "I thought she was going to shoot you," I said into his coat.

"Why would she shoot me?" He sounded mystified.

I started to giggle, although I knew it wasn't funny.

"Really, Olivia, get hold of yourself."

It took me a minute to regain my composure. "Sorry, Father."

"You must be in shock. Let's go into your flat. And I have something to tell you. Well, to ask you."

Father *ask* me something? "What is it?"

Then I heard a man's voice shout down the stairwell, "She's gone up to the roof."

"Come on." I started up the stairs, but my father held me back.

"Put a coat on. You'll freeze outside dressed like that."

I dashed into my flat, threw on my evening cloak, and ran back out past the startled constable standing guard. My father had hit the down button for the lift. "Will you be warm enough?"

"I'll be fine." The lift made the groaning noise it made going up as it stopped on the floor just above mine. It stopped for a moment and then started down again.

I was about to run upstairs when the sound of the lift stopped me. It didn't stop at my floor, or the ones below mine. From years spent waiting on the slow and creaking lift, I was almost certain it didn't stop until it reached the basement.

I started down the stairs. My father said, "Wait. The lift will be here shortly."

"She'll be gone by then. I think Fleur was in the lift going down." I ran as fast as I could in high heels down flight after flight of steps. By now, I could hear men's footsteps pounding down above us, shouting that she wasn't on the roof.

I kept hurrying down to the lobby. "Sutton, has the woman with me been through here?"

"No." He glanced at me and then turned his attention back to the constables and men from Sir Malcolm's section of the Foreign Office hurrying through his lobby. "What's going on?"

I ignored his question and raced down the final, long sections of stairs into the basement. It was dark and cold. Perfect for an assassin to hide in wait.

That thought stopped my feet as my eyes adjusted to

the poor light from a few widely spaced hanging lightbulbs.

My father, behind me, bumped into me. "There's no one here."

"She has to be."

"Why do you think she's down here?"

"Because that's how I would have escaped. Send the police past me up the stairs and take the lift down."

I heard a noise by the tradesmen's entrance and moved cautiously forward. The cement floor was cold beneath my thin-soled heels. The air chilled my face and hands, but not as much as the fear pouring icicles down my back.

There, on the empty cement ramp leading from the service entrance to the storage units, were my house keys on their ring. I picked them up and looked around.

My father walked past me and called out as if to a truant schoolgirl. "Young lady, are you down here? Please come out and show yourself."

I walked across the aisle in the center of the basement to the service entrance and glanced outside at the pavement. The area was cold and empty. If Fleur had left that way, she had disappeared into the night.

I walked back to my father's side. As he walked away, I heard a noise to one side. Looking in that direction, I saw nothing in the pale light. But then, in the deepest shadows, I thought I saw movement. So slight as to be a trick of a breeze. Except there was no breeze.

A moment later, my father turned back toward me and said, "I don't think she's here."

"I guess you're right." If Fleur escaped, I reasoned, Sir Malcolm would know who was after him. If Fleur was captured, the Nazis would send someone else, someone unknown, a classmate of Fleur's, to carry out her instructions. And Sir Malcolm would not know where to look for the danger.

My father walked to the stairs. Behind his back, I shook my head at the spot where I'd seen the motion and then joined him.

We started up the stairs just as some men, led by Sir Malcolm, raced down.

"There's no one there," my father said.

They ignored him, shining their torches around the individual storage cages. "The service entrance door is open," one of them shouted.

Running footsteps were heard to fade away, no doubt going out through the tradesmen's entrance.

My father and I went back up to my flat. I realized half of me hoped she got away without anyone getting shot, including Sir Malcolm. The other half wasn't nearly so charitable toward Sir Malcolm.

"Now," my father said, as he sat in Reggie's comfortable chair, "we need to talk."

"About?" I suspected I was in for a lecture on risk-taking or how unseemly my occupation was.

"Julia wants to meet you over a meal. She feels the two of you got off on the wrong foot while I was—unavoidably detained."

Only my father would refer to being locked in prison awaiting trial for murder as *unavoidably detained*. "Can you two be seen together in public?" I raised my eyebrows. "Is she bringing her husband?"

"He shows no inclination to return to England," Father said, not rising to my challenge. "I thought Sunday dinner after church at a hotel."

Then it dawned on me. "You called her before you called me to say you'd been released." After all I'd done to find the true killer. Steam must have been rising from my ears.

My father had the wisdom to look embarrassed.

* * *

I slept late the next morning. I awoke to find I had bundled all my covers around me in an attempt to get warm. I rose and put the kettle on to boil, then threw on a heavy sweater and wool skirt over thick stockings.

I'd only managed a single sip of tea when the phone rang. I expected to hear Sir Henry's voice at the other end of the line demanding to know why I wasn't at work, but instead, I heard Esther saying, "Your father called my father first thing this morning to tell him about your ordeal last night and that you wouldn't be coming in to work today."

"Do you want to come over? I probably won't be good company today, but this is a place to hide out from your grandmother."

I heard a sigh, and then, "I'd love to."

When Esther came over, we had tea and biscuits in the drawing room. Once we were settled, I said, "How is your grandmother adjusting to life in London?"

"She's not. She doesn't want to learn English. She

doesn't want to go out. She says she should have stayed in Berlin with my grandfather."

"Who's dead."

"Exactly. My aunts have urged her to live with them, but neither has as much room as James and I have. We drive her to Aunt Judith's before sundown on Friday and pick her up Sunday afternoon, so James is spared her doom and gloom on the weekends, but during the week, I get her all day every day."

I couldn't hide my grin. "What did you tell her to escape today?"

"She went to my aunt's yesterday and will stay there until Sunday this week, giving me a rest. Grandmother has already called me three times to make sure I'm resting, forcing me to get up each time."

I laughed at the absurdity, but then I felt guilty. I was interrupting Esther's rest, too. "Maybe I shouldn't have asked you to come over."

She rolled her eyes. "I get enough rest when she's staying with us."

"We need to find her an interest."

"I've tried." Esther sounded weary. "So, tell me what happened last night after you left us."

I told her every last detail. She oohed and gasped and made me feel very important. "Have you told Adam yet?"

"No. I owe him a letter, and this one will be difficult to write. 'Don't worry about me, she didn't fire her pistol when she had it stuck in my ribs.'"

"Well, maybe you want to leave that detail out. Where is he?"

"I don't know. They sent him somewhere, and I'm not allowed to know where. Another of those secrets between us. Of course, who knows how long it will be before he'd get any letter I'd send. And I've heard nothing from him in ages."

Eventually, Esther convinced me to put on more elegant clothes and we went out to lunch on Oxford Street. Afterward, we looked in the shop windows, which were newly decorated for Christmas.

As we crossed a side street where the traffic waited their turn to pull out into Oxford Street, I glanced in the windscreen of the first car and saw Fleur Bettenard staring at me. There was a gap in the traffic and the car leaped forward. I jumped out of the way, but not before I saw her wiggle her fingers and give me a little wave.

I looked around for a constable, but there was none to be found. I might not want Fleur caught, but Scotland Yard needed to be aware she was still nearby and a danger.

"Did you see her?" I demanded of Esther.

"Who?"

"Fleur Bettenard."

"That's impossible. Everyone's looking for her. She should be in hiding."

"No. She waved to me as she rode by." I shook my head. "Where's a phone box? I must call Sir Malcolm."

That proved to be easier to locate than a constable. When I finally got through, I heard Sir Malcolm grumble, "We're busy just now, Mrs. Denis."

"I just saw the French assassin on Oxford Street. You need to be careful."

"Why should I be careful? Everyone is looking for her. And where did you see her?"

"In a car pulling onto Oxford Street. Do you have a photo of her to circulate?"

"Yes. The one you gave us when we first searched for the French assassin. And we obtained a copy of her passport photo from the French. Blurry thing. Terrible."

"You need to be careful. You're her target."

"And she's mine. What kind of car was it?"

"Large. Black. A Rolls, I think. Maybe a Phantom. And I didn't see who was driving. I was too shocked to see Fleur sitting there to notice anything else."

Esther, standing next to me half inside the callbox, said, "It was a man driving. An older man, but not elderly. He was in uniform. A chauffeur, perhaps? And the car was a saloon. It looked expensive. I don't know the make."

I relayed this to Sir Malcolm, who repeated it to someone in his office.

"We have an escaped assassin and we have no decent photograph of her. We can't charge her with anything except attempted murder of both you and me. We don't have sufficient evidence to link her to Whittier's death or Helene's. We can't find her to bring her in to answer charges. And we don't know who might be helping her. There will be an investigation into this disaster." His last words were weighed with menace.

"Do you think she'll go to Little Hedges?"

"No. Palmer knows he's under surveillance and Mrs. Palmer is locked up. We've made doubly sure she won't escape."

"Then you might want to keep an eye on the Duke of Marshburn. I think Fleur escaped with him before."

"A duke? That's more difficult because of his position, but we'll check around his residences."

Sir Malcolm hung up, and I turned to Esther. "That was good work, noticing the driver and the car."

"It was the car that grabbed my attention. Very expensive. Now, would you like to come to dinner tonight? I'm sure my father wants to hear all about your latest escape from death."

I had to smile. "I bet he wants to know when he can count on me showing up for work."

I sent Esther home in a taxi. When I returned home, Adam was asleep in my drawing room. His stockinged feet were up on the ottoman and his head had rolled to one side as he emitted a small snore.

I watched him for only a moment before he woke up. He nearly leaped to his feet as he surrounded me in a ferocious hug. "Oh, Livvy. I talked to your father. She could have shot you. She did try to stab you."

"Well, she didn't succeed, and the danger is past for me." Then all my fears and anxiety from the last weeks poured out. "But what about you? You're in the army and Hitler's going to start a war at any time. What...?"

Anything else I might have said was silenced by his kiss.

It was a while before we began discussing what I thought of as our "situation" again. And this time, he brought it up.

He led me into the drawing room and sat us both on

the sofa. "I hope you won't be doing any more work for Sir Malcolm."

"I hope so, too, but I don't think I have any more choice in what he expects me to do than you have in your assignments for General Alford. It's our duty." I thought that was much better than admitting it was exciting.

"He doesn't pay your salary."

"No, but Sir Henry does. And Sir Henry is happy to cooperate with Sir Malcolm if it means exclusives for his newspaper." I couldn't resist telling him what I'd seen one more second. "By the way, while carrying out an assignment for Sir Henry, I saw you in Paris."

"What?" He seemed genuinely startled.

"I was making a connection between train stations and I saw you on the streets of Paris."

"When?"

"November tenth."

He bowed his head, but I could sense he was frantically trying to think of an answer.

"Don't lie to me. That was you."

He nodded, still looking down. "Don't ask me anything."

"I won't. I understand about government secrets."

He looked into my eyes. "Quit."

"What?" I couldn't believe my ears.

"Quit. Marry me and stay home and do whatever you want."

I thought of my marriage to Reggie and how bored I had been. "I tried that once. It didn't work out for me. I guess I like to be busy. To never know what tomorrow will bring. Perhaps it's the excitement." I put my arms around his shoulders. "You're the same way, and I would never ask you to leave the army. To leave a job you enjoy."

"I'm not sure enjoy is the right word," he said as he made a face. "But your latest run-in with the French assassin could have been the last for you. These people are dangerous."

I pulled away from him. "So are the people you'll be facing."

"That's my job. It's what I'm trained to do. You haven't been studying war and espionage half your life."

"I think we'll all be taking a practical course in war and espionage soon. I just have a head start on a lot of people."

He took a deep breath and let it out slowly. "Will you ever marry me, Livvy?"

"Yes, I will. When I can be married and work, and I suspect that day is coming. At the moment, there's no rush and I can keep working. Doing my bit for England."

"Or for Sir Henry," Adam said. He was scowling.

"Some days it amounts to the same thing." I gave him a smile. "Will you accept a long engagement? Until it's obvious I won't be of any further use? Or until they'll want me even if I'm married."

I held my breath as I waited for his reply. I really wanted to marry him. It was just the loneliness, the empty days, while he was away with the army that kept me from saying yes immediately. And when I wasn't being scared out of my wits, I loved my secret assignments.

"You think Sir Henry and the government will hire married women once the war starts?" At least he didn't scoff at the idea.

I nodded. "There were some married women brought into the workforce in the last war."

"On the farms." He smiled at me.

I glared back at him. "And in the government. Those with special talents."

"And you think you have special talents."

I drew away from him. "I know I do. I've been displaying them for the past year."

He looked down and nodded. When he glanced back up, he was somber. "You've been terrifying me with your talent for finding spies and killers. You've been driving me mad. Livvy, the day the war starts, let's get married. Please."

I kissed him with a passion he should have felt to his socks. "We may be the only two people in England looking forward to the war."

He kissed me back. "If that's what it takes to get you to say 'I do,' I'll take on the whole German army."

I hope you've enjoyed Olivia's newest adventure. I'm giving away a novella to readers of my newsletter. **The Mystery at Chadwick House** is a contemporary mystery with a friendly ghost set in eastern North Carolina. If you'd like a **FREE** novella, type in https://dl.bookfunnel.com/tkb6dig4pw and sign up for my infrequent newsletter. In between newsletters, keep up with my latest news at www.kateparkerbooks.com and www.facebook.com/Author.Kate.Parker.

Author's Notes

I've heard complaints that Olivia doesn't sound British enough. Since I sound American, I knew I needed help to give Olivia her voice. Marcia Wheeler has been kind enough to read over a draft of this book and correct my troubling habit of using American terms for Olivia's world. In the process, Marcia has introduced me to some domestic details I hadn't found anywhere else. I am deeply indebted to her generous assistance. Any mistakes in terminology are mine.

Deadly Deception was born of the *what if* questions that plague the life of writers. In this case, it was *what must it be like to have to flee your homeland* and *what would Olivia do if her father was in serious trouble?* Then came the fun part, creating chaos and danger to follow Olivia. This story was a long time in coming, but I'm proud of it.

I'd like to thank Hannah Meredith, Jen Parker, Elizabeth Flynn and Jennifer Brown for their help in making Deadly Deception the best it could be. As with Marcia, the mistakes are all mine.

I hope you've enjoyed Olivia's adventures. If you do, tell someone. Word of mouth is still the best way to discover good new reads. Reviews are also a good way to tell others about books that you've enjoyed.

About the Author

Kate Parker caught the reading bug early, and the writing bug soon followed. She's always lived in a home surrounded by books and dust bunnies. After spending twelve years in New Bern, North Carolina, the real-life location for the town in The Mystery at Chadwick House, she packed up and moved to Colorado to be closer to family. Now instead of seeing the rivers and beaches of the Atlantic coast, she has the Rocky Mountains for scenery.

Along with the fourth in the Deadly series, Deadly Deception, she has put up The Mystery at Chadwick House for sale this spring. She's already at work on the next Milliner Mystery while researching the fifth in the Deadly series. She reports she is having fun creating new stories to entertain readers and chaos to challenge her characters.

Follow Kate and her deadly examination of history at www.KateParkerbooks.com

and www.Facebook.com/Author.Kate.Parker/

and www.Bookbub.com/authors/kate-parker

Printed in Great Britain
by Amazon